Audrey Craven

May Sinclair

AUDREY CRAVEN

BY

MAY SINCLAIR

AUTHOR OF "THE DIVINE FIRE," ETC.

"Made subject to vanity"

1906

AUTHOR'S EDITION

TO

MY MOTHER

CHAPTER I

Everybody knew that Miss Audrey Craven was the original of "Laura," the heroine of Langley Wyndham's masterpiece. She first attracted the attention of that student of human nature at Oxford, at a dinner given by her guardian, the Dean of St. Benedict's, ostensibly in honour of the new Master of Lazarus, in reality for his ward's entertainment and instruction in the bewildering art of life.

It was thunder-weather. Out of doors, a hot and sleepy air hung over the city; indoors, the forecast was no less heavy and depressing. Not so, however, to Miss Audrey Craven. The party was large and mixed; and to the fresh, untutored mind of a tyro, this in itself was promising. The Dean pursued the ruinous policy of being all things to all men; and to-night, together with nonentities and Oxonians of European renown, there was a sprinkling of celebrities from the outside world. Among these were Mr. Langley Wyndham, the eminent novelist, and his friend Mr. Percival Knowles, the critic who had helped him to his eminence. Having collected these discordant elements around him, the Dean withdrew from the unequal contest, and hovered, smiling ineffectually, on the outskirts of his little chaos. Perhaps he tried to find comfort in a conscience satisfied for a party spoiled. But for Audrey this wild confusion was rich in possibility. However baffling to those officially responsible, it offered a wider field for individual enterprise; and if she did not possess that fine flow of animal spirits which sometimes supports lesser minds under such circumstances, she had other qualities which stood her in good stead. Conspicuous amongst these was an indomitable moral courage. She prepared to hurl herself into the breach.

Wyndham was standing a little apart from the herd, leaning against the wall, as if overcome by an atmosphere too oppressive for endurance, when he saw his friend approaching him. Knowles was looking about him with eyes alert, and that furtive but uncontrollable smile which made ladies say, "Yes; but Mr. Knowles is so dreadfully cynical, you know."

"By the way, Wyndham—I don't want to startle you, but there is a lady here who particularly wants me to introduce you to her."

Wyndham turned on him a look terrible in its dignified reproach.

"Anything but that, my dear fellow. No more introductions to-night, please. I've just suffered torture from an unspeakable youth from Aberdeen, who expected me to rejoice with him because Oxford is at last recognising the 'exeestence of a metapheesical principle in the wur-r-ld and mon— —'"

"I admit that the party is dull, from a mere worldling's point of view. But it's a glorious field for the student of human nature. And here's an opportunity for exceptional research—something quite off the beaten track. The admirer of you and all your works is the lovely Miss Craven, and I assure you she's creating a sensation at the other end of the room."

"Which is she?"

"There, the girl with the copper-coloured hair, talking to Broadbent."

"Ah, that one. No, thanks. I know what you're going to tell me—she *writes*."

"She doesn't, but she's pretty enough to do that or anything else she chooses. Scandal says she's looking for a religion. She must be a simple soul if she thinks she can pick up the article in Oxford."

"Oh, I don't know. Religions are cheap everywhere nowadays, the supply being so remarkably in excess of the demand, and Miss Craven's soul may be immortal (we'll give it the benefit of the doubt), but its simplicity is *un grand peut-être*. What's the matter?"

"It makes me ill to see the way these fellows go about leading captive silly women. Do look at Broadbent cramming his spiritual pabulum into that girl's mouth. Moral platitudes—all the old crusts he can lay his hands on, soaked in the milk-and-water of sentiment."

"And a little new wine—with the alcohol extracted by the latest process; no possible risk of injury to the bottles. Don't be uneasy; I've been watching her all evening, ever since I found her in a corner with the unspeakable youth, talking transcendentalism. A woman who can look you in the face and ask you if you have ever doubted your own existence, and if it isn't a very weird and unaccountable sensation, would be capable of anything. Five minutes afterwards she was complimenting Flaxman Reed on the splendid logic of the Roman Faith, and now I've no doubt she's contributing valuable material to Broadbent's great work on the Fourth Gospel."

He was wrong. At that moment the earnest seeker after truth was gazing abstractedly in his direction, and had left the Canon lecturing to empty benches, balancing himself on his toes, while he defined his theological position with convincing emphasis of finger and thumb. What he said is neither here nor there. Then Wyndham repented of his rudeness. He waited till Knowles was looking another way, and made for the Dean in a bee-line, approaching him from the rear to find him introducing a late arrival to his niece. He heard the name Mr. Jackson, and noted the faint shade of annoyance on the girl's face, as the interloper sat down beside her with a smile of dreamy content. It was enough to quench Wyndham's languid ardour. He was not going to take any more trouble to get an introduction to Miss Audrey Craven.

He saw her once more that evening as he turned to take leave of his host. She was still sitting beside Mr. Jackson, and Wyndham watched them furtively. Mr. Jackson was a heavy, flaxen-haired young man, with a large eye-glass and no profile to speak of. To judge by Miss Craven's expression, his conversation was not very interesting, though he was evidently exerting himself to give it a humorous turn. Wyndham smiled in spite of himself.

"Hard lines, wasn't it?" said Knowles at his elbow. "Brilliant idea of the Dean's, though—introduce the biggest bore in the county to the prettiest girl in the room."

The unconscious Mr. Jackson burst into laughter, and Audrey raised her eyebrows; she looked from Mr. Jackson to Wyndham, and from Wyndham to Mr. Jackson, and laughed a low musical laugh, without any humour in it, which echoed unmusically in the memory. Wyndham turned abruptly away, and Audrey looked after him as he turned. Her face was that of one who sees her last hope disappearing. Poor Audrey! Who would not have pitied her? After hovering all evening on the verge of an introduction to his

Eminence, it was hard to bear the irony of this decline, unsustained by any sense of its comedy. He had avoided her in the most marked manner; but all the same, she wondered whether he was thinking about her, and if so, what he was thinking.

What he thought that night, and the next, and the next after that, was something like this: "My dear lady, you think yourself remarkably clever. But really there is nothing striking about you except the colour of your hair. Biggest bore in the county—prettiest girl in the room? If it weren't for your prettiness—well, as yet that may have saved you from being a bore." After that he laughed whenever he caught himself trying to piece together the image which his memory persistently presented to him in fragments: now an oval face tinged with a childlike bloom, now grey eyes ringed with black, under dark eyebrows and lashes; or a little Roman nose with a sensitive tip, or a mouth that to the best of his recollection curled up at the corners, making a perpetual dimple in each cheek. They were frivolous details, but for weeks he carried them about with him along with his more valuable property.

CHAPTER II

Scandal was mistaken. Miss Audrey Craven was not in search of a religion, but she had passed all her life looking for a revelation. She had no idea of the precise form it was to take, but had never wavered in her belief that it was there, waiting for her, as it were, round a dark corner. Hitherto the ideal had shown a provoking reticence; the perfectly unique sensation had failed to turn up at the critical moment. Audrey had reached the ripe age of ten before the death of her father and mother, and this event could not be expected to provide her with a wholly new emotion. She had been familiarised with sorrow through fine gradations of funereal tragedy, having witnessed the passing of her canary, her dormouse, and her rabbit. The end of these engaging creatures had been peculiarly distressing, hastened as it was by starvation, under most insanitary conditions.

The age of ten is the age of disenchantment—for those of us who can take a hint. For Audrey disenchantment never wholly came. She went on making the same extravagant demands, without a suspicion of the limited resources of life. It was the way of the Cravens. Up to the last her father never lost his blind confidence in a world which had provided him with a great deal of irregular amusement. But the late Mr. Craven could be wise for others, though not for himself, and he had taken a singular precaution with regard to his daughter. Not counting the wife whom he had too soon ceased to care for, he had a low opinion of all women, and he distrusted Audrey's temperament, judging it probably by his own and that of his more intimate acquaintance. By a special clause in his will, she had to wait for her majority four years longer than the term by law appointed. Further, until she reached her majority she was to spend six months of the year at Oxford, near her guardian, for the forming and informing of her mind—always supposing that she had a mind to form. And now, at the age of five-and-twenty, being the mistress of her own person, her own income, and her own house in Chelsea, she was still looking out for a revelation.

Her cousin, Mr. Vincent Hardy, believed that he had been providentially invented to supply it. But in the nature of things a cousin whom you have known familiarly from childhood cannot strike you as a revelation. He is really little better than a more or less animated platitude.

Vincent Hardy would have been unaffectedly surprised if you had told him so. To himself he seemed the very incarnation of distinguished paradox. This simply meant that he was one of those who innocently imagine that they can defy the minor conventions with a rarer grace than other men.

Certainly his was not exactly the sort of figure that convention expects to find in its drawing-rooms at nine o'clock in the evening. It was in Audrey's house in Chelsea, the little brown house with discreet white storm-shutters, that stands back from the Embankment, screened by the narrow strip of railed plantation known as Chelsea Gardens. Here or hereabouts Hardy was to be met with at any hour of the day; and late one July evening he had settled himself, as usual, near a certain "cosy corner" in the big drawing-room. His face, and especially his nose, was bronzed with recent exercise in sun and wind, his hair was limp with the steam of his own speed, and on his forehead his hat had left its mark in a deep red cincture. His loose shooting jacket, worn open, displayed a flannel shirt, white, but not too white. This much of Hardy was raised and supported on his elbow; the rest of him, encased in knickerbockers, stockings, and exceedingly muddy boots, sprawled with a naïve abandonment at the feet of the owner of the drawing-room. Lying in this easy attitude, he delivered himself of the following address—

"Life in London is a life for lunatics. And life in England generally is a glorious life for clergymen and counter-hoppers, but it's not the life for a man. It was all very well in the last century, you know, when Englishmen were men first, and lunatics, if they chose, or clergymen or counter-hoppers, afterwards. Ah! if that wasn't exactly our golden age, it was the age of our maturity, of our manhood. If you doubt it, read the literature of the eighteenth century. Take Fielding—no, don't take Fielding. Anyhow, since then we have added nothing to the fabric of life. To pile it on above, we've simply been digging away like mad from below, and at last our top-heavy civilisation is nodding to its fall; and its fall will sweep us all back into barbarism again. Then, when we are forced back into natural conditions, the new race will be born. No more of your big-headed, spindle-shanked manikins: we shall have a chance then of seeing a *man*—that is, a perfect animal. You may turn up your nose, my superfine lady: let me tell you that this glorious animalism means sanity, and sanity means strength, and strength means virtue. *Vis—vir—virtus*, ma'am."

Hardy sat up and caressed the calves of his legs with thoughtful emotion, as if he recognised them as the sources of the moral law within him. His cousin had not followed his precipitate logic. With woman's well-known aversion from the abstract, she was concentrating her attention on the concrete case, the glorious animal before her. Now it would be very wrong to suppose that Hardy was in the least tainted with socialism, anarchism, or any such pestilent heresies, or that he had read "Emile" and "Walden." He had never heard of either of these works, and had no desire whatever for the restoration of society on a primitive basis of animalism, modified by light literature, clothing, and the moral law. For all modern theories he had a withering contempt, his own simple creed being that in the beginning God made man a Tory squire. His quarrel with the social order was a purely private and particular one. In our modern mythology, Custom, Circumstance, and Heredity are the three Fates that weave the web of human life. Hardy did not wholly sympathise with this belief. He had too profound a respect for his own pedigree to lay his sins at his great-grandfather's door. As the nephew of a Tory squire, he was but two degrees removed from original righteousness. In spite of this consideration, he was wont to describe himself with engaging candour as a "bad hat." In doing so he recognised that he was a dependent part of a vast and complicated system. If he, Vincent Hardy, was a bad hat, who was to blame for it? Obviously, civilisation for providing him with temptation, and society for supplying encouragement. As a consequence he owed both civilisation and society a grudge.

"Therefore I say that a return to barbarism will be our salvation. You and I mayn't live to see the day, but— —"

Here the impassioned orator, who had been making charges at his boots with the point of his walking-stick, succeeded in detaching a large cake of mud, which he immediately ground to powder on the carpet. Civilisation personified in Audrey Craven gazed at him in polite reproach.

"My new carpet will certainly not live to see it. It may be part of the detestable social order, but it is not responsible for it, any more than I am."

"Never mind, Audrey. It's honest Hertfordshire mud—clean from the country as God made it, if I hadn't had to cross your filthy London in order to get here."

Audrey smiled, though she knew that brown streaks of the honest Hertfordshire mud marked the hero's passage from the doorway to her feet. She was naturally long-suffering, and seldom repulsed any one, save a few of the more impertinent of her own sex. She lay back in her cosy corner, outwardly contemplating the unusual length of muscular humanity extended before her, inwardly admiring her own smile, a smile of indulgent lips and arch eyebrows, in which the eyes preserved a languid neutrality.

Being thus pleasantly preoccupied, she may be supposed ignorant of her cousin's broad gaze of unreflecting admiration, and totally unprepared for his rapid change of theme.

"Audrey," he began, with alarming suddenness, "some people would lead up to the subject cautiously. That would only waste time, and time's everything now. Is Miss Craven at home?"

"Miss Craven is always at home when I am. Would you like to see her?"

"See her? Good heavens, no! Do you know positively where she is secreting herself, or must I lock the door?"

"That is unnecessary. She will not come in—she never does."

A suspicious look darted from the corners of Hardy's eyes.

"Except when I ask her," added Audrey, sweetly.

"Well, then, if you can ensure me against the sort of interruption that annoyed me before, we will return to the question we were discussing when——"

"Please don't go over any old ground. That would bore me."

"It would bore *me*. I will begin where we left off. The problem, if you remember, was this—to put it baldly—do you care for me, or do you not?"

"Didn't we get any farther than that?"

"No, we didn't."

"Do I—or—do I not? Really I cannot tell you, Vincent, for I don't know myself."

"Nonsense! there's no logical dilemma. You can't go on for ever treating it as an open question."

"Well—you draw such absurdly hard-and-fast lines."

"Audrey, do you honestly suppose that I've walked here thirty miles, parboiled between sun and rain, in order to be made a fool of?" (in his excitement Hardy forgot that twenty miles was the precise distance, and that he had much better have taken the train). "How much longer are you going to keep up this fiendish cat-and-mouse sort of game?"

"What do you mean?"

"I mean that ten years is a devil of a time to keep a man waiting for his answer."

"Ten years?—ten days, you mean."

"Excuse me, I broached this subject for the first time ten years ago."

"Oh, I daresay, when we were both children."

"We are neither of us children now, Audrey."

"Speak for yourself. I was an infant in the eyes of the law till the other day."

"You are—let me see—five-and-twenty. If you have any mind at all, you must have made it up by this time."

"The case would be much easier if you were not such a mass of inconsistency yourself."

"I've been consistent enough in one respect. Do you remember the first time you stayed with us at Woodford, when you weren't much higher than that table, and how you and I set off together for Wanstead Woods?"

"Yes—before breakfast. I have never forgotten it."

"Nor I. You did rile me that day, Audrey. You waited till we came within a stone's-throw of the woods, and then you sat down in a turnip field and cried because you couldn't go any farther."

"After running at your heels for two miles, like a dog."

"Yes—and, with the irresponsibility of the inferior animal, eating up the whole of the cake I provided for us both."

"It was perfectly fair; you dragged me out against my will."

"So you argued at the time, but I couldn't follow your reasoning. Perhaps you have forgotten how I carried you on my back to Woodford, and then gave the milkman sixpence to drive us the rest of the way home. And you were such a contemptible little snob that you cried again because you had to sit next the milkman."

"I remember perfectly. You only carried me as far as Red Bridge, in a position the most comfortable for yourself and the most undignified for me. You borrowed that sixpence from me and never paid me again; and we were *both* punished with dry bread for breakfast, because we were seen in the milk-cart."

"The abominable injustice of my parents was of a piece with the whole system I complain of. You will observe that we were punished, not for disobedience, but for riding in a milk-cart, and not so much for being in it as for being seen in it."

"Exactly, otherwise the reminiscence would be slightly irrelevant."

"Not at all. It illustrates my thorough-going consistency. I loved you then, in spite of your detestable conduct in the matter of that cake, and I have loved you ever since in spite of your other faults."

"Thank you."

"I suppose you would prefer some hypocrite who told you that you had none?"

"On the contrary, I enjoy being told of my faults."

This was true. If it came to the point, Audrey would boldly offer her own character for dissection rather than suffer conversation to be diverted to a less interesting topic. Hardy had rather neglected these opportunities for psychological study, and herein lay the secret of his failure. He continued, adopting a more practical line of argument suggested by the episode of the sixpence —

"It's not as if you were a millionaire and I a grovelling pauper. I shall have Lavernac and two thousand a-year when my uncle, Sir Theophilus Parker, dies." Hardy rolled out the title with a certain proprietary unction; his cousin had no share in this enviable relationship. "I give the old bird five years at the very worst, and it's a moral impossibility that he should leave me in the lurch. But I don't count on that. My own property has kept me idle all my life; but I've sold it at last, and, as I said just now, I am going out to Canada to farm."

Audrey blushed, and punished her blush with a frown. If she had been playing the amusing game that Hardy suggested, it was one thing to give the mouse a little run in order to renew the pleasures of the chase, another thing to let him escape altogether from her paws. Hardy saw his advantage and followed it up.

"When I told you that I had done with civilisation, I suppose you thought it was a joke?"

"I did. Only I couldn't see the point."

"The point is this, that I'm going down to Liverpool to-morrow, and shall sail for Canada this day week. I can't stand it any longer. I can't breathe here. Town or country, it's all the same—the air chokes me, it's teeming with moral bacilli. You never thought I was so particular? No more did I——". He paused, knitting his brows. "I admit frankly that I'm a bad hat. This place has been my ruin, as it has of many a better man than me. Perhaps, if it hadn't been for you, Audrey—but I won't press that point; it wouldn't be generous, however just. Anyhow, whatever my past has been, my future lies in your hands. I would say your love was life or death to me, but that wouldn't be anywhere near the truth. It's not so much a question of death as a question of damnation."

Hardy was desperately in earnest, but not so much so as to be careless of rhetorical effect. In his desire to represent himself as a fallen angel he had done himself no little injustice, as well as grossly exaggerated the power of Audrey's regenerative influence.

She was evidently moved. She took no pains to restrain the trembling of her lips, more than was necessary to preserve their delicate outline. Hardy had paid homage to her as the superior being.

It marked an epoch in the history of his passion.

He rose to his feet and looked down on her as from a height. A fallen angel is not without his epic sublimity.

The lady hesitated. She pulled out the tremolo stop, and then spoke.

"You say that if it hadn't been for me—I don't quite understand you, but you are mistaken if you think I never cared for you—never cared, I mean to say, for your good." She also rose, with an air of having made a statement as final as it was clear and convincing. He laid his hand on her shoulder and looked steadily in her face. There was no evasion in her eyes, but her eyelids quivered.

"It's all right, Audrey; you never have denied that you love me, and you can't for the life of you deny it now."

She did not attempt to; for the entrance of the footman with coffee made denial indecent at the moment, if not impossible. That *deus ex machina* from below the stage retired, unconscious of the imminent catastrophe he had averted. But he had brought into the little drama a certain prosaic element. Coffee and romantic passion do not go hand in hand.

Then it seemed to Audrey that the welcome interval of commonplace lapsed into a dream, in which Hardy's voice went sounding on in interminable monologue.

"I shall hear the wind, Audrey, rushing over prairies infinite as the sea; I shall see the great wall of the Rockies rising sky-high. And England will seem like a little piece of patchwork, with a pattern of mole-hills for mountains, and brooks for rivers. And when I've set our Canadian farm going, I shall hunt big game. And when I've exterminated the last bison off the face of the boundless prairie, I shall devote myself to literature."

"Literature?" she echoed faintly. It was all so grotesquely strange that even this announcement brought only a dreamlike surprise.

"Yes, literature. Do you think literature is only produced by the miserable noodles who sit in their studies at home, till their muscles wither and their hearts get flabby? *My* book will be a man's book, with a man's blood and a man's brains in it. It will be a book that will make posterity sit up. And when you have enjoyed the fame of it a little, we'll go out again together. In Canada we shall find a new heaven and a new earth."

She sat silent and passive. The situation had a charm which she was powerless to break. It seemed as if the mere brute force through which Hardy had dominated her intellect hitherto, had become refined by some extraordinary process, and was exerting a moral influence over her. In order to assert herself against the intolerable fascination she rose hastily and crossed the room to where her piano stood open in the corner.

She played loud and long,—wild Polish music, alive with the beating pulses of love and frenzy and despair. It would have roused another man to sublime enthusiasm or delirious rapture.

It sent Hardy to sleep.

Stretched on the hearthrug, with slackened jaw, and great chest heaving with regular rise and fall, he slept like a tired dog. She played on, and as she played he dreamed that he stood with her in the midst of the burning prairie, they two on a little ring of charred black earth, an island in a roaring sea of fire. The ring grew smaller and smaller, till they could only find standing-room by clinging close together. As he turned to her she thrust him from her into the sea of fire, crying, "It's perfectly fair, Vincent, for you dragged me here against my will!"

He woke with a snort as the music suddenly ceased. It was midnight. He had to start from home early next morning, and if he delayed longer he would lose the last train out.

He parted from Audrey as only the traveller outward bound parts from his betrothed. In fact, as she remarked afterwards, "For the fuss he made about it he might have been going to the North Pole with his life in his hands. So like Vincent!" As for Hardy, he felt already the wind of the new heaven and the sweetness of the new earth.

Audrey was staring abstractedly into the looking-glass, when she heard the front-door shut with a violent bang, and the sound of his quick footsteps on the pavement below. She came to herself with a cold shiver.

What had she done? Surely she had not gone and engaged herself to Vincent? bound herself in the first year of her liberty to a man she had known all her life, and her own cousin too?

It was impossible; for, you see, it would have argued great weakness of mind and a total want of originality.

CHAPTER III

Whether Audrey did or did not understand herself, she was a mystery to all about her, and to none more than her father's cousin and her own chaperon, Miss Craven. This unfortunate lady, under stress of circumstances, had accepted the charge of Audrey after her parents' death, and had never ceased to watch her movements with bewildered interest and surprise. The most familiar phenomena are often the least understood, and Miss Craven's intelligence was daily baffled by the problem of Audrey. Daily she renewed her researches, with enthusiasm which would have done credit to a natural philosopher, but hitherto she had found no hypothesis to cover all the facts. The girl was either a rule for herself, or the exception that proved other people's rules; and Miss Craven was obliged to rest satisfied in the vague conclusion that she had a great deal of "character." Strange to say, that is how Audrey struck most of her acquaintance, though as yet no one had been known to venture on further definition. Miss Craven was repaid for her affectionate solicitude by an indifference none the less galling because evidently unstudied. Audrey rather liked her chaperon than otherwise. The "poor old thing," as she called her, never got in her way, never questioned her will, and made no claims whatsoever on her valuable time; besides relieving her of all those little duties that make us wonder whether life be worth living.

Under the present dispensation chaperons were a necessary evil; and Audrey was not one to fly heedlessly in the face of her Providence, Society.

All the same, Miss Craven had her drawbacks. If you, being young and vivacious, take a highly nervous old lady and keep her in a state of perpetual repression, shutting her out from all your little confidences, you will find that the curiosity so natural to her age will be sure to burst out, after such bottling, in alarming effervescence. As soon as Hardy's unmistakable footsteps were heard on the stairs, she had left the drawing-room on a hint from Audrey. In her room above she had heard the alternate booming and buzzing of their voices prolonged far into the night, but could make out no intelligible sounds. To ears tingling with prophetic apprehension the provocation was intense.

The old lady passed a restless night, and came down to breakfast the next morning quivering with suppressed excitement. Audrey's face did not inspire confidence; and it was not until she had touched lightly on the state of the weather, and other topics of general interest, that Miss Craven darted irrelevantly to her point.

"My dear, is there anything between you and your—er—cousin Mr. Hardy?"

The awful question hung in the air without a context, while Audrey went on making tea. This she did with a graceful and deliberate precision, completing the delicate operation before answering.

"Yes, there is a great deal between me and my cousin Mr. Hardy, which neither of us can get over."

There was a freezing finality in the manner of the reply, in spite of the smile which accompanied it; and even Miss Craven could not fail to understand. She bridled a little, wrapping herself closer in her soft shawl as in an impenetrable husk of reserve, and began nervously buttering toast. The whole thing was very odd; but then the ways of Audrey were inscrutable.

Audrey herself felt an unspeakable relief after that question and her own inspired answer. Last night she had possibly been ambiguous; to-day, at any rate, her words had a trenchant force which severed one of the thousand little threads that bound her to Hardy. After all, when it came to the point, there was an immense amount of decision in her character. And as the days went on, and Hardy with them, leaving league after league of the Atlantic behind him, the load at her heart grew lighter; and when at last the letter came which told her that he had crossed the Rocky Mountains, she felt with a little tremor of delight that she was a free woman once more. Her world was all before her, vaguely alluring, as it had been a month ago.

The letters which Hardy sent from time to time had no power to destroy this agreeable illusion; for of course letters were bound to come, and she answered them all with cousinly affection, as she would have answered them in any case. At last one came which roused her from her indifference, for it had a postscript:—

"By the way, there's a Miss Katherine Haviland living near you, at 12 Devon Street, Pimlico. She's a sort of little half-sister of mine, so I'd be glad if you'd go and look her up some day and be kind to her. There's a brother knocking about somewhere, but he doesn't count, he's only a baby. Ripping sport—shot a moose and two wapiti this morning."

Audrey read the letter with languid attention. She was not in the least interested to hear that he had taken up land and put it into the hands of an agent to farm. She was tired of the long highly-coloured descriptions of Canadian scenery and the tales of Vincent's adventures, and she had got into the way of skipping his vain repetitions of all the absurd things he had said to her on the night of his departure; but the postscript stirred strange feelings in her breast. His mother was married a second time, but to Audrey's certain knowledge Vincent had no little half-sisters; it followed that for some reason he had used a figure of speech. She was not in the least in love with him, but at the same time she felt all the dignity of her position as empress of his heart, and could bear no little half-sisters near the throne. She would certainly look Miss Haviland up. She would go and be kind to her that afternoon; and she put on her best clothes for the occasion.

A few minutes' walk brought her to No. 12 Devon Street, one of a row of gloomy little houses—"full of dreadful city clerks and dressmakers," she said to herself in a flight of imagination.

She lifted the knocker gingerly in her white gloved hand, and felt by no means reassured when she was shown in, and followed the servant up the narrow staircases to the attics. As she neared the top she heard a voice above her sounding in passionate remonstrance.

"Three baths in the one blessed dy, a-splashin' and a-sloogin' somethin' orful—'e didn't ought for to do it, m'm, not if it was ever so!"

Here the voice was cut short by a mingled roar and ripple of laughter, and Miss Audrey Craven paused before announcing herself. Through the half-open doorway she saw a girl standing before an easel. She had laid down her palette and brushes, and with bold sure strokes of the pencil was sketching against time, leaning a little backwards, with her head in a critically observant pose. The voice reasserted itself in crushing peroration—

"I tell you wot it is, Mr. 'Aviland—*you're no gentleman.*"

And Audrey's entrance coincided with the retreat of a stout woman, moving slowly with an unnatural calm.

The girl doubled back her sketch-book and came forward, apologising for the confusion. Face to face with the object of her curiosity, Audrey's first feeling was one of surprised and reluctant admiration. Miss Haviland was dark, and pale, and thin; she was also a little too tall, and Audrey did not know whether she quite liked the airy masses of black hair that curled high up from her forehead and low down on it, in crisp tendrils like fine wire. Yet, but for her nose, which was a shade too long, a thought too *retroussé*, Miss Haviland would have been beautiful after the Greek type. (Audrey's own type, as she had once described it in a moment of introspection, was the "Roman *piquante*," therefore she made that admission the more readily.) There was a touch of classic grace, too, in the girl's figure and her dress. She had rolled up the sleeves of her long blue overall, and bound it below her breasts and waist with a girdle of tape—not for the sake of effect, as Audrey supposed, but to give her greater freedom as she worked and moved about the studio. At this point Audrey found out that all Miss Haviland's beauty lay in the shape of her head and neck. With "that nose" she might be "interesting," but could never be beautiful; in fact, her mouth was too firm and her chin stuck out too much even for moderate prettiness.

Audrey did not arrive at these conclusions in the gradual manner here set forth. The total impression was photographed on her sensitive feminine brain by the instantaneous process; and with the same comprehensive rapidity she began to take in the details of her surroundings. The attic was long, and had one window to the west, and another to the north under the roof, looking over the leads. At the far end were a plain square table and a corner cupboard. That was the dining-room and the pantry. Before the fireplace were a small Persian rug bounded by a revolving book-case, a bamboo couch, a palm fern, a tea-table. That was the library and drawing-room. All the remaining space was the studio; and amongst easels, stacks of canvases, draperies, and general litter, a few life-size casts from the antique gleamed from their corners.

From these rapid observations Audrey concluded that Miss Haviland was poor.

"You were busy when I came in?" she asked sweetly.

"No; I was only taking a hurried sketch from the life. It's not often that our landlady exhibits herself in that sublime mood; so I seized the opportunity."

"And I interrupted you."

"No; you interrupted Mrs. Rogers, for which we were much obliged—she might have sat for us longer than we liked. I am very pleased to see you."

Certainly Audrey was a pleasant sight. There was no critical afterthought in the admiring look which Miss Haviland turned on her visitor, and Audrey felt to her finger-tips this large-hearted feminine homage. To compel another woman to admire you is always a triumph; besides, Miss Haviland was an artist, and her admiration was worth something—it was like having the opinion of an expert. Audrey pondered for a moment, with her head at a becoming angle, for she had not yet accounted for herself.

"My cousin Vincent Hardy asked me to call on you. I believe he is a very old friend of yours?"

"Yes; we have known each other since we were children."

"What do you think of his going out to Canada to farm?"

"I didn't know he had gone."

(Then Vincent had not thought it worth while to say good-bye to his "little half-sister." So far, so good.)

"Oh, didn't you? He went six weeks ago."

"I never heard. It's an unlikely thing for him to do, but that's the sort of thing he always did do."

"He hated going, poor fellow. He came to say good-bye to me the night before he went, and he was in a dreadful state. I've heard from him every week since he sailed, and he's promised to send me some bearskins. Isn't it nice of him?" ("She won't like *that*!")

Miss Haviland assented gravely, but her eyes smiled.

"I suppose you've seen a good deal of Vincent? He wrote to me about you from the Rocky Mountains."

"Did he? We used to be a good deal together when we were little. Since then we have been the best of friends, which means that we ignore each other's existence with the most perfect understanding in the world. I always liked Vincent."

This was reassuring. Miss Haviland's manner was candour itself; and depend upon it, if there had been any self-consciousness about her, Audrey would have found it out at once. She dropped the subject, and looked about her for another. The suggestions of the place were obvious.

"I see you are a great artist. My cousin didn't prepare me for that."

Miss Haviland laughed.

"Vincent is probably unaware of the interesting fact, like the rest of the world."

"That picture is very beautiful; may I look at it?" said Audrey, going up to the easel.

"Certainly. It's hardly finished yet, and I don't think it will be particularly beautiful when it is. I can't choose my subjects."

"It looks—interesting," murmured Audrey, fatuously. (What *was* the subject, after all?) "Have you done many others?"

"Yes, a good many."

"May I——?" she hesitated, wondering whether her request might not be a social solecism, like asking a professional to play.

"If you care about pictures, I will show you some of my brother's some day. His are better than mine—more original, at least."

"Your brother? Oh, of course. Vincent told me you had a brother, a baby brother. Surely——"

Miss Haviland laughed again.

"How like Vincent! He is unconscious of the flight of time. I suppose he told you I was about ten years old. But you must really see the baby; he will be delighted with your description of him." She called through the skylight, and Audrey remembered the gentleman who was "no gentleman," and who must have been responsible for half the laughter she had overheard.

"You see," Miss Haviland explained, "we've only one room for everything; so Ted always climbs on to the leads when we hear people coming—he's bound to meet them on the stairs, if he makes a rush for the bedrooms. If any bores come, I let him stay up there; and if it's any one likely to be interesting, I call him down."

"He must have great confidence in your judgment."

"He has. Here he comes."

Audrey looked up in time to see the baby lowering himself through the skylight. With his spine curved well back, his legs hanging within the room, and his head and the upper part of his body laid flat on the leads outside it, he balanced himself for a second of time. It was a most undignified position; but he triumphed over it, as, with one supple undulation, he shot himself on to the floor, saving his forehead from the window by a hair's-breath.

After this fashion Ted Haviland was revealed to Audrey. She was, if anything, more surprised by his personal appearance than by the unusual manner of his entrance. The baby could not have been more than nineteen or twenty, and there could be no dispute as to his beauty. Nature had cast his features in the same mould as his sister's, and produced a very striking effect by giving him the same dark eyebrows and lashes, with blue eyes and a mass of light brown hair. Detractors complained that the type was too feminine for their taste; but when challenged to show a single weak line in his face, they evaded the point and laid stress on the delicate pallor of his complexion. Not that it mattered, for Ted soon made you think as little of his good looks as he did himself. But Audrey never forgot him as she first saw him, glowing with exercise and the midday bath which had roused his landlady's indignation.

"I'm extremely sorry," he began airily, "for disappearing in that rude way."

"Perhaps I ought to apologise," said Audrey, "for I frightened you away."

"Not at all, though I was desperately frightened too. I was flying before Mrs. Rogers when you came in. You'll probably think I ought to have braved it out, just for the look of the thing—especially after her reflections on my social position—but unfortunately my sister has imbued that terrible woman with the belief that art can't possibly flourish anywhere outside this attic of hers. Ever since then she's kept us in the most humiliating subjection. I don't want you to think badly of Mrs. Rogers: there's no malice about her; she wouldn't raise your rent suddenly, or leave pails of water on the stairs, or anything of that kind, and she's capable of really deep feeling when it's a question of dinner."

"Ted—if you *can* forget Mrs. Rogers for a minute—I told Miss Craven that you would show her some of your sketches and things some day."

"All right; we'll have the exhibition to-day, if Miss Craven cares to stop. Plenty of time before the light goes."

Audrey hesitated: but Miss Haviland had moved aside her own easel to make room for her brother's; she seconded his invitation, and Miss Craven stopped.

Three months ago, in an Oxford drawing-room, she had found herself absorbing metaphysics, as it were through the pores of her skin, without any previous discipline in that exacting science; now, in a London studio, she became aware of a similarly miraculous influx of power. Yesterday she would have told you that she knew nothing about art, and cared less. To-day it seemed that she had lived in its atmosphere from her cradle, and learned its language at her nurse's knee. But, though familiar with art, she was not prepared for the behaviour of the artist. Ted treated his works as if he were the last person concerned with them. He would pass scathing judgment on those which pleased Audrey best; or he would stand, like a self-complacent deity, aloof from his own creations, beholding them to be very good, and not hesitating to say so.

"Well," said Audrey at last, "you've shown me a great many lovely things, but which is your masterpiece?"

"They were all masterpieces when I first finished them."

"Yes; but seriously, which do you consider your best? I want to know."

Ted hesitated, and then turned to a stack of larger canvases.

"I wonder," she murmured, "if *I* shall think it your best."

"Probably not."

"Why not?"

Ted did not answer: he hardly liked to say, "Because hitherto you have persistently admired my worst."

"This," he said, laughing, as he lifted a large canvas on to the easel, "is the only masterpiece that has withstood the test of time."

"He means," struck in his sister, "that he finished it a week ago, and that in another week he'll want to stick a knife into it."

"Probably. I've always noticed that when people call you an idealist, it's a polite way of saying you're a failure. I may be an idealist; I don't know, and I'm afraid I don't much care."

"I'm sure you do care; and you *must* have your ideals."

"Oh, as for that, I've kept as many as seven of them at a time. But I never could tame them, and when it comes to taking their portraits the things don't know how to sit properly. Look at that woman's soul, for instance"—and Ted pointed to his masterpiece with disgust.

"Why, what's wrong with it? It's beautiful."

"Yes; I got on all right with the upper half, but, as you see, I've been a little unfortunate with the feet and legs."

"Of course!" interrupted Katherine, "because you got tired of the whole thing. That's what a man's idealism comes to!"

Audrey looked up with a quick sidelong glance.

"And what does a woman's idealism come to?"

"Generally to this—that she's tried to paint her own portrait large, with a big brush, and made a mess of the canvas."

There was a sad inflection in the girl's voice, and she looked away as she spoke. The look and the tone were details that lay beyond the range of Audrey's observation, and she felt hurt, though she hardly knew why. She rose, carefully adjusting her veil and the lace about her throat.

"I adore idealists—I can't help it; I'm made that way, you see."

She shrugged her shoulders, in delicate deprecation of the decrees of Fate.

Katherine did not see, but she went down with Miss Craven to the door. Ted had proposed tea on the leads, and Audrey had agreed that it would have been charming—idyllic—if she could have stayed. But she had looked at the skylight, and then at her own closely fitting gown, and Propriety, her guardian angel, had suggested that she had better not.

"Ted," said Katherine an hour later, "I've got an idea. What a magnificent model Miss Craven would make!"

Ted made no answer; but he flung his sketch-book to the other end of the room, where it took Apollo neatly in the eye.

"I've failed miserably in my Mrs. Rogers," said he, and went off for solitary contemplation on the leads.

Katherine picked up the book and looked at it.

He *had* failed in his Mrs. Rogers; but in a corner of a fresh page he had made a little sketch of a face and figure which were not those of Mrs. Rogers. And that was a failure too.

CHAPTER IV

There was a certain truth in Hardy's description of Ted Haviland. Ted had all a baby's fascination, a baby's irresponsibility, and a baby's rigid tenacity of purpose. There perhaps the likeness ended. At any rate, Ted had contrived to plan a career for himself at the age of seven, had said nothing about it for ten years, and then quietly carried it through in spite of circumstances and the influential members of his family. These powers had been against him from the first. His mother had died in giving him birth; and as his father chose to hold him directly responsible for the tragedy, his early years were passed somewhat under a cloud. Katherine was his only comfort and stay. The girl had five years the start of him, which gave her an enormous advantage in dealing with the uncertain details of life. Her method was simplicity itself. It was summed up in the golden rule: Take your own way first, and then let other people take theirs. It was in this spirit that, mounted on a table, she painted the great battle-piece that covered the north wall of the nursery; and with equal heroism she met the unrighteous Nemesis that waits upon mortal success, and skipped off to bed at three o'clock in the afternoon as if to a tea-party. Ted worshipped his sister, because of her courage and resource, because of her fuzzy black hair cut short like a boy's, for the strength of her long limbs, and for a hundred other reasons. And Katherine loved Ted with a passion all the more intense because he was the only creature she knew that would let itself be loved comfortably; for "Papa" was an abstraction, and "Nurse" erred on the opposite extreme, being a terribly concrete reality, with a great many acute angles about her, which was a drawback to demonstrations of affection.

One day Katherine mixed some colours for Ted and taught him how to manage a pencil and paint-brush. That was just before she went to school, and then Ted said to himself, "I too will paint battle-pieces"; and he painted them in season and out of season, and was obliged to hide them away in drawers and cupboards and places, for there was no one to care for them now that Kathy was gone. As for that headstrong young person, her method was so far successful that when she was eighteen it began to be rumoured in the family that

Katherine would do great things, but that Ted was an idle young beggar. The boy had shown no talent for anything in particular, and nobody had thought of his future: not Katherine—she was too busy with her own—and certainly not his father, who at the best of times lived piously in the past with the memory of his dead wife, and was day by day loosening his hold upon the present. For Ted "Papa" became more and more an abstraction, until a higher Power withdrew him altogether from earthly affairs.

Mr. Haviland had lived in a melancholy gentility on a pension which died with him, and at his death the children were left with nothing but the pittance they inherited from their mother. When the family met in solemn conclave to decide the fate of Katherine and Ted, it learned that Katherine, true to her old principles, had taken the decision into her own hands. She meant to live for art and by art, and Uncle James was much mistaken if he thought that an expensive training was to be flung away upon a "niggling amateur." At any rate, she had taken a studio in Pimlico and furnished it, and as she had come of age yesterday, there was really no more to be said. Ted, of course, would live with her, and choose his own profession. But Ted's profession was not so easily chosen. The boy had brought a perfectly open mind to the subject, and discussed the reasons for and against the Church, the Bar, the Bank, and a trade, with admirable clearness and impartiality; but when invited to make a selection from among the four, he betrayed no enthusiasm. Finally he was asked if he had any objection to the medical profession, and replied that he had none, having, indeed, never thought about it. On the whole, he considered that the idea was not a bad one, and he would try it. He tried it for a year and a half, but not altogether with success. He had been advised to take up surgery, for a great man had noticed his long sensitive fingers, and told him that he had the hands of a born surgeon. He managed to get through the hours in the dissecting-room, standing on his head from time to time as a precaution against faintness; but his heroism gave way before the horrors of the theatre. Soon, with indignation naturally mingled with pleasure at this fulfilment of its own predictions, the family heard that Ted had flung up the medical profession. That the boy had the hands of a born surgeon was considered to be an aggravation of his offence; it constituted it flying in the face of Providence. When Ted drew attention to the fact that he had passed first in Comparative Anatomy, his uncle James told him that stupidity was excusable, and that his abilities only proved him a lazy good-for-nothing fellow. He then offered him a berth in his office, with board and lodging in his own house; and as Ted was in low water, there was nothing for it but to accept. Mr. James Pigott remained master of the situation, without a suspicion of its pathetic irony. Ted, whose intellect was incapable of adding two and two together, had to sit on a high stool and work endless sums in arithmetic. Ted, whose soul was married *sub rosa* to ideal beauty, had to live in a house where every object had the same unwinking self-complacent ugliness, and where the cook was the only artist whose genius was appreciated. Ted was a little bit of a Stoic, and he could have borne the long impressive dinners and the unstudied malice of the furniture, if only his uncle would have let him alone. But Mr. Pigott was nothing if not conscientious; and now that he had him under his thumb, he made superhuman efforts to understand his nephew's character and to win his confidence. The poor gentleman might just as well have tried to understand the character of an asymptote, or to win the confidence of a Will-o'-the-wisp; and nothing but misery can come of it when a middle-aged city merchant, born without even a rudimentary sense of humour, suddenly determines to cultivate that gift for the benefit of a boy who can detect humour in the wording of an invoice.

Well, he never knew how it happened—his mind might have been running on an illustrated edition of the cash accounts of Messrs. Pigott & Co.—but at last Ted made an arithmetical blunder so unprecedented, so astounding, that a commercial career was closed to him for ever. "Stupidity is excusable," said Uncle James. "If you had been stupid, I would have forgiven you; but you have ability enough, sir, and it follows that you are careless—criminally careless—and I wash my hands of you." And, like Pilate, he suited the action to the word.

So it happened that as Katherine was putting the last touches to her great picture "The Witch of Atlas," and to her sketch of an elaborate future, Fate stepped in and altered all her arrangements. She called it Fate, for she never could bring herself to say it was Ted. For months she had been living in a dream, in which she was no longer a poor artist toiling in a London garret: she was on the highest peak of Atlas, in the land where, as you know, dreams last forever, where the light comes down unfiltered through the transcendental air, and where, owing to the unmelting ice and snow, the shadows are always colours. To live for art and by art—she had not yet realised the incompatibility of these two aims; for Katherine was as uncompromising in this as in everything else, and refused to work in a liberal and enlightened spirit. She believed that beauty is the only right or possible or conceivable aim of the artist, and she was ready to sacrifice a great deal for this belief. For this she slept and worked in one room, which she left bare of all but necessary furniture—under which head, in defiance of all laws of political economy, she included a small Pantheon of plaster deities: for this she stinted herself in everything except air and exercise, which were cheap; and for this she refused to join housekeeping with her cousin Nettie, thereby giving lasting offence to an influential branch of the family. At the end of three years she had begun to hope, and to feel the quickening of new powers; and as her nature expanded, her art took on a subtler quality, a subdued and delicate sensuousness, which, it must be owned, had very little in common with the flesh and blood of ordinary humanity.

She was painting steadily, in a pallid fervour of concentrated excitement, the ease of her pliant hands contrasting with her firm lips and knitted brows, when Ted burst into the studio, with a thin Gladstone bag in one hand and a fat portfolio in the other. His face told her of a crisis in his history; it was humorous, pathetic, deprecating, and determined, all at once,—not the face of a boy dropping in casually at tea-time. When asked if anything had gone wrong at the office, he replied, "Probably—by this time. They lost their brightest ornament this morning. You see they said—among other things—that it wasn't the least use my stopping, as I hadn't any head for figures,—which was odd, considering that it's just with figures I've been most successful." But Katherine was to judge for herself. He sat down leisurely and began untying his portfolio. Then he caught sight of "The Witch of Atlas." "That's going to be a stunning picture, Kathy," said he. He stood before the canvas for a moment, and then turned abruptly away. When he looked at Katherine again, his face was set and a little flushed. He seemed to be making a calculation—a thing he had always some difficulty in doing. "You've been at it practically all your life; but it took you—one—two—three—five years' real hard work, didn't it, before you could paint like that?"

"Yes, Ted, five years' hard labour, with costs."

"It'll take me four. Thank heaven, I've learnt anatomy!"

Katherine said nothing: she had opened the portfolio and spread out the drawings, and was hanging over them in amazement. How, when, and where the boy had done the things, she could not imagine. There were finished studies in anatomy, of heads and limbs in every conceivable attitude. There were shilling drawing-books crammed with illustrations of most possible subjects and some impossible ones; loose sketches done on the backs of envelopes, the fly-leaves of books, and (fearful revelation of artistic depravity!) the ruled pages of ledgers. And in every one of them there was power and wild exuberant vitality. It was genius, rampant and undisciplined, but unmistakable; and she told him so. Her first feeling sent the blood to her cheeks for pure joy; her second drove it back to her heart again. Katherine was one of those people who can see a thing instantly, in all its possible bearings; and at the present moment she saw clearly, not only that Ted was a genius, but that his genius had everything to learn, and that it would take the whole of his tiny income to teach it, while the necessities of his board and lodging in the meanwhile would more than double her own expenses. She saw herself doomed to the production of an unbroken succession of pot-boilers, and for the next few years at least Ted's career was only possible at the sacrifice of her own. "Yes," she said at last, sitting down and tying the strings of the portfolio tenderly, "you'll have to work hard for four or five years or so; and then you'll have to wait. Art is long, you know, and high art's the longest of all." And when she told him that it would be a great help to her if they clubbed together, Ted actually believed her, so unaware was he of the complexities of life.

Katherine understood why Ted had gone to Guy's Hospital; but when she asked him—idiot!—why he had wasted a year at his uncle Pigott's office, he said that he wanted to prove to his uncle Pigott's limited capacity that he was utterly incapable of managing anybody's business but his own. Katherine asked no more questions, for she was trying to think. Then when she had done thinking, she took the Witch and turned her with her face to the wall. And when she looked at Ted again it was with a choking sensation, and for the first time for three years she was aware that she had a heart beating under the blue overall. She had come down from Atlas faster than she had gone up. After all, the climate there is frightfully cold, and there are passes on that lonely mountain which overhang the bottomless pit, where some have perished very miserably. Katherine had escaped the abyss, and left behind her the dreams and the golden mists and the starry peaks of ice. It was dark in the studio, and a voice was heard inquiring whether the young gentleman was going to stay for supper, "*Because*, if a bysin of hoatmeal porridge yn't enuff for one— —"

Mrs. Rogers was great in the argument *a fortiori*.

CHAPTER V

Audrey had never been able to enjoy the friendship of her own sex for more than ten minutes at a time. Her own society bored her inexpressibly, and that of the women she had known hitherto was uninteresting because it was like her own. But Katherine was unlike all other women, and she had taken Audrey's fancy. Audrey was always devising pretty little excuses for calling, always bringing in hothouse flowers, or the last hothouse novel, which Katherine positively *must* read; until, by dint of a naïve persistency, she won the right to come and go as she pleased. As for Katherine, she considered that a beautiful woman is exempt from criticism; and so long as she could watch Audrey moving about, arranging flowers with dainty fastidious touches, or lying back on the couch in some reckless but perfect pose, she reserved her judgment. She rejoiced in her presence for its beauty's sake. She loved the curves of her limbs, the play of her dimples, the shifting lights in her hair. But she had to pay for the pleasure these things afforded her, and "man's time" became a frequent item in the account. Katherine had set her heart on Ted's studying in Paris for six months, and was trying hard to make enough money to send him there. With this absorbing object in view, she herself worked equally well whether Audrey were in the studio or out of it; but it seemed that Ted's powers were either paralysed or diverted into another channel from the moment she came in. The baby was trying to solve a problem which had puzzled wiser heads than his. But he had no clue to the labyrinth of Audrey's soul; he was not even certain whether she was an intelligent being, though to doubt it was blasphemy against the divine spirit of beauty.

His researches took him very often to Chelsea Gardens, and most of his spare time not spent there was employed in running errands to and fro. Owing to these distractions his nerves became quite unhinged, and for the first time in his life he began to show signs of a temper. He had been full of the Paris scheme at first, but he had not spoken of it now for at least a month.

He had just sat down for the twentieth time to a study of Katherine's head as "Sappho," and had thrown down his palette in disgust, exclaiming—

"What's the use of keeping your mouth still, if your confounded eyes giggle?" when a note arrived from Miss Craven.

You can't step out of a violent passion all in a minute, and perhaps that was the reason why Ted's hands trembled a little as he tore open the envelope and read—

"Dear Mr. Haviland,—Do come over at once. I'm in a dreadful fix, and want your advice and help badly. I would ask your sister, only I know she is always busy.—Sincerely yours,

"Audrey Craven."

Audrey wrote on rough-edged paper, in the bold round hand they teach in schools. She had modelled hers on another girl's, and she signed her name with an enormous A and a flourish. People said there was a great deal of character in her hand-writing.

Ted crammed the note hastily into his pocket, and did his best to hide the radiance of his smile.

"It's only Miss Craven. I'm just going over for half an hour,—I'll be back for tea."

And before Katherine had time to answer he was gone.

Ted's first thought as he entered Miss Craven's drawing-room was that she was in the midst of a removal. The place was turned topsy-turvy. Curtains had been taken down, ornaments removed from their shelves, pictures from their hangings; and the grand piano stood where it had never yet been allowed to stand, in a draught between the window and the door. Tripping over a Persian rug, he saw that the floor was littered with tapestries and rich stuffs of magnificent design. On his left was a miscellaneous collection of brass and copper ware, on his right a heap of shields and weapons of barbarous warfare. On all the tables and cabinets there stood an array of Venetian glass, and statuettes in bronze, marble, and terra-cotta. He was looking about for Miss Craven, when that lady arose from a confused ocean of cushions and Oriental drapery—Aphrodite in an "Art" tea-gown. She greeted him with childlike effusion.

"At last! I'm so glad you've come—I was afraid you mightn't. Help me out of this somehow—I'm simply distracted."

And she pointed to the floor with a gesture of despair.

"Yes; but what do you want me to do?"

"Why, to offer suggestions, advice, anything—only speak."

Ted looked about him, and his eyes rested on the grand piano. "Is it a ball, a bazaar, or an auction? And are we awake or dreaming, alive or dead?"

"Can't you see, Mr. Haviland?"

"Yes, I see a great many things. But what does it all mean?"

Audrey sank on to an ottoman, and answered slowly and incisively, looking straight before her—

"It means that I'm sick of the hideousness of life, of the excruciating lower middle-class arrangement of this room. I don't know how I've stood it all these years. My soul must have been starved—stifled. I want to live in another atmosphere, to be surrounded by beautiful things. Don't laugh like that,—I know I'm not an artist; I couldn't paint a picture—how could I? I haven't been taught. But I know that Art is the only thing worth caring about. I want to cultivate my sense of beauty, and I don't want my room to look like anybody else's."

"It certainly doesn't at present."

"Please be serious. You're not helping me one bit. Look at that pile of things Liberty's have sent me! First of all, I want you to choose between them. Then I want you to suggest a colour-scheme, and to tell me the difference between Louis Quinze and Louis Quatorze (I *can't* remember), whether it'll do to mix Queen Anne with either. And whether would you have old oak, real old oak, or Chippendale, for the furniture? and must I do away with the cosy corner?"

Ted felt his head going round and round. Artistic delight in Audrey's beauty, pagan adoration of it, saintly belief in it, the first tremor of crude unconscious passion, mingled with intense amusement, reduced him to a state of utter bewilderment. But he had sufficient presence of mind to take her last question first and to answer authoritatively—

"Certainly. A cosy corner is weak-minded and conventional."

"Yes, it is. I'm not in the least conventional, and I don't think I'm weak-minded. And I want my room to express my character, to be a bit of myself. So give me some ideas. You don't mind my asking you, do you? You're the only artist I know."

"Am I really? And if you knew six or seven artists, what then?"

"Why, then—I should ask you all the same, of course."

Boy-like he laughed for pure pleasure, and boy-like he tried to dissemble his emotion, and did her bidding under a faint show of protest. He gave his vote in favour of Venetian glass and a small marble Diana, against majolica and a French dancing-girl in terra-cotta; he made an intelligent choice from amongst the various state-properties around him, and avoided committing himself on the subject of Louis Quatorze. On one point Audrey was firm. For what reasons nobody can say, but some Malay creeses had caught her fancy, and no argument could dissuade her from arranging them over the Neapolitan Psyche which she had kept at Ted's suggestion. The gruesome weapons, on a background of barbaric gold, hung above that pathetic torso, like a Fate responsible for its mutilation. Audrey was pleased with the effect; she revelled in strong contrasts and grotesque combinations, and if Liberty's had sent her a stuffed monkey, she would have perched him on Psyche's pedestal.

"I know a man," said Ted, when he had disposed the last bit of drapery according to an ingenious colour-scheme, in which Audrey's hair sounded a brilliant staccato note—"a first-rate artist—who was asked to decorate a lady's room. What do you think he did? He made her take all the pictures off the walls, and he covered them over with little halfpenny Japanese fans, and stuck little halves and quarters of fans in the corners and under the ceiling. Then he put a large Japanese umbrella in the fireplace, and went away smiling."

"Was the lady pleased?"

"Immensely. She asked all her friends to a Japanese tea-party in Mr. Robinson's room. The rest of the furniture was early Victorian."

This anecdote was not altogether to Audrey's taste. She walked to a shelf where Ted had put some bronzes, looked at them with a decided air of criticism, and arranged them differently. Having asserted her independence, she replied severely—

"Your friend's friend must have been an extremely silly woman."

"Not at all; she was a most intelligent, well-informed person, with—er—a deep sense of religion."

"And now, Mr. Haviland, you're making matters worse. You care nothing about her religion; you simply think her a fool, and you meant that I'm like her. Else why did you tell such a pointless story?"

"Forgive me; the association of ideas was irresistible. You *are* like her—in your utter simplicity and guileless devotion to an ideal."

He looked all round the room again, and sank back on the sofa cushions all limp with laughter.

"I—I never saw anything so inexpressibly sad as this afternoon's work; it's heartrending."

His eye fell on the terra-cotta Parisienne dancing inanely on her pedestal, and he moaned like one in pain. Audrey's mouth twitched and her cheeks flamed for a second. She turned her back on Ted, until his fit had spent itself, dying away among the cushions in low gurgles. Then there was silence.

Ted raised his head and looked up. She was still standing in the same place, but one hand was moving slowly towards her pocket.

He sprang to his feet and faced her. She walked to the window, convulsively grasping her pocket-handkerchief.

He followed her.

"Miss Craven—dear Miss Craven—on my soul—I swear—I never—— Can't you—won't you believe me?"

Still there was silence and an averted head.

"Speak, can't you!"

He leant against the window and began to giggle again. Audrey turned at the sound, and looked at him through eyes veiled with tears; her lips were trembling a little, and her fingers relaxed their convulsive grasp. He darted forward, seized her hand, and kissed it an indefinite number of times, exclaiming incoherently—

"Brute, hound, cur that I am! Forgive me—only say you'll forgive me! I know I'm not fit to live! And yet, how could I tell? Good heavens! what funny things women are?" Here he took possession of the little lace pocket-handkerchief, and wiped her eyes very gently. Then he kissed her once on the mouth, reverently but deliberately.

To do Audrey justice, she had meant to sustain her part with maidenly reserve, but she was totally unprepared for this acceleration of the march of events. She said nothing, but went back submissively to her sofa, hand in hand with Ted. There they sat for a minute looking rather stupidly into each other's faces.

The lady was the first to recover her self-possession. She raised her hand with a benedictory air and let it rest lightly, ever so lightly, on Ted's hair.

"My dear boy," she murmured, "I forgave you all the time."

Now there is nothing that will dwarf the proportions of the grand passion and bring you to your sober senses sooner than being patted on the head and called "My dear boy" by the lady of your love. Ted ducked from under the delicate caress, and rose to his feet with dignity. His emotion was spent, and he was chiefly conscious of the absurdity of the situation. Every object in that ridiculous room accentuated the distasteful humour of the thing. Psyche looked downcast virgin disapproval from her pedestal under the Malay creeses, and the frivolous little Parisienne flung her skirts abroad in the very abandonment of derision.

If only he hadn't made a fool of himself, if only he hadn't told that drivelling story about the Japanese umbrella, if only he hadn't laughed in that frantic manner, and if only — — But no, he could not look back on the last five minutes. The past was a grey blank, but the flaming episode of the kiss had burnt a big black hole in his present consciousness. He felt that by that rash, unpardonable act he had desecrated the holy thing; and with it all, had forestalled, delayed, perhaps for ever prevented, the sanction of some diviner opportunity. If he had only waited another year, she could not have called him her dear boy.

"I'm fully aware," he said, ruefully, "that I've behaved like a heaven-afflicted idiot, and I'd better go."

"No, you shall not go. You shall stay. I wish it. Sit down—here."

She patted the sofa beside her, and he obeyed mechanically.

"Poor, poor Ted! I *do* forgive you. We will never misunderstand each other again—never. And now I want to talk to you. What distressed me so much just now was not anything that you said or thought about *me*, but the shocking way you treat yourself and what is best in you. Can't you understand it? You know how I believe in you and hope for you, and it was your affectation of indifference to things which are a religion to me—as they are to you—that cut me to the heart."

She had worked herself up till she believed firmly in this little fiction. Yes, those tears were tears of pure altruism—tears not of wounded vanity and self-love, but of compassion for an erring genius.

She drew back her head proudly and looked him full in the face. Then she continued, in a subdued voice, with a certain incisive tremor in it, the voice that is usually expressive of the deeper emotions—

"You know, and I know, that there is nothing worth caring about except art. Then why pretend to despise it as you do? And Katherine's every bit as bad as you are,—she encourages you. I know—what perhaps she doesn't—that you have great enthusiasms, great ideals; but you are unfaithful to them. You laughed at me; you know you did— —"

("I didn't," from Ted.)

"— —because I'm trying to make my life beautiful. You're led away by your strong sense of humour, till you see something ridiculous in the loveliest and noblest things" (Ted's eyes wandered in spite of himself to the little lady in terra-cotta). "I know why: you're afraid of being sentimental. But if people have feelings, why should they be ashamed of them? Why should they mind showing them? Now I want you to promise me that, from this day forth, you'll take yourself and your art seriously; that you'll work hard—you've been idling shamefully lately" (oh, Audrey! whose fault was that?)—"and finish some great picture before the year's out" (he had only five weeks to do it in, but that was a detail). "Now promise."

"I—I'll promise anything," stammered the miserable Ted, "if only you'll look at me like that—sometimes, say between the hours of seven and eight in the evening."

"Ridiculous baby! Now we must see about the pictures; we've just time before tea."

The mention of tea was a master-stroke; it brought them both back to the world of fact, and restored the familiar landmarks.

Ted, solemnly penitent, gave his best attention to the pictures: there was not a trace of his former abominable levity in the air with which he passed sentence on each as Audrey brought them up for judgment. But when he came to the family portraits he suspended his verdict, and Audrey was obliged to take the matter into her own hands.

She took up a small picture in a square frame and held it close to Ted's face.

"Portrait of my uncle, the Dean of St. Benedict's. What shall I do with it?"

"That depends entirely on the amount of affection you feel for the original."

"H'm—does it? He's a dear old thing, and I'm very fond of him, but—what do you think of him?—from an artistic point of view?"

She stood with her body curved a little backwards, holding the Dean up high in a good light. Her attitude was so lovely that it was impossible to disapprove of her. Ted's reason tottered on its throne, and he laughed, which was perhaps the best thing he could have done.

"He is not, strictly speaking, handsome."

"No," said Audrey; "I'm afraid he'll have to go."

She knelt down beside the portrait of a lady. It was evidently the work of an inferior artist, but his most malignant efforts had failed to disguise the beauty of the face. It bore a strong resemblance to Audrey, but it was the face of an older woman, grave, intelligent, and refined by suffering.

"I've been obliged to take this down," she said, as if apologising more to herself than Ted, "because I want to hang my large photo of the Sistine Madonna in its place."

"What is it?"

"It's—my mother's portrait. She died when I was a very little girl, and I hardly ever saw her, you know. I'm not a bit like her."

He stood silent, watching her intently as she spoke.

"Family portraits," she continued, "may be interesting, but they are not decorative. Unless, of course," she added, hastily, being at a loss to account for the peculiar expression of Ted's face, "they're very old ones—Lelys and Sir Joshua Reynoldses."

"That face does not look old, certainly."

"No. She died young."

She had not meant to say that; a little shiver went through her as the words passed her lips, and she felt a desire to change the subject. But the portrait of the late Mrs. Craven was turned to the wall along with the Dean.

"Hullo!" exclaimed Ted, taking up a photo in a glass frame, hand-painted, "here's old Hardy! What on earth is he doing here?"

Audrey blushed, but answered with unruffled calm.

"Vincent? Oh, he's a family portrait too. He's my cousin—first cousin, you know."

"What are you going to do with *him*?"

"I—I hardly know."

She took the photo out of his hands and examined it carefully back and front. Then she looked at Ted.

"What *shall* I do with him? Is he to go too?"

"Well, I suppose he ought to. He's all very well in his own line, but—from an artistic point of view—he's not exactly—decorative."

"Poor old Vincent! No, he's not."

And Vincent was turned face downward among the ruins of the cosy corner, and Audrey and Ted rested from their labours.

When Ted had gone, the very first thing Audrey did was to get a map and to look out the Rocky Mountains. There they were, to be sure, just as Vincent had described them, a great high wall dividing the continent. At that moment Hardy was kneeling on the floor of his little shanty, busy sorting bearskins and thinking of Audrey and bears. He had had splendid sport—that is, he had succeeded in killing a grizzly just before the grizzly killed him. How nervous Audrey would feel when she got the letter describing that encounter! Then he chose the best and fluffiest bearskin to make a nice warm cape for her, and amused himself by picturing her small oval chin nestling in the brown fur. And then he fell to wondering what she was doing now.

He would have been delighted if he could have seen her poring over that map with her pencilled eyebrows knit, while she traced the jagged outlines of the Rockies with her finger-nail, congratulating herself on the height of that magnificent range.

Yes, there was a great deal between her and her cousin Mr. Hardy.

CHAPTER VI

One fine morning in latter spring, about four months after the day of the transformation scene in Audrey's drawing-room, Ted Haviland was lying on his back sunning himself on the leads. There are many lovelier places even in London than the leads of No. 12 Devon Street, Pimlico, but none more favourable to high and solitary thinking. Here the roar of traffic is subdued to a murmur hardly greater than the stir of country woods on a warm spring morning—a murmur less obtrusive, because more monotonous. It is the place of all others for one absorbed in metaphysical speculation, or cultivating the gift of detachment. The very chimney-pots have a remote abstracted air; the slopes of the slates rise up around you, shutting you in on three sides, and throwing you so far back on yourself; while before you lies the vast, misty network of roofs, stretching eastward towards the heart of the city, and above you is the open sky. It is even pleasant here on a day like this, a day with all the ardour of summer in it, and all the languor of spring, with the sun warming the slates at your back, and a soft breeze from the river fanning your face. You must go up on to the leads on such a day to feel the beauty and infinity of blue sky, the only beautiful and boundless thing here, where there is no green earth to rival heaven.

Ted had certainly no taste for detachment, but he was so far advanced towards metaphysical speculation that he was engaged in an analysis of sensation. Off and on, ever since that day of unreasonable mirth and subsequent madness, he had been a prey to remorse. He had kept away from Audrey for a fortnight, during which time his imagination had run riot through past, present, and future. Audrey had been sweet and confiding from the first; she had believed in him with childlike simplicity, and when she had trusted to his guidance in her innocent æstheticism, he, like the coarse-minded villain that he was, had made fun of all her dear little arrangements, those pathetic efforts to make her life beautiful. He had made her cry, and then taken a brutal advantage of her tears. To Ted's conscience, in the white-heat of his virgin passion, that premature kiss, the kiss that transformed a boyish fancy into full-grown love, was a crime. And yet she had forgiven him. All the time she had been thinking, not of herself, but of him. Her words, hardly heeded at the moment, came back to him like a dull sermon heard in some exalted mood, and henceforth transfigured in memory. She had done well to reproach him for his frivolity and want of purpose. She was so ready to say pleasant things, that blame from her mouth was sweeter than its praise. It showed that she cared more. By this time he had forgotten the traits that had impressed him less pleasantly.

Happily for him, his passion for Audrey was at first altogether bound up with his art. We are not all geniuses, but to some of us, once perhaps in a lifetime, genius comes in the form of love. To Ted love came in the form of genius, quickening his whole nature, and bringing his highest powers to a sudden birth. He had begun and almost finished the work which Audrey had urged him to undertake, and nobody could say that he had approached his subject in a frivolous spirit. It was a portrait of herself. Ted had been rather inclined to affect the romantic antique: Audrey had been a revelation of the artistic possibilities of modern womanhood, and he turned in disgust from his languid studies of decadent renaissance, or renaissant decadence, to this brilliant type. One corner of the studio was stacked with sketches and little full-length portraits of Audrey. Audrey from every point of view. Audrey in a black Gainsborough hat, Audrey with brown fur about her throat, Audrey half-smothered in billowy silk and chiffon, Audrey as she appeared at a dance in a simple frock and sash, and Audrey in a tailor-made gown, in the straight lines of which Ted professed to have discovered new principles of beauty. In fact, he dreamed of founding a New Art on portraits of Audrey alone. From which it would appear that he was taking himself and his art very seriously indeed.

Audrey had just left him after a protracted sitting, and up among the dreamy chimney-pots he was reviving in fancy the sensations of the morning. He was brought back from his ecstasy by Katherine's voice calling, "Ted, come down this minute—I've got something to show you"; and, rousing himself very much against the grain, he dropped languidly into the room below.

Katherine had come in all glowing with excitement. She pushed back her broad-brimmed hat from her forehead, and thrust both hands into her coat-pockets, bringing out two loose heaps of gold.

"There!" she said, letting sovereigns and half-sovereigns drip on to the table with an impressive chink, "aren't you thankful that I wasn't murdered, walking through the great sinful city with all that capital about me?"

"What's up? Has our uncle climbed down, or have you been robbing a till?"

"Neither. I've been to the bank, cashing real live cheques. Five pounds for my black-and-white for the Saint Abroad, I mean the "Woman at Home." Fifteen pounds for Miss Maskelyne's prize bull-dog (I idealised him). Twenty pounds for Lady Stodart's prize baby. Total, forty pounds." She arranged the sovereigns in neat little piles on the table. "That's enough to take you to Paris and set you going." Ted started, and his face fell a little. "It's positively my only dream that ever came true. Picture it, think of it, just on the brink of it. You can start next week, to-morrow if you like!"

Ted's face turned a deep crimson, and he was silent.

"Then Audrey's promised me twenty for a copy of the Botticelli Madonna; I began it yesterday. That'll be enough to keep you on another month, if you want it, and bring you home again."

Still Ted said nothing. He sat down and buried his face in his hands. Katherine knelt down and put her arm tight round his neck.

"Ted, you duffer, do you really care so much? I *am* so glad. I didn't know you'd take it that way."

He drew back and looked her mournfully in the face.

"Kathy, you're an angel; it's awfully good of you; but I—I can't take it, you know."

"Why not? Too proud?"

"No—rubbish! It does seem an infernal shame not to, when you've scraped it together with your dear little paws; but—well—don't think me a brute—I don't know that I want to go to Paris now."

"Not to go to Paris?"

"No."

"Idiot!"

"Kathy, which Botticelli did she ask you to do for her?"

"The one you got so excited about, with St. John and the angel—right-hand side opposite you as you go in. Come, I can see through that trick, and I'm not going to stand any nonsense."

"It isn't nonsense."

"It is. Why, you were raving about Meissonier last year."

"Yes, last year; but——"

"Well?" Katherine rose and gazed at him with the austerity of an inquisitor. Ted gave an uneasy laugh.

"I've been thinking that you and I between us could found a school of our own this year. I've got the eccentricity, and you've got the cheek. We should build ourselves an everlasting name."

"Do be serious; I shall lose my temper in another minute. Is it the wretched money you're thinking of?"

"No, it isn't the money altogether." He got up and walked to his easel.

"Then, oh Ted, you know that Paris—Paris in May—must be simply divine!"

"Why don't you go yourself?"

"No, no; that's not the same thing at all. I don't want to go; besides, I can't. I haven't the time."

"Well, to tell you the truth, Kathy, no more can I. I haven't the time either." He took up his palette and brushes and began carefully touching up the canvas before him.

"Oh—h!" She stared at him for a minute in silence. Ted looked up suddenly; their eyes met, and he set his face like a flint.

"Kathy," he said, slowly, "I've behaved in the most ungrateful and abominable manner. I should like to go to Paris very much, and I—I think I'll start next week."

"Thank you, dear boy; it's the very least you can do."

And they dropped the subject. Ted was the first to speak again.

"By-the-bye, what's on to-morrow morning, Kathy?"

"National Gallery for me." She looked up from her work and saw Ted standing with his hands in his pockets, gazing with an agonised expression at his portrait of Audrey.

"I suppose *she* is going to sit again?"

"Well, yes; she may look in for another hour in the morning perhaps."

Ted was not skillful in deceit, and something in his manner told Katherine that the sitting somehow depended on her absence. She began to see dimly why he had been so frightened at the idea of going to Paris. She looked over her shoulder.

"You haven't made the corners of her mouth turn up enough. It's just as well, they turn up too much."

"No, they don't; that's what makes her so pretty."

Katherine went to her work next morning in anything but a cheerful spirit. She had set her heart on Ted's studying abroad; and now Audrey had come in between, frittering away his time, and making him restless and unlike himself. To be sure, his powers had expanded enormously of late; but she was not happy about him, and was half afraid to praise his work. To her mind there was something feverish and unhealthy in its vivid beauty. It suggested genius outgrowing its strength. If Audrey really had anything to do with it, if she was coming in any way between him and the end she dreamed for him, why, then, she could hate Audrey with a deadly hatred. That was what she said to herself just before she opened the front-door and found Audrey standing on the doorstep, looking reprehensibly pretty in a gown of white lawn over green silk. Her wide hat was trimmed with bunches of white tulle and pale green poppies, and she had a little basket full of lilies of the valley hanging from her wrist.

"You wretch!" she cried, shaking a bunch of lilies at Katherine, as she stood in the narrow passage; "you're always going out when I'm coming in."

"And you're always coming in when I'm going out. Isn't it funny?"

Audrey said nothing to that, but she kissed Katherine on both cheeks, and pinned a bunch of lilies at her throat with a little gold pin that she took from her own dress. Then she tripped lightly upstairs, with a swish, swish, of her silk skirts, wafting lilies of the valley as she went. Katherine watched her up the first flight, and the hate died out of her heart. After all, Audrey was so perfect from an artistic point of view that moral disapproval seemed somehow beside the point.'

"May I come in?" asked Audrey, tapping at the open door of the studio. Ted rose with a reverent alacrity, very much as you rise to the musical parts of a solemn service in church. He arranged her chair carefully, with soft cushions for her back and feet. "If you don't mind," said he, "we must work hard, for I want to finish you this morning, or perhaps to-morrow, if you can give me another sitting," and he patted a cushion and held it up for her head.

"You can have any number of sittings," said Audrey, ignoring these preparations for her comfort; "but first of all, I'm going to make your room pretty."

Ted dropped his cushion helplessly and followed her as she moved about the room. First she took off her gloves in a leisurely manner and laid them down among Ted's wet brushes. Then she began to arrange the lilies of the valley in a little copper bowl she found on the chimneypiece. Then she caught sight of her gloves and exclaimed, "Oh, look at my beautiful new gloves, lying among your nasty paints! Why didn't you tell me, you horrid boy?" Then Ted and she tried to clean them with turpentine, and made them worse than ever, and between them they wasted half an hour of the precious morning. After that, Audrey took off her hat and settled herself comfortably among the cushions; she drew her white fingers through her hair till it stood up in a great red aureole round her head, and the sitting began.

Ted's heart gave a bound as he set to work. He had learnt by this time to control the trembling of his hands, otherwise the portrait would never have reached its present perfection. He had painted from many women in the life school, and always with the same emotions, the same reverence for womanhood, and the same delight in his own power, tempered by compassion for the model. But these were so many studies in still life compared with the incarnate loveliness before him—Audrey: it made him feel giddy to paint the edge of the ruffles about her throat, or the tip of her shoe. Her beauty throbbed like pulses of light, it floated in air and went to his head like the scent of her lilies. He had reproduced this radiant, throbbing effect in his picture. It was a head, the delicate oval of the full face relieved against a background of atmospheric gold into which the golden surface tints of the hair faded imperceptibly. The eyebrows were arched a little over the earnest, unfathomable eyes; the lips were parted as if with impetuous breath; the whole head leaned slightly forward, giving prominence to the chin, which in reality retreated, a defect chiefly noticeable in profile. Ted had painted what he saw. It might have been the head of a saint looking for the Beatific Vision; it was only that of an ordinary pretty woman.

As a rule, they both chattered freely during the sittings. This is, of course, necessary, if the artist is to know his sitter's face with all its varying expressions; and Audrey had given Ted a great many to choose from. This morning, however, he worked steadily and in a silence which she was the first to break.

"What do you mean by talking about one more sitting in that way? You said you'd want six yesterday."

"I did, but——" He leaned back and began tilting his chair to and fro. "The fact is—I'm awfully sorry, but I'm afraid I'm going to leave England." The young rascal had chosen his words with a deliberate view to effect, and Audrey's first thoughts flew to America, though not to Hardy. She moved suddenly in her chair.

"To emigrate? You, with your genius? Surely not!"

"No, rather not; it's not as bad as all that. But—I'm afraid I have to go to Paris for six months or so."

"Whatever for?"

"Well—I must, you see."

"Must you? And for six months, too; why?"

"Because I—that is—I want to study for a bit in the schools there."

"Oh,"—she leaned back again among her cushions, and looked down at her hands clasped demurely,—"if you want to go, that's another thing."

"It isn't another thing; and I don't want to go, as it happens."

"Then I am sure you needn't go and study; what can they teach you that you don't know?" she leaned forward and looked into his face. "You're not going in for that horrid French style, surely?"

"Well, I'd some thoughts——" he hesitated, and Audrey took courage.

"It can't be—it mustn't be! Oh, do, do give up the idea—for *my* sake! It'll be your ruin as an artist." She had risen to her feet, and was gazing at him appealingly.

"You dear little thing, what do you know about the French school or any other?"

"Everything. I take in 'Modern Art,' and I read all the magazines and things, and—I know all about it."

"You don't know anything about it. All the same——" he paused, biting his lip.

"All the same, what?"

"If I thought you cared a straw whether I went or stayed——"

"Haven't I shown you that I care?"

"No, you haven't."

"Ted!" Audrey made that little word eloquent of pleading, reproachful pathos; but he went on—

"For heaven's sake, don't talk any more rot about art and my genius! Anybody can do it. Do you think that's what I want to hear from you?" He checked himself suddenly. "I beg your pardon. Now I think we'll go on, if you don't mind sitting a little longer."

"But I do mind. Either you're very rude, or—I can't understand you. Why do you speak to me like this?" She had picked up her hat and begun playing with its long pins. As she spoke she stabbed it savagely in the crown. The nervous action of her hands contrasted oddly with the pensive Madonna-like pose of her head, but the corners of her mouth were turned up more than ever, and the tip of her little Roman nose was trembling. Then she drew the pins slowly out of her hat, and made as if she would put it on. Ted tried to reason, but he could only grasp two facts clearly—that in another second she would be gone, and that if he left things as they stood he would have to exchange London for Paris. He leaned against the wall for support, and looked steadily at Audrey as he spoke.

"You think me a devil, and I can only prevent that by making you think me a fool. I don't care. I'm insane enough to love you—my curious behaviour must have made that quite obvious. If you'll say that you care for me a little bit, I won't go to Paris. If you won't, I'll go to-morrow and stay there."

Audrey had known for some time that something like this would happen. She had meant it to happen. From the day she first saw Ted Haviland, she had made up her mind to be his destiny; and yet, now that it had happened, though Ted's words made her heart beat uncomfortably fast, a little voice in her brain kept on saying, "Not yet—not yet—not yet." She sat down and tried to collect her thoughts. Ted would be sure to begin again in another second. He did.

"Or if you don't care now, if you'll only say that you might care some day, if you'll say that it's not an utter impossibility, I won't go. I'll wait five years—ten years—on the off chance, and hold my tongue about it too, if you tell me to."

Not yet—not yet—not yet.

"Audrey!"

She started as if a stranger had called her name suddenly, for the voice was not like Ted's at all. Yet it was Ted, Ted in the shabby clothes she had seen him in first, which never looked shabby somehow on him; but it was not the baby as she knew him. He was looking at her almost defiantly, a cloud had come over his eyes, and the muscles of his face were set. Audrey saw the look of unrelenting determination, which is only seen to perfection in the faces of the very young, but it seemed to her that Ted had taken a sudden leap into manhood.

"Audrey," he said again, and their eyes met. She tried to speak, but it was too late. The boy had crouched down on the floor beside her, and was clasping her knees like a suppliant before some marble divinity.

"Don't—Ted, don't," she gasped under her breath.

"I won't. I don't ask you to do it now, before I've made my name. It may take years, but—I shall make it. And then, perhaps——"

She tried to loosen his fingers one by one, and they closed on her hand with a grip like a dying man's. Through the folds of her thin dress she could feel his heart thumping obtrusively, and the air throbbed with the beating of a thousand pulses. Her brain reeled, and the little voice inside it left off saying "Not yet." She stooped down and whispered hurriedly—

"I will—I will."

The suppliant raised his head, and his fingers relaxed their hold.

"You *will*, Audrey? So you don't—at the present moment?"

"I do. It wasn't my fault. I didn't know what love was like. I know now."

Passion is absolutely sincere, but it is not bound to be either truthful or consistent. What has it to do with trains of reasoning, or with the sequence of events in time? Past and future history are nothing to it. For Audrey it was now—now—now. All foreshadowings, all dateless possibilities, were swept out of her fancy; or rather, they were crowded into one burning point of time. Now was the moment for which all other moments had lived and died. Life had owed her some great thing, and now with every heart-beat it was paying back its long arrears. Henceforth there would be no more monotony, no more measuring of existence by the hands of the clock, no more weighing of emotion by the scruple. The revelation had come. Now and for ever it was all the same; for sensation that knows nothing about time is always sure of eternity.

CHAPTER VII

When Katherine came back from the National Gallery she found Ted alone: he had drawn up the couch in front of his easel, and lay there gazing at his portrait. The restless, hungry look had gone from his eyes. There was no triumph there, only an absolute satisfaction and repose. Face and attitude said plainly, "I have attained my heart's desire. I am young in years, but old in wisdom. I know what faith and hope and love are, which is more than you do. I am not in the least excited about them, as you see; I can afford to wait, for these things last for ever. If you like, you may come and worship with me before my heavenly lady's image; but if you do, you must hold your tongue." And Katherine, being a sensible woman, held her tongue. But she took up a tiny pair of white gloves, stained with paint and turpentine, that lay folded on the easel's ledge, and after examining them critically, laid them on Ted's feet without a word. A faint smile flickered across his lips. That was all their confession.

After some inward debate, Katherine determined to go over and see Audrey. She had no very clear notion of what had happened that morning; but she could only think that the ridiculous boy had proposed to Audrey and been accepted. The idea seemed preposterous; for though she had been by no means blind to all that had been going on under her eyes for the last few months, she had never for a moment taken Audrey seriously, or supposed that Ted in his sober senses could do so either. This morning a horrible misgiving had come over her, and she had gone to her work in a tumult of mixed feelings. For the present she had made Ted's career the end and aim of her existence. What she most dreaded for him, next to the pain of a hopeless attachment, was the distraction of a successful one. A premature engagement is the thing of all others to blast a man's career at the outset. What good was it, she asked herself passionately, for her to pinch and save, to put aside her own ambition, to do the journeyman's work that brings pay, instead of the artist's work that brings praise, if Ted was going to fling himself away on the first pretty face that took his fancy? Again the feeling of hatred to Audrey surged up in her heart, and again it died down at the first sight of its object.

Audrey was standing at the window singing a little song to herself. She turned as the door opened, and when she saw Katherine she started ever so slightly, and stood at gaze like a frightened fawn. She was attracted by Katherine, as she was by every personality that she felt to be stronger than her own. Among all artists there is a strain of manhood in every woman, and of womanhood in every man. Katherine fascinated her weaker sister by some such super-feminine charm. At the same time, Audrey was afraid of her, as she had been afraid of Hardy in his passion, or of Ted in his boisterous mirth. There were moments when she thought that Katherine's direct unquestioning gaze must have seen what she hid from her own eyes, must have penetrated the more or less artistic disguises without which she would not have known herself. Now her one anxiety was lest Katherine knew or guessed her treatment of Vincent, and had come to reproach her with it. Owing to some slight similarity of detail, the events of the morning had brought the recollection of that last scene with Hardy uppermost in her mind. She had persuaded herself that her love for Ted was her first experience of passion, as it was his; but at the touch of one awkward memory the bloom was somehow brushed off this little romance. For these reasons there was fear in her grey eyes as she put up her face to Katherine's to be kissed.

"Do you know?" she half whispered. "Has he told you?"

"No, he has told me nothing; but I know."

There was silence as the two women sat down side by side and looked into each other's faces. Katherine's instinct was to soothe and protect the shy creatures that shrank from her, and Audrey in her doubt and timidity appealed to her more than she had ever done in the self-conscious triumph of her beauty. She took her hand, caressing it gently as she spoke.

"Audrey—you won't mind telling me frankly? Are you engaged to Ted?"

True to her imitative instincts, Audrey could be frank with the frank. "Yes, I am. But it's our own little secret, and we don't want anybody to know yet."

"Perhaps you are wise." She paused. How could she make Audrey understand what she had to say? She was not going to ask her to break off her engagement. In the first place, she had no right to do so; in the second place, any interference in these cases is generally fatal to its own ends. But she wanted to make Audrey realise the weight of her responsibility.

"Audrey," she said at last, "do you remember our first meeting, when you thought Ted was a baby?"

"Yes, of course I do. That was only six, seven months ago; and to think that I should be engaged to him now! Isn't it funny?"

"Very funny indeed. But you were perfectly right. He is a baby. He knows no more than a baby does of the world, and of the men in it. Of the women he knows rather less than an intelligent baby."

"I wouldn't have him different. He needn't know anything about other women, so long as he understands *me*."

"Well, the question is, does he understand himself? What's more, are you sure you understand him? Ted is two people rolled into one, and very badly rolled too. The human part of him has hardly begun to grow yet; he's got no practical common-sense to speak of, and only a rudimentary heart."

"Oh, Katherine!"

"Quite true,—it's all I had at his age. But the ideal, the artistic side of him is all but full-grown. That means that it's just at the critical stage now."

"Of course, I suppose it would be." Audrey always said "Of course" when she especially failed to see the drift of what was said to her.

"Yes; but do you realise all that the next few years will do for him? That they will either make or ruin his career as an artist? They ought to be years of downright hard work, of solitary hard work; he ought to have them all to himself. Do you mean to let him have them?"

Audrey lowered her eyes, and sat silent, playing with the ribbons of her dress, while Katherine went on as if to herself—

"He is so young, so dreadfully young. It would have been soon enough in another ten years' time. Oh, Audrey, why did you let it come to this?"

"Well, really, Katherine, I couldn't help it. Besides, one has one's feelings. You talk as if I was going to stand in Ted's way—as if I didn't care a straw. Surely his career must mean more to his wife than it can to his sister? I know you think that because I haven't been trained like you, because I've lived a different life from yours, that I can't love art as you do. You're mistaken. To begin with, I made up my mind ten years ago that whatever I did when I grew up, I wouldn't marry a nonentity. What do you suppose Ted's fascination was, if it wasn't his genius, and his utter unlikeness to anybody else?"

"Geniuses are common enough nowadays; there are plenty more where he came from."

"How cynical you are! You haven't met many people like Ted, have you?"

"No, I haven't. Oh, Audrey, do you *really* care like that? I wonder how I should feel if I were you, and knew that Ted's future lay in my hands, as it lies in yours."

Audrey's cheeks reddened with pleasure. "It does! It does!" She clasped her little hands passionately, as if they were holding Ted and his future tight. "I know it. All I want is to inspire him, to keep him true to himself. Haven't I done it? You know what his work was like before he loved me. Can you say that he ever painted better than he does now, or even one-half as well?"

Katherine could not honestly say that he had; but she smiled as she answered, "No; but for the last six months he has done nothing from anybody but yourself. You make a very charming picture, Audrey, but you can hardly want people to say that your husband can only paint one type."

"My husband can paint as many types as he pleases." Katherine still looked dubious. "Anything more?"

"Yes, one thing. You say you want to keep Ted true to himself, as you put it. He made up his mind this morning to go to Paris to study hard for six months. It means a lot of self-sacrifice for you both, to be separated so soon; but it will be the making of him. You won't let him change his mind? You won't say anything to keep him back, will you?"

Audrey's face had suddenly grown hard, and she looked away from Katherine as she answered, "You're not very consistent, I must say. You can't think Ted such an utter baby if you trust him to go off to Paris all by himself. As to his making up his mind this morning, our engagement alters all that. After all, how can it affect Ted's career if he goes now or three years hence?"

"It makes all the difference."

"I can't see it. And yet—and yet—I wouldn't spoil Ted's chances for worlds." She rose and walked a few paces to and fro. "Let me think, let me think!" She stood still, an image of abstract Justice, with one hand folded over her eyes, and the other clenched as if it held the invisible scales of destiny, weighing her present, overcharged with agreeable sensations, against her lover's future. Apparently, after some shifting of the weights, she had made the two balance, for she clapped her hands suddenly, and exclaimed, with an emphasis on every other word—

"Katherine! An inspiration! We'll go to Paris for our honeymoon, and Ted shall stay there six months—a year—for ever, if he likes. Paris is the place I adore above all others. I shall simply live in that dear Louvre!" She added in more matter-of-fact tones, "And I needn't order my trousseau till I get there. That'll save no end of bother on this side. I hate the way we do things here. For weeks before your wedding-day to have to think of nothing but clothes, clothes, clothes—could anything be more revolting?"

"Yes," said Katherine, "to think of them before a funeral."

Audrey looked offended. Death, like religion, is one of those subjects which it is very bad taste to mention under some circumstances.

Katherine went away more disheartened than ever, and more especially weighed down by the consciousness that she had made a fool of herself. She knew Audrey to be vain, she divined that she was selfish, but at least she had believed that she could be generous. By letting her feel that she held Ted's future in her hands, she had roused all her woman's vague cupidity and passion for power, and henceforth any appeal to her generosity would be worse than useless. With a little of her old artistic egoism, Katherine valued her brother's career very much as a thing of her own making, and the idea of another woman meddling with it and spoiling it was insupportable. It was as if some reckless colourist had taken the Witch of Atlas and daubed her all over with frightful scarlet and magenta. But the trouble at her heart of hearts was the certainty that Audrey, that creature of dubious intellect and fitful emotions, would never be able to love Ted as his wife should love him.

CHAPTER VIII

All true revelations soon seem as old as the hills and as obvious. Yesterday they were not, to-day they have struck you dumb, to-morrow they will have become commonplaces, and henceforth you will be incapable of seeing anything else. So it was with Audrey. Her engagement was barely a week old before she felt that it had lasted for ever. Not that she was tired of it; on the contrary, she hoped everything from Ted's eccentricity. She was sick to death of the polished conventional type—the man who, if he came into her life at all, must be introduced in the recognised way; while Ted, who had dropped into it literally through a skylight, roused her unflagging interest and curiosity. She was always longing to see what the boy would say and do next. Poor Audrey! Her own character was mainly such a bundle of negations that you described her best by saying what she was not; but other people's positive qualities acted on her as a powerful stimulant, and it was one for which she perpetually craved. She had found it in Hardy. In him it was the almost physical charm of blind will, and she yielded to it unwillingly. She had found it in Ted under the intoxicating form of vivid emotion. Life with Vincent would have been an unbroken bondage. Life with Ted would have no tyrannous continuity; it would be a series of splendid episodes. At the same time, it seemed to her that she had always lived this sort of life. Like the "souls" in Ted's ingenious masterpiece, Audrey had suffered a metempsychosis, and her very memory was changed. The change was not so much shown in the character of her dress and her surroundings (Audrey was not the first woman who has tried to be original by following the fashion); these things were only the outward signs of an inward transformation. If her worship of the beautiful was not natural, it was not altogether affected. She really appreciated the things she saw, though she only saw them through as much of Ted's mind as was transparent to her at the moment. It never occurred to her to ask herself whether she would have chosen to stand quite so often on the Embankment watching the sun go down behind Battersea Bridge, or whether she would have sat quite so many hours in the National Gallery looking at those white-faced grey-eyed Madonnas of Botticelli that Ted was never tired of talking about. It was so natural that he should be always with her when she did these things, that it was impossible to disentangle her ideas and say what was her own and what was his. She was not given to self-analysis.

But there were limits to Audrey's capacity for receiving impressions. Between her and the world where Katherine always lived, and which Ted visited at intervals now becoming rarer and rarer, there was a great gulf fixed. After all, Audrey had no grasp of the impersonal; she could only care for any object as it gave her certain emotions, raised certain associations, or drew attention to herself. She was at home in the dim borderland between art and nature, the region of vanity and vague sensation. Here she could meet Ted halfway and talk to him about ideals for the hour together. But in the realm of pure art, as he had told her when she once said that she liked all his pictures because they were his, personalities count for nothing; you must have an eye for the thing itself, and the thing itself was the one thing that Audrey could not see. In that world she was a pilgrim and a stranger; it was peopled with shadowy fantastic rivals, who left her with no field and no favour; flesh and blood were powerless to contend against them. They excited no jealousy—they were too intangible for that; but in their half-seen presence she had a sense of helpless irritation and bewilderment—it baffled, overpowered, and humiliated her. To a woman thirsting for a great experience, it was hard to find that the best things lay always just beyond her reach; that in Ted's life, after all of it that she had absorbed and made her own, there was still an elusive something on which she had no hold. Not that she allowed this reflection to trouble her happiness long. As Katherine had said, Ted was two people very imperfectly rolled into one. Consciously or unconsciously, it became more and more Audrey's aim to separate them, to play off the one against the other. This called for but little skill on her part. Ted's passion at its white-heat had fused together the boy's soul and the artist's, but at any temperature short of that its natural effect was disintegration. Audrey had some cause to congratulate herself on the result. It might or might not have been flattering to be called a "clever puss" or an "imaginative minx" (Ted chose his epithets at random), whenever she pointed out some novel effect of colour or picturesque grouping; but it was now July, and

Ted had not done a stroke of work since he put the last touches to her portrait in April.

It was now July, and from across the Atlantic came the first rumours of Hardy's return. Within a month, or six weeks at the latest, he would be in England, in London. The news set Audrey thinking, and think as she would the question perpetually recurred, Whether would it be better to announce her engagement to Ted, or still keep it a secret, still drift on indefinitely as they had done for the last four months? If Audrey had formed any idea of the future at all, it was as a confused mirage of possibilities: visions of express trains in which she and Ted were whirled on for ever through strange landscapes; visions of Parisian life as she pictured it—a series of exquisite idyls, the long days of quivering sunlight under blue skies, the brief languid nights dying into dawn, coffee and rolls brought to you before you get up, strawberries eaten with claret instead of cream because cream makes you ill in hot climates, the Paris of fiction and the Paris of commonplace report; and with it all, scene after scene in which she figured as doing a thousand extravagant and interesting things, always dressed in appropriate costumes, always making characteristic little speeches to Ted, who invariably replied with some delicious absurdity. The peculiarity of these scenes was, that though they succeeded each other through endless time, yet neither she nor Ted ever appeared a day older in them. As Audrey's imagination borrowed nothing from the past, it had no sense of the demands made by the future. Now, although in publicly announcing her engagement to Ted she would give a fixity to this floating phantasmagoria which would rob it of half its charm, on the other hand she felt the need of some such definite and stable tie to secure her against Vincent's claim, the solidity of which she now realised for the first time. Unable to come to any conclusion, she continued to think.

The news from America had set old Miss Craven thinking too. She had at first rejoiced at Audrey's intimacy with the Havilands, for various reasons. She was glad to see her settling down—for the first time in her volatile life—into a friendship with another girl; to hear of her being interested in picture-galleries; to find a uniform gaiety taking the place of the restless, captious moods which made others suffer besides herself. As for the boy, he was a nice clever boy who would make his way in the world; but he was only "the boy." Three months ago, if anybody had told Miss Craven that there was a possibility of an engagement between Audrey and Ted Haviland, she would have laughed them to scorn. But when it gradually dawned on her that Katherine hardly ever called at the house with her brother, that he and Audrey went everywhere together, and Katherine never made a third in their expeditions, it occurred to her that she really ought to speak a word in season. Her only difficulty was to find the season. After much futile watching of her opportunity, she resolved to trust to the inspiration of the moment. Unfortunately, the moment of the inspiration happened to be that in which Audrey came in dressed for a row up the river, and chafing with anxiety because Ted was ten minutes behind time. This at once suggested the subject in hand. But Miss Craven began cautiously—

"Audrey, my dear, do you think you've enough wraps with you? These evenings on the river are treacherous."

Audrey gave an impatient twitch to a sort of Elizabethan ruff she wore round her neck.

"How tiresome of Ted to be late, when I particularly told him to be early!"

"Is Miss Haviland going with you? Poor girl, she looks as if a blow on the river would do her good."

"N-no, she isn't."

"H'm—you'd better wait and have some tea first?"

"I've waited quite long enough already. We're going to drive to Hammersmith, and we shall get tea there or at Kew."

"I don't want to interfere with your amusements, but doesn't it strike you as—er—a little imprudent to go about so much with 'Ted,' as you call him?"

"No, of course not. He's not going to throw me overboard. It's the most natural thing in the world that I should go with him."

"Yes—to you, my dear, and I daresay to the young man himself. But if you are seen together, people are sure to talk."

"Let them. I don't mind in the least—I rather like it."

"*Like* it?"

"Yes. You must own it's flattering. People here wouldn't take the trouble to talk if I were nobody. London isn't Oxford."

"No; you may do many things in Oxford which you mayn't do in London. But times have changed. I can't imagine your dear mother saying she would 'like' to be talked about."

"Please don't speak about mother in that way; you know I never could bear it. Oh, there's a ring at the front door! That's Ted." She stood on tiptoe, bending forward, and held her ear to the half-open door. "No, it isn't; it's some wretched visitor. Don't keep me, Cousin Bella, or I shall be caught."

"Really, Audrey, now we are on the subject, I must just tell you that your conduct lately has given me a great deal of anxiety."

"My conduct! What *do* you mean? I haven't broken any of the seven commandments. (Thank goodness, they've gone!)"

"I mean that if you don't take care you'll be entangling yourself with young Mr. Haviland, as you did ——"

"As I did with Vincent, I suppose. That *is* so like you. You're always thinking things, always putting that and that together, and doing it quite wrong. You were hopelessly out of it about Vincent. Whether you're wrong or right about Mr. Haviland, I simply shan't condescend to tell you." And having lashed herself into a state of indignation, Audrey went on warmly—"I'm not a child of ten. I won't have my actions criticised. I won't have my motives spied into. I won't be ruled by your miserable middle-class, provincial standard. What I do is nobody's business but my own."

"Very well, very well; go your own way, and take the consequences. If it's not my business, don't blame me when you get into difficulties."

Audrey turned round with a withering glance.

"Cousin Bella, you are really *too* stupid!" she said, with a movement of her foot that was half rage, half sheer excitement. "Ah, there's Ted at last!" She ran joyously away. Miss Craven sank back in her chair, exhausted by her unusual moral effort, and too deeply hurt to return the smile which Audrey flashed back at her, by way of apology, as she flew.

The bitter little dialogue, at any rate, had the good effect of wakening Audrey to the practical aspects of her problem. Before their engagement could be announced, it was clear that Ted ought to be properly introduced to her friends. However she might affect to brave it out, Audrey was sensitive to the least breath of unfavourable opinion, and she did not want it said that she had picked up her husband heavens knows how, when, and where. If they had been talked about already, no time should be lost before people realised that Ted was a genius with a future before him, his sister a rising artist also, and so on. Audrey was busy with these thoughts as she was being rowed up the river from Hammersmith. At Kew the room where they had tea was full of people she knew; and as she and Ted passed on to a table in a far corner, she felt, rather than saw, that the men looked after them, and the women exchanged glances. The same thing happened at Richmond, where they dined; and there a little knot of people gathered about the river's bank and watched their departure with more than friendly interest. If she had any lingering doubts before, Audrey was ready now to make her engagement known, for mere prudence' sake. And as they almost drifted down in the quiet July evening, between the humid after-glow of the sunset and the dawn of the moonlit night, Audrey felt a wholly new and delicate sensation. It was as if she were penetrated for the first time by the indefinable, tender influences of air and moonlight and running water. The mood was vague and momentary—a mere fugitive reflection of the rapture with which Ted, rowing lazily now with the current, drank in the glory of life, and felt the heart of all nature beating with his. Yet for that one instant, transient as it was, Audrey's decision was being shaped for her by a motive finer than all prudence, stronger than all sense of propriety. In its temporary transfiguration her love for Ted was such that she would have been ready, if need were, to fix Siberia for their honeymoon and to-morrow for their wedding-day. As they parted on her doorstep at Chelsea, between ten and eleven o'clock, she whispered, "Ted, that row down was like heaven! I've never, never been so happy in all my life!" If she did not fix their wedding-day then and there, she did the next best thing—she fixed the day for a dinner to be given in Ted's honour. Not a tedious, large affair, of course. She was only going to ask a few people who would appreciate Ted, and be useful to him in "the future."

As it was nearly the end of the season Audrey had no time to lose, and the first thing she did after her arrival was to startle Miss Craven by the sudden question—

"Cousin Bella, who was the man who rushed out of his bath into the street shouting 'Eureka'?"

"I never heard of any one doing so," said Cousin Bella, a little testily; "and if he did, it was most improper of him."

"Wasn't it? Never mind; he had an idea, so have I. I think I shall run out on to the Embankment and shout 'Eureka' too. Aren't you dying to know? I'm going to give a grand dinner for Te—for Mr. and Miss Haviland; and I'm not going to ask one—single—nonentity,—there! First of all, we must have Mr. Knowles—of course. Then—perhaps—Mr. Flaxman Reed. H'm—yes; we haven't asked him since he came up to St. Teresa's. If he isn't anybody in particular, you can't exactly call him nobody." Having settled the question of Mr. Flaxman Reed, Audrey sat down and sent off several invitations on the spot.

Owing to some refusals, the dinner-party gradually shrank in size and importance, and it was not until within four days of its date that Audrey discovered to her dismay that she was "a man short." As good luck would have it, she met Knowles that afternoon in Regent Street, and confided to him her difficulty and her firm determination not to fill the gap with any "nonentity" whatever. Audrey was a little bit afraid of Mr. Percival Knowles, and nothing but real extremity would have driven her to this desperate course. "If you could suggest any one I know, who isn't a nonentity, and who wouldn't mind such ridiculously short notice: it's really quite an informal little dinner, got up in a hurry, you know, for Mr. Haviland, a very clever young artist, and his sister."

Knowles smiled faintly: he had heard before of the very clever young artist (though not of his sister). He was all sympathy.

"Sorry. I can't think of any one you know—*not* a nonentity—but I should like to bring a friend, if I may. You don't know him, I think, but I believe he very much wants to know you."

"Bring him by all means, if he won't mind such a casual invitation."

"I'll make that all right."

Knowles lifted his hat, and was about to hurry away.

"By-the-bye, you haven't told me your friend's name."

He stopped, and answered with a sibilant incoherence, struggling as he was with his amusement. But at that moment Audrey's attention was diverted by the sight of Ted coming out of the New Gallery, and she hardly heard what was being said to her.

"I shall be delighted to see Mr. St. John," she called back, making a random shot at the name, and went on her way with leisurely haste towards the New Gallery.

CHAPTER IX

On the evening of her dinner Audrey had some difficulty in distributing her guests. After all, eight had accepted. Besides the Havilands, with Mr. Knowles and his friend Mr. St. John, there was Mr. Flaxman Reed, who, as Audrey now discovered, greatly to her satisfaction, was causing some excitement in the religious world by his interesting attitude mid-way between High Anglicanism and Rome. There were Mr. Dixon Barnett, the great Asiatic explorer, and his wife; and Miss Gladys Armstrong, the daring authoress of "Sour Grapes" and "Through Fire to Moloch," two novels dealing with the problem of heredity. Audrey had to contrive as best she might to make herself the centre of attraction throughout the evening, and at the same time do justice to each of her distinguished guests. The question was, Who was to take her in to dinner? After weighing impartially the claims of her three more or less intimate acquaintances, Audrey decided in favour of the unknown. She felt unusual complacence with this arrangement. Her fancies were beginning to cluster round the idea of Mr. St. John with curiosity. It was to be herself and Mr. St. John, then. Mr. Knowles and Miss Armstrong, of course: the critic was so cynical and hard to please that she felt a little triumphant in having secured some one whom he would surely be delighted to meet. Mr. Flaxman Reed and Katherine—n-no, Mrs. Dixon Barnett, Mr. Dixon Barnett falling to Katherine's share. For Ted, quite naturally, there remained nobody but Cousin Bella. "Poor boy, he'll be terribly bored, I'm afraid, but it can't be helped."

The Havilands were the first to arrive.

"How superb you look!" was Audrey's exclamation, as she kissed her friend on both cheeks and stepped back to take a good look at her. Katherine's appearance justified the epithet. Her gown, the work of her own hands, was of some transparent black stuff, swathed about her breasts, setting off the honey-like pallor of her skin; her slight figure supplied any grace that was wanting in the draperies. That black and white was a splendid foil for Audrey's burnished hair and her dress, an ingenious medley of flesh-pink, apple-green, and ivory silk.

"One moment, dear; just let me pin that chiffon up on your shoulder, to make your sleeves look wider—there!" She hovered round Katherine, spying out the weak points in her dress, and disguising them with quick, skillful fingers. A woman never looks more charming than when doing these little services for another. So Ted thought, as he watched Audrey laying her white arms about his sister, and putting her head on one side to survey the effect critically. To the boy, with his senses sharpened to an almost feverish subtilty by the incessant stimulus of his imagination, Audrey was the epitome of everything most completely and joyously alive. Roses, sunlight, flame, with the shifting, waving lines of all things most fluent and elusive, were in her face, her hair, the movements of her limbs. Her body was like a soul to its clothes; it animated, inspired the mass of silk and lace. He could not think of her as she was—the creature of the day and the hour, modern from the surface to the core. Yet never had she looked more modern than at this moment; never had that vivid quality, that touch of artificial distinction, appeared more stereotyped in its very perfection and finish. But Ted, in the first religious fervour of his passion, had painted her as the Saint of the Beatific Vision; and in the same way, to Ted, ever since that evening on the river, she recalled none but open-air images. She was linked by flowery chains of association to an idyllic past—a past of four days ago. Her very caprices suggested the shy approaches and withdrawals of some divinity of nature. It was by these harmless fictions, each new one rising on the ruins of the old, that Ted managed to keep his ideal of Audrey intact.

There was a slight stir in the passage outside the half-open door. Audrey, still busy about Katherine's dress, seemed not to hear it.

"My dear Audrey!" protested Miss Craven from her corner.

"There, that'll do!" said Katherine, laughing; "you've stuck quite enough pins into me for one night."

"Stand still, and don't wiggle!" cried Audrey, as the door opened wide. For a second she was conscious of being watched by eyes that were not Ted's or anything like them. At the same time the footman announced in a firm, clear voice, "Mr. Knowles and Mr. Langley Wyndham!"

She had heard this time. The look she had seen from the doorway was the same look that had followed her in the Dean's drawing-room at Oxford. All the emotions of that evening thronged back into her mind—the vague fascination, the tense excitement, the mortification that resulted from the wound to her self-love and pride.

So this was Mr. St. John!

A year ago he had refused an introduction to her, and now he wanted to know her; his friend had said so. He was seeking the acquaintance of his own accord, without encouragement. How odd it all was! Well, whether his former discourtesy had been intentional or not, he knew how to apologise for it gracefully.

She had no time to think more about the matter, for her remaining guests came in all together; and in another five minutes Audrey was suffering from that kind of nightmare in which some grave issue—you don't know precisely what—hangs on the adjustment of trifles, absurdly disproportionate to the event, and which disarrange themselves perversely at the dramatic moment. Everything seemed to go wrong. She had relied on Knowles and Miss Gladys Armstrong for a brilliant display of intellectual fireworks; but beyond the first casual remarks absolutely required of them, they had not a word to say to each other. Miss Armstrong managed cleverly enough to strike a little spark of epigram from the flinty dialogue. It flickered and went out. Knowles smiled politely at the abortive attempt; but at her first serious remark he shook his head, as much as to say, "My dear lady, this is a conundrum; I give it up," and finally turned to Katherine on his left. In fact, he monopolised her during the rest of dinner, much to the annoyance of Mr. Dixon Barnett, who spent himself in futile efforts to win back her interest,—his behaviour in its turn rousing the uneasy attention of Mrs. Dixon Barnett. She, again, was so preoccupied in watching the movements of her lord, that she almost forgot the existence of Mr. Flaxman Reed, who sat silent and depressed under her shadow.

Wyndham gave Audrey credit for great perspicacity in pairing these two off together. "Poor fellow," he said to himself; "to preserve him from the temptations of the world and the flesh, she's considerately sent him in with the devil." For his own part, he devoted himself to Audrey and his dinner. From time to time he glanced across the table, and whenever he did so the corners of Knowles's mouth twitched nervously and he began to stroke his upper lip—a provoking habit of his, seeing that he had no moustache to account for it. Evidently there was some secret understanding between the two, and Wyndham was gravely and maliciously amused.

Katherine was enjoying herself too, but without malice. She had so few acquaintances and lived so much in the studio, that it was all fresh life to her. She was pleased with that unconscious irony of Audrey's which had thrown Knowles and Miss Armstrong together; pleased with the by-play between Knowles and Wyndham, and with the behaviour of the married couple. It was always a delight to her to watch strange faces. Mrs. Dixon Barnett was a big woman, with a long head, and she looked something like a horse with its ears laid back, her hair being arranged to carry out that idea. The great Asiatic explorer, whose round face wore an expression of permanent surprise, suggested a man who has met with some sudden shock from which he has never recovered. Katherine felt sorry for the Asiatic explorer. She felt sorry for Miss Gladys Armstrong too, a little pale woman with a large gaze that seemed to take you in without looking at you. Her face, still young and childlike, was scored with the marks of hard work and eager ambition, and there was bitterness in the downward droop of her delicate mouth. Yet the authoress of "Sour Grapes" was undeniably a successful woman. And Wyndham too, the successful man—Wyndham's face attracted Katherine in spite of herself, it was full of such curious inconsistencies. Altogether it was refined, impressive, almost noble; yet each of the features contradicted itself, the others, and the whole. The general outline was finely cut, but it looked a little worn at the edges. The shaven lips were sensitive, but they had hard curves at the corners; they were firm, without expressing self-restraint. In the same way the nose was fine at the bridge, and coarse towards the nostrils. The iris of the eyes was beautiful, with its clear brown streaks on an orb of greenish grey; yet his eyes were the most disagreeable feature in Wyndham's face. As for Knowles, he interested her with his genial cynicism; but it was a relief to turn from these restless types to Mr. Flaxman Reed. He had the face of the ideal ascetic—sweet in its austerity, militant in its renunciation. What in heaven's name was he doing at Audrey Craven's dinner-table?

Katherine was not too much absorbed in these speculations to see that Ted was behaving very prettily to old Miss Craven, and making himself useful by filling up awkward pauses with irrelevant remarks. The boy looked perfectly happy. Audrey's mere presence seemed to satisfy him, though she had not spoken a dozen words to him that evening, and was separated from him by the length of the table. At last she rose, and as he held the door open for her to go out, she turned to him with arched eyebrows and a smile that was meant to say, "You've been shamefully neglected, I know, but I had to attend to these tiresome people." Katherine saw Mr. Wyndham making a mental note of the look and the smile. She had taken an instinctive dislike to that man.

Upstairs in the drawing-room the five women settled down in a confidential group, and with one accord fell to discussing Mr. Wyndham. Miss Craven began it by mildly wondering whether he "looked so disagreeable on purpose, or because he couldn't help it." On the whole, she inclined to the more charitable view.

"What do you say, Kathy?" asked Audrey, without looking up.

"I agree with Miss Craven in thinking nature responsible for Mr. Wyndham's manners."

Mrs. Dixon Barnett disapproved of Katherine, but she joined in here with a guttural assent.

"Poor man," said Miss Gladys Armstrong, "he certainly hasn't improved since that affair with Miss Fraser."

Audrey looked up suddenly,—"What affair?"

"Don't you know? They were engaged a long time, wedding-day fixed and everything, when she broke it off suddenly, without a word of warning."

"Why?"

"Why indeed! She left her reasons to the imagination."

"When did it happen?"

"Just about this time last year. I can't think what made her do it, unless she had a turn for psychical research—raking in the ashes of his past, and that sort of thing."

"Was he very much cut up about it?"

"He didn't whine. But he's got an ugly wound somewhere about him. Curious man, Langley Wyndham. I haven't got to the bottom of him yet; and I flatter myself I know most men. My diagnosis is generally pretty correct. He's a very interesting type."

"Very," said Audrey below her breath. The novelist knitted her brows and fell into a reverie. Her interest in Langley Wyndham was not a purely professional one. Audrey reflected too. "Just about this time last year. That might account for things." She would have liked to ask more; but further discussion of his history was cut short by the entrance of Wyndham himself, followed by the rest.

Mr. Flaxman Reed was the first to take the empty seat by Audrey's side. He remembered the talk he had with her at Oxford—that talk which had provoked Wyndham's sarcastic comments. Himself a strange compound of intellectual subtilty and broad simplicity of character, he had taken Audrey's utterances in good faith. She had spoken to him of spiritual things, in one of those moments of self-revelation which, he knew well, come suddenly to those—especially to women—whose inner life is troubled. But this was not the atmosphere to revive such themes in. He had no part in Audrey's and in Wyndham's world,—the world which cared nothing for the principles he represented, those two great ideals which he served in his spirit and his body—the unity of the Church and the celibacy of the priesthood. But Audrey interested him. He had first met, last seen her, during a spiritual and intellectual crisis. He had stood alone then, severed from those dearest to him by troubled seas of controversy; and a word, a look, had passed which showed that she, this woman, sympathised with him. It was enough; there still clung to her the grave and tender associations of that time.

To-night the woman was unable to give him her whole-hearted attention. Audrey was disturbed and preoccupied. Ted was lounging at the back of her chair, hanging on her words; Wyndham and Miss Armstrong were sitting on the other side of her, and she felt herself straining every nerve to catch what they were saying.

"Yes," said Miss Armstrong in the tone of a proud parent, "'Through Fire to Moloch' was my first. In that book I threw down the gauntlet to Society. It shrugged its shoulders and took no notice. My second, 'Sour Grapes,' was a back-hander in its face. It shrieked that time, but it read 'Sour Grapes.'"

"Which at once increased the demand for 'Through Fire to Moloch.' I congratulate you."

Miss Armstrong ignored the impertinent parenthesis. "The critics abused me, but I expected that. They are men, and it was the men I exposed — —"

Knowles, who was standing near, smiled, and blushed when he caught himself smiling. Wyndham laughed frankly at his confusion, and Audrey grew hot and cold by turns. What was the dreadful joke those two had about Miss Armstrong? She leaned back and looked up at Ted sweetly.

"Ted, I should like to introduce you to Mr. Knowles. He'll tell you all about that illustrated thing you wanted to get on to."

"I'm afraid," said Knowles, "that's not in my line: I don't know anything about any illustrated things."

"Well, never mind; I want you to know something about Mr. Haviland, anyhow."

This was just what Knowles wanted himself. He was deeply interested in the situation as far as he understood it, and he looked forward to its development. This little diversion created, Miss Armstrong continued with imperturbable calm. But Audrey, listening with one ear to Mr. Flaxman Reed, only heard the livelier parts of the dialogue.

"Life isn't all starched linen and eau-de-Cologne," said Miss Armstrong, sententiously.

"Did I ever say it was?" returned Wyndham.

"Virtually you do. You turn your back on average humanity."

"Pardon me, I do nothing of the kind. I use discrimination."

"Nature has no discrimination."

"Exactly. And Nature has no consideration for our feelings, and very little maidenly reserve. Therefore we've invented Art."

Audrey leaned forward eagerly. She felt an unusual exaltation. At last she was in the centre of intellectual life, carried on by the whirl of ideas. She answered her companion at random.

"Yes," Mr. Flaxman Reed was saying, "my work *is* disheartening. Half my parish are animals, brutalised by starvation, degraded out of all likeness to men and women."

"How dreadful! What hard work it must be!"

"Hard enough to find decent food and clothing for their bodies. But to have to 'create a soul under those ribs of death'— —" he paused. His voice seemed suddenly to run dry.

"Yes," said Audrey in her buoyant staccato, "I can't think how you manage it."

There was a moment of silence. Wyndham had turned from Miss Armstrong; Knowles and Ted had long ago joined Miss Haviland at the other end of the room, where Mr. Dixon Barnett, still irresistibly attracted by Katherine, hovered round and round the little group, with the fatal "desire of the moth for the star." Audrey stood up; Miss Armstrong was holding out her hand and pleading a further engagement. The little woman looked sour and ruffled: Wyndham's manner had acted on her like vinegar on milk. She was followed by Mr. Flaxman Reed. Wyndham dropped into the seat he left.

"Dixon," said Mrs. Barnett in a low voice which the explorer knew and obeyed. They were going on to a large "At Home."

Audrey turned to Wyndham with a smile, "I hope you are not going to follow them, Mr. Wyndham?"

"No; I'm not a person of many engagements, I'm thankful to say. Barnett hasn't much the cut of a great explorer, has he?"

"No; but those wiry little men can go through a great deal."

"A very great deal. Is Mrs. Barnett a friend of yours?"

"No, not especially. Why?"

"Mere curiosity. That mouth of hers ought to have a bit in it. It's enough to send any man exploring in Central Asia. I can understand Barnett's mania for regions untrodden by the foot of man—or woman."

Audrey laughed a little nervously. "I made a mistake in introducing him to Miss Haviland."

"It was a little cruel of you. But not half so unkind as asking Miss Armstrong to meet Knowles. That was a refinement of cruelty."

"Why? What have I done? Tell me."

"Didn't you know that Knowles went for Miss Armstrong in last week's 'Piccadilly'? Criticised, witticised, slaughtered, and utterly made game of her?"

"No? I'd no idea! I thought they'd be delighted to meet each other; and I know so few really clever people, you know" (this rather plaintively). "He does cut up people so dreadfully, too."

"He cut her up into very small pieces. Knowles does these things artistically. He's so urbane in his brutality; that's what makes it so crushing. Are you an admirer of Miss Armstrong?"

He looked her full in the face, and Audrey blushed. She had read Miss Armstrong's works, and liked them, because it was the fashion; but not for worlds would she have admitted the fact now.

"I don't think I am. I've not read *all* her books."

"*Did* you like them?"

"I—I hardly know. She's written so many, and I can't understand them—at least not all of them."

Wyndham smiled. She had read all of them, then.

"I'm glad to hear it. I can't understand them myself; but I detest them, all the same."

"I thought so. I saw you were having an argument with her."

"Oh, as for that, I agreed with her—with her theory, that is, not with her practice; that's execrable. But whatever she says I always want to support the other side."

He changed the subject, much to Audrey's relief.

"I think you knew Mr. Flaxman Reed at Oxford?"

"Yes, slightly. He's an old friend of my uncle's."

"There's something infinitely pathetic about him. I've an immense respect for him—probably because I don't understand him. I was surprised to meet him here."

"Really, you are very uncomplimentary to me."

"Am I? Mr. Reed has renounced all the pleasant things of life—hence my astonishment at seeing him here. Do you find him easy to get on with?"

"Perfectly." She became absorbed in picking the broken feathers out of her fan. She took no interest in Mr. Flaxman Reed. What she wanted was to be roused, stimulated by contact with a great intellect; and the precious opportunity was slipping minute by minute from her grasp. Wyndham was wasting it in deliberate trivialities. She longed to draw him into some subject, large and deep, where their sympathies could touch, their thoughts expand and intermingle. She continued tentatively, with a suggestion of self-restrained suffering in her voice, "I don't think I have any right to discuss Mr. Reed. You know—I have no firm faith, no settled opinions."

It was an opening into the larger air, a very little one; she had no knowledge or skill to make it bigger, but she was determined to show herself a woman abreast of her time. Wyndham leaned back and looked at her through half-opened eyelids.

"You are no longer convinced of the splendid logic of the Roman faith?"

She started. His words recalled vividly that evening at Oxford, though she would not have recognised them as hers but for the quotation marks indicated by Wyndham's tone.

"No—that was a year ago. What did you know about me then?"

"Nothing. I divined much."

"You are right. How well you remember!" She leaned forward. Her face was animated, eager, in its greed of sympathy, understanding, acknowledgment. Clear and insistent, with a note as of delicate irony, the little porcelain clock in the corner sounded eleven. Knowles and others were making a move. Wyndham rose.

"I remember most things worth remembering."

Five minutes afterwards Audrey, wrapt in thought, was still standing where Wyndham had left her. Miss Craven and Katherine had gone upstairs, and she was alone with Ted. Suddenly she clenched her hands together, at the full length of her white arms, and turned to him in an agony of tenderness, clinging to him like an overwrought child, and lavishing more sweetness on him than she had done since the day of their engagement. Ted was touched with the unusual pathos of her manner. He put it down to sorrow at their separation during the whole of a long evening.

CHAPTER X

It was the third week in August; summer was dying, as a London summer dies, in days of feverish sunlight and breathless languor. Everywhere there was the same torpor, the same wornout, desiccated life in death. It was in the streets with their sultry pallor, in the parks and squares where the dust lay like a grey blight on every green thing. Everywhere the glare accentuated this toneless melancholy. It was the symbol of the decadence following the brilliant efflorescence of the season, the exhaustion after that supreme effort of Society to amuse itself. This lassitude is felt most by those who have shared least in the amusement, the workers who must stay behind in the great workshop because they are too busy or too poor to leave it.

There was one worker, however, who felt nothing of this depression. Langley Wyndham had reasons for congratulating himself that everybody was out of town, and that he was left to himself in his rooms in Dover Street. For one thing, it gave him opportunity for cultivating Miss Craven's acquaintance. For another, he had now a luxurious leisure in which to polish up the proofs of his last novel, and to arrange his ideas for its successor. Compared with this great work, all former efforts would seem to the taste they had created as so much literary trifling. Hitherto he had been merely trying his instrument, running his fingers over the keys in his easy professional way; but these preliminary flourishes gave no idea of the constructive harmonies to follow. And now, on a dull evening, some three weeks after Audrey's dinner-party, he was alone in his study, smoking, as he leaned back in his easy-chair, in one of those dreamy moods which with him meant fiction in the making, the tobacco-smoke curling round his head the Pythian fumes of his inspiration. The study was curiously suggestive of its owner's inconsistencies. With its silk cushions, Oriental rugs, and velvet draperies, its lining of books, and writing-table heaped with manuscripts and proofs, it witnessed to his impartial love of luxury and hard work. It told other secrets too. The cigar-case on the table beside him was embroidered by a woman's hand, the initials L. W. worked with gold thread in a raised monogram. Two or three photographs of pretty women were stuck by their corners behind the big looking-glass over the fireplace, together with invitation cards, frivolous little notes, and ball programmes. On one end of the mantel-board there was a photograph of Knowles; on the other, the one nearest Wyndham's chair, an empty frame of solid silver. The photograph and the frame represented the friendship and the love of his life.

To-night he had left his proofs untouched on the writing-table, and had settled himself comfortably to his pipe, with the voluptuous satisfaction of a man who has put off a disagreeable duty. He felt that delicious turmoil of ideas which with him accompanied the building up of a story round its central character. Not that he yet understood that character. Wyndham had his intuitions, but he was not the man to trust them as such; it was his habit to verify them by a subsequent logic. His literary conscience allowed nothing to take the place of the experimental method, the careful observation, and arranging of minute facts, intimate analytical study from the life. No action was too small, no emotion too insignificant, for his uncompromising realism. He had applied the same method to his own experience. Whatever came in his way, the tragedy or comedy of his daily life, his moods of passion and apathy, the aspirations of his better moments, all underwent the same disintegrating process. He had the power of standing aloof from himself, of arresting the flight of his own sensations, and criticising his own actions as a disinterested spectator. Thus he made no experiment on others that he had not first tried on his own person. If any man ever understood himself, that man was Langley Wyndham. He was by no means vain of this distinction; on the contrary, he would have said that as a man's inner consciousness is the only thing he has any direct knowledge of, he must be a fool if he can live with himself—the closest of all human relations—for thirty-five years without understanding his own character.

What he really prided himself on was his knowledge of other people, especially of women. Unfortunately, for the first few years of his literary life he knew no women intimately: he had many acquaintances among them, a few enemies, but no friends; and the little he knew of individuals had not tended to raise his opinion of women in general. Consequently he drew them all, as he saw them, from the outside; the best sort with a certain delicacy and clearness of outline, the result of unerring eyesight and the gift of style; the worst sort with an incisive, almost brutal touch that suggested the black lines bitten out by some powerful acid. His work "took" because of its coarser qualities, the accentuated bitterness, the startling irony, the vigorous, characteristic phrase. Those black strokes were not introduced to throw up the grey wash or pencilled shading; Wyndham's cynicism was no mere literary affectation, it was engrained in his very nature. He had gone through many phases of disillusionment (including disgust at his own success) before that brief crisis of feeling which ended in his engagement to Miss Fraser. Then, for the first time in his life, a woman's nature had been given to him to know. It was a glorious opportunity for the born analyst; and for the first time in his life he let an opportunity go. He loved Alison Fraser, and he found that love made understanding impossible. He never wanted to understand her; the relentless passion for analysis was absorbed in a comprehensive enthusiasm which embraced the whole of Alison and took no count of the parts. To have pulled her to pieces, even with a view to reconstruction, would have been a profanation of her and of his love. For a whole year the student of the earthly and the visible lived on the substance of things unseen—on faith in the goodness of Alison Fraser. By a peculiar irony it was her very goodness—for she was a good woman—which made her give up Wyndham. As Miss Gladys Armstrong had guessed (or as she would have put it, diagnosed), a detail of Wyndham's past life had come to Miss Fraser's knowledge, as these details always come, through a well-meaning friend. It was one which made it difficult for her to reconcile her marriage with Wyndham to her conscience. And because she loved him, because the thought of him, so hard to other women, so tender to herself, fascinated her reason and paralysed her will—flattering the egoism inherent even in the very good—because she was weak and he was irresistibly strong, she cut herself from him deliberately, open-eyed, and with one stroke. She had just sufficient strength for the sudden breaking off of their engagement, none for explanation, and none, alas! to save her from regretting her act of supererogatory virtue.

Wyndham gave no sign of suffering. He simply sank back into himself, and became the man he had been before, plus his experience of feeling, and minus the ingenuousness of his self-knowledge. He took instead to self-mystification, trying to persuade himself that because he could not have Alison, Alison was not worth having. After that, it was but a step to palming off on his reason the monstrous syllogism that because Alison was unworthy, and Alison was a woman, therefore all women were unworthy. Except for purely literary purposes, he had done with the sex. He became if anything more intently, more remorselessly analytical, more absolutely the student of human nature. He lived now in and for his work.

He struck out into new paths; he was tired of his neutral washes, and striking effects in black and white. He had begun to dream of glorious subtilties of design and colour. Novels were lying in his head ten deep. He had whole note-books full of germs and embryos, all neatly arranged in their separate pigeon-holes. In some he had jotted down a name and a date, or a word which stood for a whole train of ideas. In others he had recorded some illustration as it occurred to him; or a single sentence stood flanked by a dozen variants—Wyndham being a careful worker and sensitive to niceties of language. To-night he was supremely happy. He saw his way to a lovely little bit of psychological realism. All that had been hitherto wanting to this particular development of his art had been the woman. In Audrey Craven he had found the indispensable thing— intimacy without love, or even, as he understood the word, friendship. She was the type he had long desired, the feminine creature artless in perpetual artifice, for ever revealing herself in a succession of disguises.

He was beginning to adjust his latest impressions to his earlier idea of her. He recalled the evening when he had first seen her—the hot, crowded drawing-room, the heavy atmosphere, the dull faces coming and going, and the figure of Audrey flashing through it all. She had irritated him then, for he had not yet classified her. He had tried not to think of her. She dogged his thoughts with most unmaidenly insistence; her image lay in wait for him at every crossroad of association; it was something vivid yet elusive, protean yet persistent. He recalled that other evening of her dinner-party—their first recognised meeting. Her whole person, which at first sight had impressed him with its emphatic individuality, now struck him as characterless and conventional. And yet—what was she like? She was like a chameleon. No, she wasn't; he recollected that the change of colour was a vital process in that animal. She was like an opal—all sparkle when you move it, and at rest dull, most undeniably dull. No, *that* wasn't it exactly. She was a looking-glass for other people's personalities (he hated the horrid word, and apologised to himself for using it), formless and colourless, reflecting form and colour. After a moment's satisfaction with this last fancy, he became aware that he was being made the fool of metaphor. That was not his way. To find out what lay at the bottom of this shifting personality, what elemental thoughts and feelings, if any, the real Audrey was composed of; to see for himself the play of circumstances on her plastic nature, and know what reaction it was capable of—in a word, to experimentalise in cold blood on the living nerve and brain tissue, was his plan of work for the year 1896.

Making a mental note of several of the above phrases for future use, Wyndham knocked the ashes out of his pipe and went to bed, where he dreamed that the Devil, in evening dress, was presenting him with Audrey's soul—done up in a brown wrapper marked "MS. only"—for dissection.

CHAPTER XI

It was in no direct accordance with his literary plans, though it may have been preordained in some divine scheme of chances, that Wyndham found himself next Sunday attending evensong at St. Teresa's, Lambeth. It so happened that Audrey and the Havilands had chosen that very evening to go and hear, or, as Ted expressed it, see Flaxman Reed. He wanted Flaxman Reed's head for a study. Ted seldom condescended to enter any church of later date than the fifteenth century, and, architecturally speaking, he feared the worst from St. Teresa's. Indeed, smoke, fog, and modern Gothic genius have made the outside of that building one with the grimy street it stands in, and Ted was not prepared for the golden beauty of the interior. His judgment halted as if some magic effect of colour had blinded it to stunted form and pitiful perspective. But the glory of St. Teresa's is its music. The three late-comers were shown into seats in the chancel as the choir were singing the *Magnificat*. Music was the one art to which Audrey's nature responded spontaneously after its kind. She knelt down and covered her face with her hands for a prayer's space, while the voices of the choir and organ shook her on every side with a palpable vibration. She was conscious then of a deep sense of religion merging in a faint expectancy, a premonition of things to follow. She rose from her knees and found an explanation of this in the fact that Langley Wyndham was standing in the opposite seat below the choir. She was not surprised; for her the unexpected was always about to happen. It had happened now.

She tried not to see or think of him; but she felt him as something illuminating and intensifying her consciousness. She heard the vicar's voice like a fine music playing in the background. Then organ and choir burst into the anthem. It was a fugue; the voices seemed to have gathered together from the ends of the world, flying, pursuing and flying, doubled, trebled, quadrupled in their flight, they met and parted, they overtook and were overtaken. And now it was no longer a fugue of sounds—it was a fugue of all sensations. The incense rose and mingled with the music; the music fled and rose, up among the clustering gas-jets, up to the chancel roof where it lost itself in a shimmering labyrinth of gold and sapphire, and died in a diminuendo of light and sound. Audrey looked up, and as her eyes met Wyndham's, it seemed as if a new and passionate theme had crashed into her fugue, dominating its harmonies, while the whole rushed on, more intricate, more tumultuous than before. Her individuality that had swum with the stream became fluent and coalesced with it now, soul flooded with sense, and sense with soul. She came to herself exhausted and shivering with cold. Flaxman Reed was in the pulpit. He stood motionless, with compressed lips and flashing eyes, as he watched the last deserters softly filing out through the side-aisles. The lights were turned low in nave and chancel; Ted wriggled in his seat until he commanded a good view of the fine head, in faint relief against a grey-white pillar, stone on stone; and Flaxman Reed flung out his text like a challenge to the world: "The things which are seen are temporal; but the things which are not seen are eternal." The words suggested something piquantly metaphysical, magnificently vague, and Audrey followed the sermon a little way. But Flaxman Reed was in his austerest, most militant mood. He was a master of antithesis, and to Audrey there was something repellent in his steel-clad thoughts, his clear diamond-pointed sentences. No eloquence had any charm for her that was not as water to reflect her image, or as wind to lift and carry her along. Her fancy soon fluttered gently down to earth, and she caught herself wondering whether Wyndham would walk back to Piccadilly or go in a hansom.

She was still pursuing this train of thought as they left the church, when she proposed that they should go back to Chelsea by Westminster instead of Lambeth Bridge. Wyndham overtook them as they turned down to the river by St. Thomas's Hospital. He stopped while Audrey pointed out the beauty of the scene with her little air of unique appreciation. "Isn't it too lovely for words? The suggestion—the mystery of it!" Her voice had a passionate impatience, as if she chafed at the limitations of the language. "Who says London's cold and grey? It's blue. And yet what would it be without the haze?" Wyndham smiled inscrutably: perhaps he wondered what Miss Audrey Craven would be without the haze?

"What did you think of the service?" she asked presently. By this time she and Wyndham were walking together a little in advance of the others.

"I didn't hear it. I was watching Flaxman Reed all the time." This statement, as Audrey well knew, was not strictly correct.

"So was I. My uncle says if he stays in the church he'll be the coming man."

"The coming man? H'm. He's been going back ever since I knew him. At present he's got to the thirteenth century; he may arrive at the Nicene age, but he'll never have a hold on his own. He's nothing but a holy anachronism."

"Oh? I thought you didn't understand him?"

"In one way I do, in another I don't. You see I knew him at Oxford when I was a happy undergraduate." (Audrey could not imagine Langley Wyndham ever being an undergraduate; it seemed to her that he must always have been a Master of Arts.) "I knew the real Flaxman Reed, and he was as logical a sceptic as you or I. There was an epidemic of ideas in our time, and the poor fellow was frightened, so he took it—badly. Of course he made up his mind that he was going to die, and he was horribly afraid of dying. So instead of talking about his interesting symptoms, as you or I might do" ("You or I"—again that flattering association!), "he quietly got rid of the disease by attacking its source."

"How?"

"Well, I forget the precise treatment, but I think he took equal parts of St. Augustine and St. Thomas Aquinas, diluted with *aqua sacra*. He gave me the prescription, but I preferred the disease."

"At any rate he was in earnest."

"Deadly earnest. That's the piety of the fraud."

"You surely don't call him a fraud?"

"Well—a self-deceiver. Isn't that the completest and most fatal form of fraud? He fights and struggles to be what he isn't and calls it renouncing self."

"He renounces the world too—and everything that's pleasant."

"I'm afraid that doesn't impress me. I can't forget that he renounced reason because it was unpleasant. Rather than bear a little spiritual neuralgia, he killed the nerve of thought."

"How terrible!" said Audrey, though she had no very precise notion of what was involved in that operation.

"To us—not to him. Yet he talks about doing good work for his generation."

"Why shouldn't he? He works hard enough."

"Unfortunately his generation doesn't want his work or him either. It's too irrevocably pledged to reality. There's one thing about him though—his magnificent personality. I believe he has unlimited influence over some men and most women."

Audrey ignored the last suggestion. "You seem to find him very interesting."

"He is profoundly interesting. Not in himself so much, but in his associations. Do you know, when I saw you in church to-night it struck me that he might possibly influence *you*."

"Never! I should have to give up my intellect first, I suppose. I'm not prepared to do *that*." Wyndham smiled again. "Why, what made you think he would influence me?"

"I'd no right to think anything at all about it, but I know some women take him for a hierophant."

"Some women? Do you think I'm like them?"

"You are like nothing but yourself. I was only afraid that he might persuade you to renounce yourself and become somebody else, which would be a pity."

"Don't be alarmed. I'm not so impressionable as you think."

"Aren't you? Be frank. Didn't you feel to-night that he might have a revelation for you?"

"No. And yet it's odd you should say so. I have felt that, but—not with him. I shall never come under that influence."

"I hope not." (It was delightful to have Langley Wyndham "hoping" and being "afraid" for her.) "He belongs to the dead—you to the living."

What a thing it is to have a sense of style, to know the words that consecrate a moment! They were crossing Westminster Bridge now, and Audrey looked back. On the Lambeth end of the bridge Ted and Katherine were leaning over the parapet; she looked at them as she might have looked at two figures in a crowd. Lambeth and St. Teresa's seemed very far away. She said so, and her tone implied that she had left illusion behind her on the Surrey side.

Wyndham said good-bye at Westminster. Audrey was not quite pleased with his manner of hailing a hansom; it implied a conscious loss of valuable time.

"What fools we were to let him catch us up," said Ted as they walked towards Pimlico. Audrey made no answer. She was saying to herself that Langley Wyndham had read her, and—well, she hardly thought he would take the trouble to read anything that was not interesting.

CHAPTER XII

Audrey had made a faint protest against Wyndham's realistic presentation of Flaxman Reed. In doing so she was not guided by any insight into the character of that divine, or by any sympathy with his aims. Indeed she could not have understood him if she had tried. Her thoughts had never travelled along that avenue of time down which Wyndham had tracked his pathetic figure to the thirteenth century. She merely wanted to avoid a slavish acquiescence in Wyndham's view, to guard a characteristic intellectual attitude. Intellect has its responsibilities, and she was anxious to show herself impartial. In all this Flaxman Reed counted for nothing. It was intolerable to her that Wyndham should have classed her even for a moment with those weak emotional creatures who submitted to his influence. Why, he might just as well have said that she was influenced by Ted Haviland; the fact being that no engaged woman ever preserved her independence more completely than she had done. Had devotion to Ted interfered with her appreciation of Wyndham? Then she reflected that Wyndham did not know about her engagement any more than other people.

So when Mr. Flaxman Reed called, as he did on Monday afternoon, Audrey met him with a mind secure against any malignant charm. His most innocent remarks excited her suspicion.

"I'm glad you've found your way to St. Teresa's. We don't often get such a strong contingent from the other side." By "the other side" Mr. Reed meant Middlesex, but to Audrey the phrase was insidiously controversial. She determined to take her stand once and for all.

"I'm afraid my heterodoxy is incorrigible. So I should say is Mr. Langley Wyndham's."

The vicar raised his eyebrows in mild surprise. "I don't know why *he* came—unless it was for old acquaintance' sake."

"Ah! you knew him, didn't you? Do tell me about him. He's public property, you know."

"I daresay, but I have no right to discuss him. We hardly ever meet now; if we did we shouldn't agree. We are enigmas to each other."

"Yes," she said meditatively, and with a faint reproduction of Wyndham's manner, "I should say you would be. He belongs so essentially to the present, don't you think?"

Flaxman Reed flushed painfully. "And I to the past—is that what you mean?"

"Yes, I think I do."

"You may be right. I suppose he is very modern—a decadent who would rather die with his day than live an hour behind it—who can't see that the future may have more kindred with the past than with the present. Mind you, I'm not talking of him, but of his school."

"Then you read him? Of course—everybody reads him."

"I've not much time for any reading that lies outside my work. But I read his first book when it came out. Is it from him you get what you call your heterodoxy?"

"No. You have to think these things out for yourself."

Audrey was led into making this statement simply by the desire to please. That eternally feminine instinct told her that at the moment she would be most interesting to Flaxman Reed in the character of a forlorn sceptic. His face sharpened with a sudden distrust.

"What, have *you* got the malady of the century—the disease of thought? Surely this is something new?"

"It is. One can't go on for ever in the old grooves. One must think."

"Yes; that curse is laid upon us for our sins."

Audrey smiled a bitter smile, as much as to say that she must have committed some awful crime to be so tormented with intellect as she was.

"I suppose," he continued guilelessly, "every earnest mind must go through this sooner or later."

"Yes, but I've come out on what you call the other side. I can't go back, can I?"

"No; but you can go round."

Audrey shook her head sadly, feeling all the time how nice it was to be taken seriously.

"Why not? Why not compromise? What is life but compromise? What else is my own position as an Anglican priest? I daresay you know that my heart is not altogether with the Church I serve?" He checked himself; he had not meant to strike this personal note. And how could he explain the yearning of his heart for the great heart of the Mother-church? This would have been possible last year at Oxford, but not now. "I tell you this because I feel that it might perhaps help you."

"No; I know what you will say next. You will tell me to stop thinking because it hurts me."

"I won't. You will go on thinking in spite of me. But your intellect will be feeding on itself. You will get no farther. Thought can never be satisfied with thought."

Flaxman Reed was only a simple pure-minded priest, but Wyndham himself could not have chosen words more subtly calculated to establish the "influence." To have two such champions battling for possession of her soul was exciting enough in all conscience, but she was inexpressibly flattered by that dramatic conception of herself as a restless intellect struggling with the storms of doubt. It would be hard to say how Flaxman Reed came to believe in any real passion of thought behind Audrey's spiritual coquetry. His ministration to a living illusion was almost as touching as his devotion to a dead ideal. But Audrey herself was too completely the thrall of the illusion to feel compunction.

There was no voice to warn him that his enthusiasm was the prey of the eternal vanity. He leaned back in his meditative hieratic attitude, his elbows resting on the arm of his chair, his thin hands joined at the finger-tips, wondering what he should say to help her. After all, Audrey had stated her case a little vaguely—there was a reticence as to details. These, however, he easily supplied from his own experience, supposing hers to have been more or less like it. He said he wished he had known of this before, that he had spoken sooner, wincing perceptibly as Audrey pointed out the inexpediency of discussing eternal things on so temporal an occasion as her dinner-party. He did not mean that. His time now was short; he had a stupid parish meeting at five o'clock. He went rapidly over the ground, past immemorial stumbling-stones of thought, refuting current theories, suggesting lines of reading; in his excitement he even recommended some slight study of Patristics. There was nothing like getting to the sources—Polycarp and Irenæus were important; or he could lend her Lightfoot. But he did not want to overwhelm her with dogmas—mere matter for the intellect—he would prefer her to accept some truths provisionally and see how they worked out. After all, the working out was everything. He wanted her to see that it was a question of will. In the crisis of his own life he had helped himself most by helping others—practically, he meant—seeing after his poor people, and so on. Didn't she think it might be the same with her?

Audrey looked grave. It was good to be taken seriously, but this was going a little too far.

Didn't she think she could "do something? Other ladies——"

Flaxman Reed was doing well, very well indeed, but he had spoiled it all by that hopelessly inartistic touch. Any man of the world could have told him that to mention "other ladies" to Audrey—to take her out of the circle of supreme intelligences in which he had placed her ten minutes ago, and to confuse her with the rank and file of parochial underlings and hangers-on—was death to the "influence." It was an insult to her glorious womanhood. Some people might even have objected that such crass ignorance of the world he renounced detracted from the merit of the renunciation. Her voice was very cold and distant as she answered him. "What do you suppose I could do? If you mean slumming, I've never been down a slum in my life." No, he didn't mean slumming exactly. To tell the truth, he could not fancy Audrey mingling with the brutal side of life. He would have shrunk from giving her work that he committed without a pang to his deaconesses and sisters.

"Do you mean mothers' meetings then, and that sort of thing? I *couldn't*."

No, he didn't mean mothers' meetings either. But he thought she might like to come sometimes to their social evenings.

"Social evenings"—that was worse than all. He had plunged in his nervousness to the lowermost bathos. Audrey saw that he looked puzzled and disheartened. She crossed over to her writing-desk, wrote out a cheque for five pounds, and gave it to him with the prettiest action in the world. "I want you to take that for your poor people. I wish I could help in some other way, but I can't. I am so sorry." The apology was sweetness itself, but she had the air of having settled her account with humanity—and him. He thanked her gravely and took his leave, reminding her that whenever she needed his help, it would still be there. She remained musing some time after he had gone.

He little guessed how nearly he had won the victory. Perhaps he would have scorned any advantage gained by an appeal to her sex, though he had conceded much to it—more than he well knew.

CHAPTER XIII

August was a miserable month for Katherine in the hot attic, hard at work on her own pictures, and too often finishing the various orders for black and white which Knowles had after all managed to put in Ted's way. She could have stood the hard work if she had not been more than ever worried on Ted's account. With her feminine instinct sharpened by affection, she foresaw trouble at hand—complications which it would never have entered into the boy's head to consider. For reasons of her own Audrey was still keeping her engagement a secret. She was less regular, too, in making appointments, fixing days for Ted to go over and see her; and more often than not he missed her if he happened to call at Chelsea Gardens of his own accord. At the same time she came to Devon Street as often as, or oftener than, ever, and there her manner to Ted had all its old charm, with something added; it was more deeply, more seriously affectionate than before. And yet it was just in these tender passages that Katherine detected the change of key. That tenderness was not remorse, as she might have supposed. It had nothing to do with the past, being purely an emotion of the passing moment. Audrey was playing a new part. Her mind was swayed by a fresh current of ideas; it had suffered the invasion of a foreign personality. The evidence for this was purely psychological, but it all pointed one way. A sudden display of new interests, a startling phrase, a word hitherto unknown in Audrey's vocabulary, her way of handling a book, the alternate excitement and preoccupation of her manner, they were all unmistakable. Katherine had noticed the same signs in the days of Audrey's first absorption in Ted. She had caught his tricks, his idioms, his way of thinking. She had even begun to see, like Ted, the humour of things, and to make reckless speeches, not quite like Ted, that shocked cousin Bella's sense of propriety. Katherine had smiled at her innocent plagiarism, and wondered at the transforming power of love. And now—Audrey was actually undergoing another metempsychosis. Under whose influence? Here again Katherine's instinct was correct. It was Wyndham's presence that in three weeks had brought about the change. Yes; in that impressive affection, in the pleading tremor of her voice, in her smiles and caresses, Audrey was acting a part before one invisible spectator. She played as if Wyndham were standing by and looking on. Her love for Ted had been a reality; therefore it served as a standard to measure all emotions by—it made this new passion of the imagination a thing of flesh and blood. No wonder that she would not announce her engagement. At the best of times her fluent nature shrank from everything that was fixed and irrevocable—above all from the act of will that trammelled her wandering fancy, the finality that limited her outlook upon life. And now it was impossible. The three weeks in which she had known Wyndham had shown her that, compared with that complex character, that finished intellect, Ted was indeed little better than a baby. Not that she could have done without Ted—far from it. As yet Wyndham was still the unknown, shadowy, far-off, and unapproachable. The touch of Ted's hand seemed to make him living, to bring him nearer to her. Ted still stood between her and the void where there is no more revelation, no hope, no love—and Hardy would be in London in another week.

Katherine had not guessed all the truth, any more than Audrey had herself; but she had guessed enough to make her extremely anxious. Audrey was not the wife she could have wished for Ted: she disapproved of his marriage with her as a certain hindrance to his career; but, above all, she dreaded for him the agony of disappointment which must follow if Audrey gave him up. She had no very clear idea of what it would mean to him; but judging his nature by what she had seen of it, she feared some shock either to his moral system or to his artistic powers. She longed to speak to him about it; but Ted and she were not accustomed to handling their emotions, and of late they had avoided all personal questions not susceptible of humorous treatment. After this persistent choosing of the shallows, she shrank from a sudden plunge into the depths. She felt strongly, and with her strong feeling was a bar to utterance.

At last an incident occurred which laid the subject open to frivolous discussion.

Katherine was painting one afternoon, and Ted was leaning out of the window, which looked south-west to Chelsea, his thoughts travelling in a bee-line towards the little brown house. Suddenly he drew his head in with an exclamation.

"Uncle James, by Jove! He'll be upon us in another minute. I'm off!" And he made a rush for his bedroom.

Katherine had only time to wipe the paint from her brush, to throw a tablecloth over the Apollo and a mackintosh over the divine shoulders of the Venus—Mr. Pigott was a purist in art, and Katherine respected his prejudices—when her uncle arrived, panting and inarticulate.

"Well, uncle, this is a surprise! How are you?"

"No better for climbing up that precipice of yours. What on earth possessed you to come to this out-of-the-way hole?"

"It's a good room for painting, you see——"

"*What's* that? Couldn't you find a good room in West Kensington, instead of planting yourself up here away from us all?"

This was a standing grievance, as Katherine knew.

"Well, you see, it's nicer here by the river, and it's cheaper too; and—how's aunt Kate?"

"Your aunt Kate has got a stye in her eye."

"Dear me, I'm very sorry to hear it. And you, uncle?"

"Poorly, very poorly. I ought not to have got out of my bed to-day. One of my old attacks. My liver's never been the same since I caught that bad chill at your father's funeral."

Uncle James looked at Katherine severely, as if she had been to blame for the calamity. His feeling was natural. One way or another, the Havilands had been the cause of calamity in the family ever since they came into it. Family worship and the worship of the Family were different but equally indispensable forms of the one true religion. The stigma of schism, if not of atheism, attached to the Havilands in departing from the old traditions and forming a little sect by themselves. Mr. Pigott meant well by them; at any time he would have helped them substantially, in such a manner as he thought fit. But, one and all, the Havilands had refused to be benefited in any way but their own; their own way, in the Pigotts' opinion, being invariably a foolish one—"between you and me, sir, they hadn't a sound business head among them." As for Ted and Katherine, before the day when he had washed his hands of Ted in the office lavatory, uncle James had tried to play the part of an overruling Providence in their affairs, and the young infidels had signified their utter disbelief in him. Since then he had ceased to interfere with his creatures; and latterly his finger was only to be seen at times of marked crisis or disturbance, as in the arrangements for a marriage or a funeral.

An astounding piece of news had come to his ears, which was the reason of his present visitation. He hastened to the business in hand.

"What's this that I hear about Ted, eh?"

"I don't know," said Katherine, blushing violently.

"I'm told that he's taken up with some woman, nobody knows who, and that they're seen everywhere together——"

"'Who told you this?"

"Your cousin Nettie. She's seen them—constantly—in the National Gallery and the British Museum, carrying on all the time they're pretending to look at those heathen gods and goddesses"—Katherine glanced nervously round the studio. "They actually make assignations—they meet on the steps of public places. Nettie has noticed her hanging about waiting for him, and some young friends of hers saw them dining together alone at the Star and Garter. Now what's the meaning of all this?"

Katherine was too much amused to answer yet; she wanted to see what her uncle would say next. He shook his head solemnly.

"I knew what it would be when you two had it all your own way. As for you, Katherine, you took a very grave responsibility on your shoulders when you persuaded your young brother to live with you here, in this neighbourhood, away from all your relations. Your influence has been for anything but good."

"My dear uncle, you are so funny; but you're mistaken. I know Miss Craven, the lady you mean, perfectly well; she and Ted are great friends, and it's all right, I assure you."

"Do you mean to tell me he is engaged to this young lady he goes about with?"

Katherine hesitated: if she had felt inclined to gratify a curiosity which she considered impertinent, she was not at liberty to betray their secret.

"I can't tell you that, for I'm not supposed to know."

"Let me tell you, then, that it looks bad—very bad. To begin with, your cousin Nettie strongly disapproves of the young woman's appearance, so loud and over-dressed, evidently got up to attract. But it lies in a nutshell. If he's not engaged to her, why is he seen everywhere with her? If he is engaged to her, and she's a respectable woman—I say *if* she's respectable, why doesn't he introduce her to his family? Why doesn't he ask your aunt Kate to call on her?"

"Well, you see, supposing they are engaged, they wouldn't go and proclaim it all at once; and in any case, that would depend more on Miss Craven than Ted. I can't tell you any more than I have done; and I'd be greatly obliged if you wouldn't allow Ted's affairs to be gossiped about by cousin Nettie or anybody else."

She was relieved for the moment by the entrance of Mrs. Rogers with the tea-tray.

"Tea, uncle?"

"No, thank you, none of your cat-lap. I must see Ted himself. Where is he?"

"I'm not sure, but I *think* he's gone out."

Mrs. Rogers looked up from her tray, pleased to give valuable information.

"Mr. 'Aviland is in 'is bedroom, m'm; I 'eard 'im as I come up."

"Oh, I'll go and tell him then."

She found Ted dressing himself carefully before calling on Audrey. She wasted five minutes in trying to persuade him to see his uncle. Ted was firm.

"Give him my very kindest regards, and tell him a pressing engagement alone prevents my waiting on him."

With that he ran merrily downstairs. His feet carried him very swiftly towards Audrey.

Katherine gave the message, with some modifications; and Mr. Pigott, seeing that no good was to be gained by staying, took his leave.

Ted came back sooner than his sister had expected. He smiled faintly at the absurd appearance of the Venus in her mackintosh, but he was evidently depressed. He looked mournfully at the tea-table.

"I'm afraid the tea's poison, Ted, and it's cold."

"It doesn't matter, I don't want any."

"Had tea at Audrey's?"

"No."

He strode impatiently to the table and took up one of the illustrations Katherine had been working at.

"What's up?" said she.

"Oh—er—for one thing, I've heard from the editor of the 'Sunday Illustrated.' He's in a beastly bad temper, and says my last batch of illustrations isn't funny enough. The old duffer's bringing out a religious serial, and he must have humour to make it go down."

Katherine was relieved. To divert him, she told him the family's opinion as to his relations with Audrey. That raised his spirits so far that he called his uncle a "fantastic old gander," and his cousin Nettie an "evil-minded little beast."

"After all, Ted," said Katherine, judicially, "why does Audrey go on making a mystery of your engagement?"

"I don't know and I don't care," said Ted, savagely.

Surely it was not in the power of that harmless person, the editor of the "Sunday Illustrated," to move him so? Something must have happened.

What had happened was this. As Ted was going into the little brown house at Chelsea he had met Mr. Langley Wyndham coming out of it; and for the first time in his life he had found Audrey in a bad temper. She was annoyed, in the first place, because the novelist had been unable to stay to tea. She had provided a chocolate cake on purpose, the eminent man having once approved of that delicacy. (It was a pretty way Audrey had, this remembering the likings of her friends.) She was also annoyed because Ted's coming had followed so immediately on Wyndham's going. It was her habit now, whenever she had seen Wyndham, to pass from the reality of his presence into a reverie which revived the sense of it, and Ted's arrival had interfered with this pastime. The first thing the boy did, too, was to wound her tenderest susceptibilities. He began playing with the books that lay beside her.

"What a literary cat it is!"

She frowned and drew in her breath quickly, as if in pain. He went on turning over the pages—it was Wyndham's "London Legends"—with irreverent fingers.

"I should very much like to know——" said Audrey to Ted, and stopped short.

"What would you very much like to know, Puss?"

"What you saw in me, to begin with."

"I haven't the remotest idea—unless it was your intellect."

"I should also like to know," said Audrey to the teapot, "why people fall in love?"

"The taste is either natural or acquired. Some take to it because they like it; some are driven to it by a hereditary tendency or an unhappy home. I do it myself to drown care."

"Will you have any tea?" asked Audrey, sternly.

"No, thank you, I won't."

She laughed, as she might have laughed at a greedy child for revenging on its stomach the injury done to its heart. Poor Ted, he was fond of chocolate cake too! She would have given anything at that moment if she could have provoked him into quarrelling with her.

Instead of quarrelling, he stroked her beautiful hair as if she had been some soft but irritable animal. He said he was sure her dear little head was aching because she was so bad-tempered; he implored her not to eat too much cake, and promised to call again another day, when he hoped to find her better. So he left her, and went home with a dead weight at his heart.

Towards evening his misery became so acute that he could no longer keep it to himself. They were on the leads, in the long August twilight, Katherine sitting with her back against the tall chimney, watching the reflection of the sunset in the east, the boy lying at her feet, with his heels in the air and his head in the nasturtiums. The time, the place, the attitude were all favourable to confidences, and Ted wound up his by asking Katherine what she thought of Audrey? Now was the moment to rid herself of the burden that weighed on her; Ted might never be in so favourable a mood again. She spoke very gently.

"Ted, I am going to hurt your feelings. I don't quite know how to tell you what I think of her. She's not good enough for you, to begin with——"

"I know she's not intelligent. She can't help that."

"And she's not affectionate. Oh, Ted, forgive me! but she doesn't love you—she can't, it's not in her. She loves no one but herself."

"She *is* a little selfish, but she can't help that either. It makes no difference."

"So I fear. And then she's years older than you are, and you can't marry for ages; don't you see how impossible it all is?"

Her voice thrilled with her longing to impress him with her own conviction. His passion was wrestling with a ghastly doubt, but it was of the kind that dies hard.

"Of course it's quite impossible now"—neither he nor Katherine considered the question of Audrey's money, they had never thought of it—"but, as she said herself, in five years' time, when she's thirty and I'm twenty-five, the difference in our ages won't be so marked."

"It will be as marked as ever, even if your intellect grows at its present rate of development."

"I've admitted that she's a little deficient in parts; and, as you justly observe, stupidity, like death, is levelling. We should suit each other exactly in time."

"Ah, if you can see that, why, oh why, did you fall in love with her?"

"*She* asked me that this afternoon. I said it was because she was so clever. It was because I was a fool—stupidity came upon me like a madness—I wish to heaven I'd never done it. It's played the devil with my chances. I was sitting calmly on the highroad to success, with my camp-stool and my little portable easel, not interfering in the least with the traffic, when she came along like a steam-roller, knocked me down, crushed me, and rolled me out flat. I shall never recover my natural shape; and as for the camp-stool and the portable easel—these things are an allegory. But I love her all the same."

Katherine laughed in spite of herself, but she understood the allegory. Would he ever recover his natural shape? To that end she was determined to make him face the worst.

"Ted, what would you do, supposing—only supposing—she were to fling you over for—for some one else?"

"I should blow my brains out, if I had any left. Verdict, suicide while in a state of temporary insanity."

"Suicide of a genius! That would be a fine feather in Audrey's cap."

"She always had exquisite taste in dress. Besides, she's welcome to it—or to any little trifle of the kind."

It was useless attempting to make any impression on him. She gave it up. Ted, however, was so charmed with the idea of suicide that he spent the rest of the evening discussing ways and means. He was not going to blow his brains out, or to take poison in his bedroom, or do anything disagreeable that would depreciate Mrs. Rogers's property. On the whole, drowning was the cheapest, and would suit him best, if he could summon up spirits for it. Only he didn't want to spoil the river for *her*. It must be somewhere below London Bridge, say Wapping Old Stairs. Here Katherine suggested that he had better go to bed.

He went, and lay awake all night in a half-fever. When Katherine went into his room the next morning (ten o'clock had struck, and there was no appearance of Ted), she found him lying in a deep sleep; one arm was flung outside the counterpane, the hand had closed on a crumpled sheet of paper. It was Audrey's last note of invitation—the baby had taken it to bed with him.

"Poor boy—poor, poor Ted!"

But, for all her sympathy, love, the stupidity that comes on you like a madness, was a thing incomprehensible to Katherine.

CHAPTER XIV

The next day Audrey's head was aching to some purpose. She had been going through a course of Langley Wyndham. Yesterday he had brought her his last book, "London Legends," and she had sat up half the night to read it. She was to tell him what she thought of it, and her ideas were in a whirl.

She stayed in bed for breakfast, excused herself from lunch, left word with the footman that she was not at home that afternoon, and sent down another message five minutes afterwards that, if by any chance Mr. Wyndham were to call, he might be admitted. "Not that he's in the least likely to come after being here yesterday," she said to herself; and yet, as she sat alone in the drawing room, she listened for the ringing of bells, the opening of doors, and the sound of footsteps on the stairs. Every five minutes she looked at the clock, and her heart kept time to its ticking. Half-past two. In any case he wouldn't come before three; and yet—surely that was the front-door bell. No. Three o'clock, four o'clock—he would be more likely to drop in about tea-time. Five o'clock; tea came in on the stroke of it, and still no Wyndham. Half-past five—he had once called later than that when he wanted to find her alone. Something told her that he would come to-day. He would be anxious to know what she thought of his book. She was in that state of mind when people trust in intuitions, failing positive evidence. Surely in some past state of existence she had sat in that chair, surrounded by the same objects, thinking the same thoughts, and that train of ideas had been completed by the arrival of Wyndham. Science accounts for this sensation by supposing that one half of the brain, more agile than another, jumps to its conclusion before its tardier fellow can arrive. To Audrey it was a prophecy certain of fulfilment. And all the time her head kept on aching. The poor little brain went on wandering in a maze of its own making. How truly she had, in cousin Bella's phrase, "entangled herself" with Hardy, with Ted, and possibly, nay probably, with Wyndham. She saw no escape from the dreadful situation. And as a dark background to her thoughts there hung the shadow of Hardy's return. She only realised it in these moods of reaction that followed the exaltation of the last three weeks. And to make matters worse, for the first time in her life she was dissatisfied with herself. Not that she was in the least aware of the deterioration of her character. She took no count of the endless little meannesses and falsehoods which she was driven into by her position. Simple straightforward action was impossible. This much was evident to her, that whatever course she took now, she must end by forfeiting some one's good opinion: Hardy's first—well, she could get over that; but Ted's? Katherine's? Wyndham's?—if he came to know everything? It was there, in that last possibility, that she suffered most.

Half-past six. She had given up Wyndham and her belief in psychical prophecy, and was trying to find relief from unpleasant reflections in a book, when Wyndham actually appeared. He came in with the confident smile of the friend sure of a welcome at all hours.

"Forgive my calling at this unholy time. I knew if I came earlier I should find you surrounded by an admiring crowd. I wanted to see you alone."

"Quite right. I am always at home to friends."

They dropped into one of those trivial dialogues which were Audrey's despair in her intercourse with Wyndham.

Suddenly his tone changed. He took up "London Legends."

"As you've already guessed, my egregious vanity brings me here. I don't know whether you've had time to look at the thing——"

"I sat up to finish it last night."

"Indeed. What did you think of it?"

"Don't ask me. I didn't criticise—sympathy comes first."

"Excuse me, it doesn't. Criticism comes first with all of us. Sympathy comes last of all—when we know the whole of life, and understand it."

"What would my poor little opinion be worth?"

"Everything. A really unbiassed judgment is the rarest thing in the world, and there's always a charm about naïve criticism."

"I couldn't put the book down. Can I say more?"

"Yes, of course you can say more. You can tell me which legend you disliked least; you can criticise my hero's conduct, and find fault with my heroine's manners; you can object to my plot, pick holes in my style. No, thank goodness, you can't do that; but you can take exception to my morality."

She sat silent, waiting for her cue, and trying to collect her thoughts, which were fluttering all abroad in generalities.

He went on with a touch of bitterness in his voice—

"I thought so. It's the old stumbling-block—my morality. If it hadn't been for that, you would have told me, wouldn't you? that my figures breathe and move, that every touch is true to life. But you daren't. You are afraid of reality; facts are so immoral."

It would be impossible to describe the accent of scorn which Wyndham threw into this last word.

"I thought your book very clever—in spite of the facts."

"Facts or no facts, you'd rather have your beliefs, wouldn't you?"

"No, no; I lost them all long ago!" cried Audrey, indignantly.

"I don't mean the old vulgar dogmas, of course, but the dear little ideals that shed such a rosy light on things in general, you know. Ah! that's what you want; and when an artist paints the real thing for you, you say, 'Thank you; yes, it's very clever, I see; but I prefer the pretty magic-lantern views, and the limelight of life.'"

"Not at all. I've much too great a regard for truth."

"I know. You're always looking for Truth, with a capital T; but, when it comes to the point, you'd rather have two miserable little half-truths than one honest whole truth about anything. That's why you disliked my book."

"I didn't."

"Oh, yes, you did. What you disliked about it was this. It made you see men and women, not as you imagined them, but as God made them. You saw, that is, the naked human soul, stripped of the clumsy draperies that Puritanism wraps round it. You saw below the surface—below the top-dressing of education, below the solid layer of traditional morality—deep down to the primitive passions, the fire of the clay we're all made of. You saw love and hate, forces which are older than all religions and all laws, older than man and woman, and which make men and women what they are. And they seemed to you not commonplaces, which they are—but something worse. You don't know that these *facts* are the stuff of art, because they are the stuff of nature; that it takes multitudes of such facts, not just one or two picked out because of their 'moral beauty'—for you purists believe in the beauty of morality as well as in the immorality of beauty—to make up a faithful picture of life. And you shuddered, didn't you? as you laid down the book you sat up half the night to read, and you said it was ugly, revolting; you couldn't see any perfect characters in it—only character in the making, only wretched men and women acting according to certain disagreeable laws, which are none the less immutable because one half of the world professes to ignore their existence. You said, 'Take away the whole world of nature, take away logic and science and art, but leave me—leave me my ideals!' Isn't that it?"

The torrent of his rhetoric swept her away, she knew not whither. But in his last words she had caught her cue. If she was ever to be an influence in Wyndham's life, encouraging, inspiring his best work, she must not suffer him to speak lightly of "ideals." It seemed to her that her methods with Ted were crude compared with her management of Wyndham.

"Oh, don't, don't! It's dreadful! But you are right. I can't live without ideals. All the great artists had them. You have them yourself, or at least you *had* them. I don't know what to think about your book—I can't think, I can only feel; and I read between the lines. Surely you feel with me that there's nothing worth living for except morality? Surely you believe in purity and goodness?"

Her face was flushed, her hands were clasped tightly together in her intensity. So strong was the illusion her manner produced, that for one second Wyndham could have been convinced of her absolute sincerity. Not long—no, not long afterwards, her words were to come back to him with irony.

"Morality? I've the greatest respect for it. But after all, its rules only mark off one little corner from the plain of life. Out there, in the open, are the fine landscapes and the great highroads of thought. And if you are to travel at all, you must go by those ways. There's dust on them, and there's mud—plenty of mud; but—there are no others."

"I would be very careful where I put my feet, though. I don't like muddy boots."

"I daresay not; who does? But the traveller is not always thinking about his boots."

"Don't let's talk about boots." She made a little movement with her mouth, simulating disgust.

"Your own metaphor; but never mind. *A propos des bottes*, I should like——" he broke off and added in a deep, hieratic voice, "To the pure all things are pure, but to the Puritan most things are impure. I wish I could make you see that; but it's a large subject. And besides, I want to talk about you."

"Me?"

"Yes, you. With all your beliefs, there was a time, if I'm not much mistaken, when you were pleased to doubt the existence of your charming self?"

She looked up with a smile of pleasure and of perfect comprehension. He could hardly have said anything more delicately caressing to her self-love. It seemed, then, that every word she had uttered in his hearing had been weighed and treasured up. She could hardly be supposed to know that this power of noticing and preserving such little personal details was one of the functions of the literary organism. If a woman like Miss Fraser had been flattered by it, what must have been its effect on the susceptible Audrey?

"So you remember that too?" she said, softly.

"Yes; it impressed me at the time. Now I know you better I don't wonder at it. It's the fault of your very lovely and feminine idealism, but you seem to me to have hardly any hold on the fact of existence, to be unable to realise it. If I could only give you the sense of life—make you feel the movement, the passion, the drama of it! My books have a little of that; they've got the right atmosphere, the *smell* of life. But never mind my books. I don't want you to have another literary craze—I beg your pardon, I mean phase; you seem to have had an artistic one lately."

He rose to go.

"I've always cared for the great things of life," said she.

"Ah yes—the great things, stamped with other people's approval. I want you to love life itself, so that you may be yourself, and feel yourself being."

Her whole nature responded as the strings of the violin to the bow of the master. "Life" was one of those words which specially stirred her sensibility. As Wyndham had foreseen, it was a word to conjure with; and now, as he had willed, the idea of it possessed her. She repeated mechanically—

"Life—to love life for itself——"

"And first—you must know life in order to love it."

She sighed slightly, as if she had taken in a little more breath to say good-bye. The ideal was flown. She had received the stamp of Wyndham's spirit, as if it had been iron upon wax. It was her way of being herself and feeling herself being.

The same evening she wrote a little note to Ted that ran thus:—

"Dearest Ted,—I have been thinking it all over, ever since yesterday, and I am convinced that my only right course is to break off our engagement. It has all been a mistake—mine and yours. Why should we not recognise it, instead of each persisting in making the other miserable? I release you from your promise to me, and will always remain very affectionately yours, AUDREY CRAVEN."

She had just sent the note to the post, when a servant came in with a telegram. It was from Hardy, announcing his arrival at Queenstown. And she had trusted to her engagement to Ted for protection against Vincent's claim.

If she had only waited!

CHAPTER XV

"Great strength and safety with heaviest charges." "Absolute immunity from all risk of blowing open." "The combination of a perfect trigger action with a perfect cocking action." Ted Haviland was standing outside the window of a gunsmith's shop in the King's Road, Chelsea, reading the enticing legends in which Mr. Webley sets forth the superiority of his wares above those of all other makers. It was the second day after he had got Audrey's letter. In his least hopeful moods he had never expected that blow; and when it fell, as a bolt from the blue, he was stunned and could not realise that he was struck. He imagined all kinds of explanations to account for Audrey's conduct. It was a misunderstanding, a sudden freak; there was some mystery waiting to be solved; some one—his cousin Nettie probably—had spread some story about him which had reached Audrey. The scandal already spread in the family would have been enough; she could hardly have identified its loudly dressed heroine as herself. It only remained for him to clear his character. Anything, anything rather than believe in what all healthy youth revolts against—the irrevocable, the end.

He had tried three times to see Audrey, and she was "not at home"; though the third time he had seen her go into the house not two minutes before. That instant he had turned away with a stinging mist in his eyes and the blood surging in his brain. His thoughts now leaped to the end as blindly as they had shrunk from it before. He had no definite idea of shooting himself when he turned into the King's Road—his one object was to go in any direction rather than home; but the shop window, with its stacks of rifles and cards displaying "Mark I." revolvers, arranged on them like the spokes of a wheel, caught his attention. He was possessed with the desire to have a revolver of his own, no matter for what purpose.

He had just chosen a "Mark I.," and was going into the shop to buy it, when he heard his name called in a loud hearty voice, "Ted, you bounder! stop!" and his arm was pulled with a grip that drew him backward from the doorstep.

"Hardy!"

He knew the voice, but it was hard to recognise the man. A thick black beard, a face that might have been tanned with bark, trousers tucked into high boots, and tightened with a belt like a horse-girth, an old Norfolk jacket stained with travel and the chase, a canvas shirt laced with a red cord and tassels, and a plate-like hat of grey felt flapping about his ears, made Hardy look something like a cowboy or a bandit. So singular was the apparition that had plucked Ted back from the abyss, that the Furies and the infernal phantoms vanished into smoke before it. It brought with it a breath of Atlantic seas and of winds from the far West.

"You young rascal! so it's you, is it? I didn't know you from Satan, till I saw you turn round after flattening your nose against what's-his-name's plate-glass. I wish I were in your shoes."

"Do you?" said Ted, with a grimace. "H'm. Why?"

"Because your whole expression suggests—partridges!"

"Does it? As it happens, I was thinking about a revolver."

"Potting burglars, eh? About all the sport you poor devils of Cockneys will get on the First."

"Look here, Hardy, this is uncanny. Where did you spring from?"

"Straight from Euston this afternoon, from Queenstown yesterday morning, before that from the other side of the Rockies."

"That accounts for your amazing get-up."

"Yes; and, by Jove! after a year in a log-hut on the wrong side of a precipice, you're glad to get your feet on London pavement, and smell London smells again. And look there, Ted! There isn't a lovelier sight on God's earth than a well-dressed Englishwoman. Where are we going? How about that revolver?"

Ted had forgotten all about it. Hardy's sane, open-air spirits had infected him so far that he had let himself be dragged at a rapid pace up the King's Road, where their progress attracted considerable attention. As Hardy strode on, with his long swinging legs, he appeared to be scattering the crowd before him.

"Never mind the thing now; it'll keep. How that girl stares! Does she take us for banditti?"

"Not you, you puppy, in that coat and topper. No mistaking you for anything but what you are—the sickly product of an effete civilisation. Don't be frightened, you haven't gone off in the least; you're a little pale, but prettier than you were, if anything."

"I say *you* ought to be in the bosom of your family."

"I haven't got a family."

"Well, what brings you here of all places in the world?"

"My cousin Audrey Craven."

There was no reserve about Hardy. At the name, so unexpectedly spoken, the under-world opened again for Ted, with all its Furies. They walked on for some minutes in silence, then Hardy began again—

"I called to see her. Of course she was out. Hard lines, wasn't it?"

Ted forced himself to speak. "Oh yes, beastly hard."

"You must have met her lately. How is she looking?"

"Oh, remarkably cheerful, when I last saw her."

"When was that?" Hardy asked, a little anxiously.

"The day before yesterday."

"Ah! She'd got my telegram then."

Ted bit his lip. They were too much absorbed, he in his misery and Hardy in his joy, for either to be conscious of the other's feeling.

"Old boy," said Hardy, as they turned out of the King's Road, "what have you got to do?"

"Nothing."

"Then come and help me to hunt up some diggings. How about Devon Street?"

"I don't know; but I suppose we can look," said Ted, dismally. Hardy's spirits were beginning to pall on him.

"I may as well go and look up Katherine, while I'm about it. Dear old Sis, I suppose she'll be out too."

"Not she—she's too busy for that."

"Not too busy to see her old playfellow, you bet your boots."

He was so glad to see everybody again that he was sure everybody must be glad to see him. In his rapture at being in London, the place he loathed and execrated a year ago, he could have embraced the stranger in the street. Those miles of pavement, those towering walls that seemed to make streets of the sky as he looked up, all that world of brick and mortar was Audrey's world, the ground for her feet, the scene of all her doings. The women that went by wore the fashions she would be wearing now. At any moment she herself might turn out of some shop-door, round some corner. A faint hope that he might find her with Katherine had led him to Devon Street.

But Ted's, not Audrey's, were the first hands that touched his; and it was not Audrey, but his "little half-sister," that gave Hardy his first welcome home.

"Well, Sis?"

"Vincent! is it you?"

There was nothing in the words but the glad courtesy of the woman who had been his playfellow in the days when he was a boy and she a tomboy, but they went to Hardy's heart and dried up his speech. They were the first kind words he had heard since he left England.

Katherine put away her work and made him sit in the one comfortable chair the studio afforded; Mrs. Rogers was sent for cakes and cream at a moment's notice; and the resources of the tiny household were taxed to their utmost to do honour to the returned emigrant. Even Ted forgot his gloom for the time being, and took his part in these hospitable rites. Then came the question of Hardy's lodgings. Mrs. Rogers was consulted, and, being unable to name any landlady of greater respectability than herself, and her ground-floor happening to be to let—the rarest thing in the world for her—she suggested that "the gentleman should try it for a week or two, till 'e could suit 'isself elsewhere. But, though I sy it as shouldn't, when a gentleman comes to me, sir, 'e wants to sty. My larst gentleman, 'e'd a styd with me till 'e was took awy in 'is coffin if I'd a kep' 'im; but Lor' bless you, my dear, 'e was that pertic'ler I couldn't do with 'is fads, not at fancy prices, I couldn't. I 'ad to tell 'im to gow, for Mussy's syke, where 'e'd git 'is own French cook, and 'is own butler to black 'is 'arf-doz'n pyre o' boots all at once for 'im." This was the recognised fiction by which Mrs. Rogers accounted for the departure of any of her lodgers. Lest it should seem to speak badly for her willingness and for the quality of the attendance at No. 12, she invariably added, "Not but wot I'd work my 'ead orf to please any gentleman that *is* a gentleman; and when you've eaten one of my dinners, sir, you won't want nobody else to cook and do for you no more." And though Ted had pointed out to her the sinister ambiguity of this formula, she had never invented any other.

The ground-floor was seen; and after Mrs. Rogers, on her part, had stipulated for cold lunches three days in the week, and not more than one bath in the one day; and after Katherine, on Hardy's part, had suggested sundry innovations, involving the condemnation of all the pictures and ornaments she could lay her hands on,—a piece of sacrilege which Mrs. Rogers regarded more in sorrow than in anger, as indicating a pitiable aberration of intellect,—the rooms were taken from that date.

Was it Chance, or Necessity, or Providence, that caused Ted and Hardy to meet at the parting of the ways?—that waked Ted from the dream of self-destruction, and lodged Hardy under the same roof with Katherine Haviland?

His arrangements completed, Hardy hurried off again to Chelsea. Audrey, he thought, had expected him by a later train, and would be back by six o'clock, waiting for him. This time the footman met him with a little note from his mistress. Audrey had never dreamed that

Vincent could get up to town so quickly. She was so sorry she had missed him; especially as she had had to go to bed with a feverish cold and a splitting headache. She would be delighted to see him if he could call to-morrow afternoon, between three and four. And she was always very affectionately his.

He was bitterly disappointed, but his disappointment was nothing to his trouble about Audrey's illness. Feverish colds contracted in August often prove fatal. But he was not utterly cast down. There was still to-morrow.

He went back to Devon Street slowly, for he felt tired, out of all proportion to his muscular exertions that day. During the evening, which he spent in the Havilands' studio, his depression gave way before the prospect of seeing Audrey to-morrow. He looked at Katherine's pictures, gave her a great deal of advice, and expressed the utmost astonishment at the progress she had made. He considered "The Witch of Atlas" particularly fine.

"It was painted four years ago, and as a matter of fact I haven't made a bit of progress since. But never mind, you're quite right. It isn't half bad."

She bent over her picture lovingly, brushed away the dust from the canvas, and turned it resolutely with its face to the wall. She had not looked at it since the day of renunciation. Her work led Hardy on to talk of his, and he grew eloquent about the book, "Sport West of the Rockies," which, as he had once told Audrey, was "to make posterity sit up." He had the manuscript downstairs in his bag. Some day he would read them a chapter or two; it would give them some idea of wild virgin Nature, of what a sportsman's life really was—the best life, perhaps, take it all round, to be lived on this earth; it was to be the Pioneer-book of its subject. Hardy was always at his ease with Ted and Katherine. Self-restraint was superfluous in their company; they knew him too well, and liked him in spite of their knowledge. They were used to his tempestuous bursts of narrative, and would laugh frankly in his face, while he joined in the laugh with the greatest enjoyment. With him ornamental story-telling was an amusing game, in which, if you were clever enough to catch him lying, you had won and he had lost, that was all.

To-night he lay back in his chair and expanded gloriously. He told tales of perilous adventure by flood and field, by mountain and forest; of the wild chase of moose and wapiti among the snows of the Rockies; of the fierce delight of single-handed combat with grizzly bears, the deadliest of their kind; of how he, Hardy, had been rolled down a cañon, locked in the embrace of a furry fiend that he had stabbed in the throat one second before the fatal hug. He told of the melting of the snows in forest rivers; of the flood that swept away the lonely traveller's encampment, and bore him, astride on a log of driftwood, five miles amid wrack and boulders on its whirling current; of deliverance through a pious Indian and his canoe, which he entered as by a miracle in mid-stream, and without upsetting any of the three. He told of long wanderings in the twilight solitudes of Canadian forests; of dangers from wolves and the wild coyotes, half-dog, half-wolf, heard nightly howling round the Indian camp-fires; and from the intangible malice of the skunk, a beautiful but dreadful power, to be propitiated with bated breath and muffled footstep. He told, too, of the chip-munks, with their sharp twittering bark; and he contrived to invest even these tiny creatures with an atmosphere of terror—for it is well known that their temper is atrocious, and that a colony of them will set upon the unfortunate traveller who happens to offend one, and leave nothing of him but his bones and the indigestible portions of his clothing. And over all he cast the glamour of his fancy, as if it had been the red light of the prairie sunsets; in it he appeared transfigured, a half-mythical personage, heroic, if not indeed divine. The whole of it had appeared word for word in the pages of the Pioneer-book.

"Ah, Sis," he observed complacently at the end of it, "that's all copy for 'Sport West of the Rockies.' When that comes out you'll soon see me at the top of the tree. Why aren't you an artist in words? Why don't you use the pen instead of the brush?"

He implied that if her ambition had been literary he would have raised her to a position just below him, on the highest pinnacle of earthly fame. Then he passed, by a gentle transition, to another subject.

"By-the-bye, have you two seen much of my cousin Audrey?"

This second utterance of the name was too much for Ted's overstrained nerves. He got up, stifled a yawn, and held out his hand to Hardy.

"I say, do you mind if I go to bed now? I can't for the life of me keep awake."

"Good-night, old fellow; I'm afraid I've sent you to sleep with my yarns."

"Not a bit. We'll have some more to-morrow."

To-morrow?

"What's the matter with the boy, Kathy? He looks seedy."

"Oh, nothing. He's not over-strong, perhaps, but he's all right."

"What's he doing with himself here?"

"Painting. Oh, Vincent, I should like you to see some of his things, now he's gone!"

All her pride in her brother was roused, perhaps by Vincent's boasting. She lifted the white linen cloth that covered one of Ted's easels, and revealed the portrait of Audrey. She had not guessed the truth; if she had, she would not have looked at Vincent just then. The effect she had produced was unmistakable. The blood rose to his face in a wave that died suddenly away, leaving a yellowish pallor under its sunburn.

"How beautiful!" he said softly, more to himself than Katherine.

He gazed at the portrait as if his eyes would never be satisfied with seeing. The pathos in his face gave it a sort of spirituality; and Katherine noticed his hand trembling as he helped her to cover the picture again.

"It's like her—as only genius could make it."

Only genius? Did he think that only genius had wrought that work of transfiguration, in which Katherine found it hard to see any likeness to the woman as she knew her now? She had read the secret of Vincent's hope. Ought she to let him believe a lie? Did not she, Ted's sister, of all people owe him the truth? No. Vincent's eyes looked as if they wanted sleep before everything. Sufficient unto the night is the evil thereof. And perhaps, after all, she had been mistaken. Hardy held out his hand, said a short good-night, and was gone before she could say more.

There flashed back on her the memory of Audrey's first visit to her. She recalled her little self-conscious air of possession in speaking of her cousin. She was morally certain that Audrey had treated Vincent as she had treated Ted.

"Beware of the woman who kisses you on both cheeks; it's too much for friendship, and too little for love!"

Hardy went out of doors, turned on to the Embankment, and so on to Chelsea, for the third time that day. He wanted to assure himself of Audrey's nearness by one more sight of the brown brick shrine that held her. The house stood as he had seen it once before, asleep in the yellow gaslight, shut in from the road by the trees, screened from the lamps on the Embankment by the storm-shutters folded over its windows, guarding its secrets well, all but two windows on the second floor, which were open to the night. That was Audrey's room, he knew. Little fool! Ill with a feverish cold, and sleeping with open windows! For about half an hour he walked up and down on the Embankment opposite, like a sentry on duty, his long shadow blackening and fading as he passed from light to light.

When he got back to his rooms, he felt a sensation that had sometimes come upon him after a long day's hunting, a feeling of deadly fatigue and stifling emptiness, as if the rest of his body were drained of the blood that choked his heart. He opened his travelling-bag, took out a large silver flask, looked at it, sighed, shuddered slightly, poured about two tablespoonfuls of brandy down his throat; and then, with a gesture of indescribable disgust, emptied the remainder out of the window into the yard below. He undressed and got into bed quickly, turned over on his right side for greater ease, and was soon asleep and dreaming of to-morrow.

CHAPTER XVI

There was no sleep for Ted that night. Towards morning he fell into a doze, broken by unpleasant dreams, and woke with a confused consciousness of trouble. It had been connected in his dreams with Hardy's return, and, once awake, the knowledge that he was in the same house with him was insupportable. Not that he had yet guessed how Vincent stood to Audrey; he had simply a nervous dread of hearing him talk about her. The casual utterance of her name went through him like a sword, and in his present mood Vincent's boisterous spirit disturbed and irritated him. More to get away from him than with any definite idea of work, he spent his morning at the National Gallery, touching up the copy of the Botticelli Madonna which Katherine had begun long ago for Audrey. He had set to work almost mechanically, with a sense that whatever he did at the present moment was only provisional,—only a staving off of the intolerable future; but soon the technical difficulties of his task absorbed him, and he became interested in spite of himself. He was so passive to the spiritual influences of line and colour, that perhaps the beauty of the grey-eyed girl Madonna may have given him something of its own tranquillity.

Unfortunately the good effects of his morning's industry were undone when he got home, by finding Hardy alone in the studio, sitting before Audrey's portrait. He had dragged the easel to the light, and had been studying the canvas for some minutes before Ted came in. The boy stifled an angry exclamation.

"Ted," said Hardy, "what do you want for this picture?"

"I don't want anything for it."

"Nonsense! Every good picture has its price."

"This one hasn't, anyway."

"Look here, and don't be a young fool. This is the best thing you've done in your life or ever will do. I'm in rather low water at present, but wait till I've heard from my British Columbian agent, or, better still, wait till the Pioneer-book comes out, and I'll give you a hundred for it, honour bright, if you'll let me have it at once."

"I can't let you have it at once, and I won't let you have it at all."

"The deuce you won't! Come, fix your own price."

"I'm not a swindling dealer, and I'm not a liar, though you mightn't think it. I told you I wasn't going to let you have it at any price."

"H'm. Do you mind telling me one thing? Are you going to sell it to any one else?"

"I'm not going to sell it to any one. I'm going to keep it myself."

They looked at each other with steady eyes, each understanding and each defying the other's thought. Hardy's face was the first to soften. He put his hand on Ted's shoulders. "All right, old boy. We've hit each other hard this time. The least we can do is to hold our tongues about it." And he left him.

Hardy spoke with the magnanimity of imperfect comprehension. He had been defeated in his purpose of buying Audrey's portrait; but however great his discomfiture, he, being the successful lover, could afford a little pity for Ted as the victim of a hopeless passion. To Ted, on the other hand, the revelation of Hardy's feelings threw light on Audrey's conduct. It accounted for everything that was most inexplicable in it. It must have been the news of Hardy's return that made her break off her engagement so suddenly. His instinct told him that she had probably given her word to her cousin before he left England; jealousy suggested that she had cared for him all the time. He tried to reason it out, but stopped short of the obvious conclusion that, if these things were altogether as he supposed, her engagement to himself must have been merely an amusement hit upon by Audrey to fill up a dull interval. He preferred to regard it as a mystery. And now all reasoning gave way before the desire to see her again, and know the truth from herself once for all.

To Audrey, as the fountain of truth, he accordingly went, choosing a time between half-past two and three when she was most likely to be in. As he reached her door, it was being held open for her to go out, and she was standing in the outer hall buttoning her gloves. She drew back when she saw Ted, but escape was impossible. He saw the movement and the flash of her little white teeth as she bit her lip with annoyance.

She came forward smiling.

"Oh, is it you, Ted? As you see, I'm just going out."

"You will see me before you go?"

"I can't possibly. I've got to go and call on an uncle and aunt at the Hôtel Metropole."

"I'm very sorry. But I won't keep you more than ten minutes."

"I can't spare ten minutes. I'm late as it is, and I have to be back by half-past three. I've got an appointment."

"You've not time to get there and back. You'd better put it off."

"I can't, Ted. They're only up from Friday till Monday. Dean Craven has to preach at the Abbey to-morrow. Come again."

"I can't come again."

"Well, then— —" she hesitated. "You may walk part of the way with me."

He went with her down the short flagged path that led to the gate. Once out of the servant's hearing, he stopped, and looked firmly in her face.

"I must see you now, and it had better be in the house. I've only one question to ask you. Five minutes will be enough for that—at least it won't be my fault if it isn't."

She had laid her hand on the gate, which Ted held shut, and her mouth was obstinately set. Something in his voice conquered her self-will. She turned and led the way to the house.

"You had better come into the morning-room."

He followed her; she closed the door, and they stood facing each other a moment without speaking.

"Well, Ted?" Her voice went to his heart with its piercing sweetness.

"Audrey, why did you write that letter?"

"Because it was easier to write what I did than to say it. Do you want to hold me to my word?"

"No. I want to know your reasons for breaking it. You haven't given me any yet."

"I did, Ted. I told you it had all been a mistake—yours and mine."

"Speak for yourself. Where was my mistake?"

"The mistake was in our ever getting engaged at all—in our thinking that we cared for each other."

"I cared enough for you, didn't I?"

"No, you didn't. You only thought you did. Katherine told me——"

"What did Katherine tell you?"

"That you hadn't any feelings, that you really cared for nothing but your painting, that you'd only a ru—rudimentary heart."

"Really? That is interesting. When did she tell you that?"

"The very day we were engaged."

"And you believed her?"

"Not then. I did afterwards."

"How long afterwards—the other day?"

"Ye-yes; I think so."

"I see—when you wanted to believe it. Not before."

She was trembling, but she gathered together all her feeble forces for the defence.

"No, no; don't you remember? At the very first—the day of our engagement—we were both so miserable at the idea of your going away—we did it all so recklessly—before either of us thought. You see, Ted, you were so very young."

"It's a pity that didn't strike you before."

"It did, it did; but I wouldn't think of it. I blinded myself. The fact is, we were both as mad as hatters. You know people can't get married in that state. We should have had to wait for a—a lucid interval."

Ted recognised the miserable pleasantry; it was what he had said to her himself a day or two after their engagement. The phrase had amused Audrey at the time and lodged in her memory. She borrowed it now in her hour of need, and laughed, unconscious of her plagiarism.

"I understand perfectly. You want to get rid of me as a proof of your own sanity. Is that it?"

She looked up in the utmost surprise. "Not to get rid of you, Ted, of course not. I shall still keep you as my best friend."

"Thanks. You had better not try to do that. I'm told I've no talent for friendship."

"Then I suppose, after this, you'd rather I cut you, if we meet?"

"You can please yourself about that."

"You may be sure I shall. Oh, Ted, I didn't expect that from you! But it's quite right. Hit hard, I can't defend myself."

"Please don't attempt it, there's no occasion to. Only tell me one thing."

"Well?" She sat down as if wearied with this unnecessary trifling.

He paused.

"It's evident that you don't care about *me*. Do you care for any one else?"

"You've no right to ask me that."

"Haven't I? I thought I had; and, if you'll only think a minute, you'll agree with me."

She put her head on one side as if gravely considering the question.

"No. You've no right to ask me that."

"Let me put it differently—since your feelings are sacred, you needn't tell me anything about *them*. Were you engaged to Hardy before you knew me?"

"That question is even more impertinent than the last."

"I beg your pardon then. Don't answer it, if you don't like to."

He turned away.

"Don't go yet, Ted. I haven't done. Listen. I was thoughtless, I was mistaken" (Audrey was anxious to escape the imputation of a big fault by the graceful confession of a little one), "but I'm not as bad as you think me. You think I cared for Vincent. I didn't. I never cared a straw about him—never. You were the first."

"Was I? Not the last though, it seems."

"Perhaps not. But I deceived myself before I deceived you."

"Well, you took me in completely, if it's any satisfaction to you. Never mind, Audrey; you've done your best to remedy that now."

He had turned, and his hand was on the door to go, when he heard her calling him back softly.

"Ted——" She had followed him to the door, he felt the touch of her little gloved hand on his coat-sleeve; under the black meshes of her veil he saw her eyes shining with tears that could not fall. He hesitated.

"Forgive me," she whispered.

"Not till you have answered my question."

"Which question, Ted?"

"The impertinent one."

"About Vincent?"

"Yes."

Her eyes had been fixed on the ground, now they glanced up quickly.

"Did Vincent tell you I was engaged to him?"

"No."

Her eyelids drooped again; then, urged to desperation by her own cowardice, she raised them and looked in his face to answer. And as she looked, she saw for the first time how changed it was. Its bloom was gone, the lines were set and hard: Ted looked years older than his age.

"Don't believe him if he ever says so. I am not engaged to him, and I never was."

"Thanks. That was all I wanted to know."

He turned on his heel and left her. He knew that she had lied.

He left her in a state of vague consternation. She had been prepared for an outburst of feeling on Ted's part, in which case she would have remained mistress of the field without loss of dignity. As it had happened, the victory was certainly not with her. This was contrary to all her expectations. She had looked for protestations, emotions — in short, a scene; but not for cold, dispassionate cross-examination. It was so unlike Ted — Ted, who was always giving himself away; it was more the sort of thing she could have fancied Wyndham saying under the same circumstances. She had seen something of this impersonal manner once or twice before, in those rare moments when they had discussed some picture, or Ted had talked to her about his work or Katherine's. It had annoyed her then; she thought it showed a want of enthusiasm. Now the boy's heartless self-possession amazed and overpowered her. Audrey was incapable of imagining what she had not seen, and she had never got to the bottom of the Haviland character; never divined its gravity under the mask of frivolity; never proved its will, nor reckoned with its pride. Three days ago she would have laughed at the idea of referring any moral question to Ted's judgment, for she had taken no pains to hide her faults from him; she had been selfish, reckless, vain, capricious, by turns and altogether, and it had made no difference then. Now she felt that he had condemned her. To be sure, she had told him a lie; but what was that in the catalogue of her offences?

It was everything. He could have forgiven anything but that.

CHAPTER XVII

But Ted's notion of morality was a question Audrey had no time to go into. A violent ring at the front-door bell recalled her to herself, and made her glance at the clock. It was a quarter-past three. She had wasted half an hour in fruitless discussion with Ted, and it left her ill-prepared for the stormy interview to follow. Her nerve gave way before the prospect of that hour with Hardy. She might have escaped it if it had not been for Ted, for she had meant to call early on her uncle and aunt, and bring them back with her to Chelsea, so that it would be impossible for Vincent to see her alone. Ted's coming had made that scheme useless. She listened. Yes, it was Vincent; she had heard his voice in the hall.

"I told him between three and four. Anybody else would have known that meant half-past four."

She spent ten minutes after Hardy was announced gathering herself together to meet him. She would have thought of sending for Miss Craven, an old device of hers when she wanted to avoid explanations; but Miss Craven was away. Her only hope was in some casual caller.

Meanwhile Hardy was striding up and down the drawing-room, waiting impatiently for Audrey. He was a little hurt at being shown into an empty room; he had expected to find the small thing sitting there to welcome him. That ten minutes was the longest he had ever spent,—it was the meeting-point in time for two eternities. As his thought leaped forward to the future it was thrown back upon the past. Then, as he gazed about him half mechanically, he was aware that his eyes were looking for the things they had been used to, and could not find them. Everything was changed in that room he had run in and out of as a boy. The familiar furniture, the signs and tokens of Audrey's daily presence, the old-fashioned knick-knacks which had delighted her mother's heart, all were gone. His aunt's portrait was no longer there; in its place hung the photogravure of the Madonna di San Sisto. Instead of the cosy corner where he had lain at Audrey's feet his last night in England, there stood a polished rosewood secretary, thrown open, showing its empty pigeon-holes.

Everywhere he looked it was the same; there were new things all around him. If he could have read their secret he would have seen that that room was the picture of Audrey's soul; the persons who had by turns taken possession of it had left there each one the traces of his power. If you could have cut a vertical section through Audrey's soul, you would have found it built up in successive layers of soul. When you had dug through Wyndham, you came to Ted; when you had got through Ted, you came upon Hardy, the oldest formation of all. The room was instructive as a museum filled with the records of these changes. But the specimens were badly arranged, recent deposits lying side by side with relics of an earlier period: thus the floor was covered with the bearskin given by Hardy and the Persian rugs laid down during the Art age. The rosewood secretary and a little revolving book-case by Audrey's chair marked the change wrought by Wyndham. They were part of modern history and the memory of man. Hardy, in the midst of these curiosities of natural science, was like a lay visitor without a guide: he admired, he wondered, he recognised an object here and there, but of what it all meant he had not the ghost of an idea.

He left off wondering, and waited, listening for the feet that used to fall so lightly on the stairs.

At last the door opened softly, and Audrey stood before him. But she stood still, looking at him as if uncertain whether to go or stay.

"Audrey!" His face lit up with joy, his heart bounded.

"How do you do, Vincent?"

He held out his arms, and she came to him slowly, without a word. She let him hold her for an instant, closing her eyes to hide the fear in them; let him lift her veil and kiss her cheeks and mouth. Then she turned her face away, put out her hands against his chest, and pushed him from her.

"Audrey! What have I done?"

"Oh! I don't know, I don't know!"

She walked away to the looking-glass over the chimneypiece, and took off her gloves and veil. She wanted to gain time. Hardy followed her to the opposite side of the fireplace.

"Whatever possessed you, Vincent, to grow that horrid beard?"

He had forgotten the change in his personal appearance. He looked in the glass and was startled by his own reflection. Owing to the agony of the shock she had given him, his face was still grey and drawn. The poor fellow tried to smile, and that made matters worse.

"I daresay it was a nasty shock. Did it make you feel as if I was somebody else?"

"Oh no; it has not altered you much. It's not that. But—I hate beards, as you know."

There was silence. Hardy was struggling with the old stifling sensation in his heart. Emotion was bad for him.

"Is this all you've got to say to me, after being a year away?"

She looked at him, shook her head, and played with the ornaments on the mantel-board.

"Why can't you speak to me? Has anything happened? Is anybody dead?"

"No; but I wish I was."

"Why do you say that?"

"Because——" She was trying to wring the neck off a little china image now. "Oh, Vincent, don't think me very unkind! but I—I'd rather, another time, you didn't show your cousinly affection quite in that way. That's all."

He covered his eyes with one hand to shut out the sight of Audrey.

"No, that's not all, I see. There's something else behind that,—there must be. *Has* anything happened?"

She bowed her head and sighed, a long shivering sigh. The china image slipped through her fingers, and was broken to bits on the hearthstone.

"Audrey—what is it?"

He took her by the wrists and drew her gently to him. As he touched her he saw her face whiten and her eyes dilate.

"Do you remember last year when you said you loved me?—when you promised to be my wife? Do you remember how you said good-bye to me then? Now you won't speak to me. What have you been doing to make you hate me? Or what stupid idea have you got into your head about me?"

"Nothing—nothing. Only—I want you to understand that what you said just now is out of the question. It can't be."

"Why not? You promised; so it could be once, why not now?"

"Because—because—I never really promised, you know."

"You never promised! You little liar! You may want to break your promise, but you can hardly say you didn't make it."

"I never made it—not of my own free will. You took advantage of me; you forced me into it. You teased me till I said I cared for you, and—I didn't."

"So, then, you told me a lie? You wrote lie after lie to me in your letters for a year?"

She writhed away from him, but he still held her by the wrists, face to face with him, the length of their arms apart.

"Let me go, Vincent! You've no right to hold me in this way. You're hurting my arm!"

Unconsciously his grasp had tightened till the diamond mounted on one of her thread-like bracelets was pressed into her flesh and made it bleed.

"See there!"

He let her go. She sat down and put her pocket-handkerchief to her wrist.

"If you tell lies, Audrey, what am I to believe? What you said then, or what you say now?"

"I'm telling the truth now, because I don't want this wretched misunderstanding to go any further."

"Can't you speak plainly? Do you mean this, that you don't love me?"

"Yes. It's true. I don't love you; I can't—at least, not like that."

"I can't believe it! It's impossible! As long as I can remember, whatever you said or did, you made me think you loved me. You said last year you'd be my wife; but that's nothing. Long before that, you let me live on the hope of it, year after year. It's inconceivable that you could have done these things if you didn't care for me. Even you couldn't be such an unfeeling little fiend."

"No, no; you worked on my feelings. You wouldn't let me have any will of my own. And now you want me to marry you whether I like it or not. Whatever happens, I can't do that, Vincent."

"Why not?"

"Must I tell you?"

"Isn't that the very least you can do?"

"Well—you know, Vincent, you've been very wild; you've told me so yourself a thousand times."

"Is it that? You knew that long ago."

"I never realised it till now. Now I know that I can only really love some one strong and good, whose goodness would help me and make me good too."

Audrey's infantile irony made Hardy laugh. That laugh frightened her.

"Do you think I don't know that?" he said. "What do you suppose I went out of England for? It wasn't to shoot, or to farm either. It was to get away out of the reach of temptation, to live in a pure air, and make myself pure for your sake. Do you know, Audrey, I was out there, without a soul to speak to, a year, one horrible long year, fighting the devil, waiting till I could come back and tell you that I was fit to love you. God knows I'm not all I ought to be,—who is? At least, I'm not ashamed now to ask you to be my wife. Will you never forget the past?"

She had hesitated before, but now Hardy's humility put her in the position of the superior, and his piteous confession gave her the words she wanted.

"No. It's no use. Once for all, I do not love you; and if I did, I could not marry any man who had led the life you have."

"Very well. Remember, Audrey, if I wasn't good enough for you, I was good enough as men go. Now, I'll go to the devil, and give my whole mind to it. But I've a great deal to say to you before I go. You object to my life. Good or bad, it's your own work. It's women like you who make men like me. You knew my weakness, and played on it. You could have helped me, if you'd only given me up honestly at first, as another woman would have done; but you didn't want to do that. I'd have left England long before, if you'd let me go: you knew it, and you kept me here, though you saw me going to the bad. Oh, you were an artist in your own line! You knew the effect of every word, every touch, every movement of yours, and you went out of your way to—to make goodness impossible for me. God knows why, but you liked—you *liked* to see me longing for what you never meant to give me. And because I didn't come out of that ordeal quite clean, you talk to me about my life, and tell me you are too good and pure to marry me. Are you really so very much better than I am, after all?"

She sat still at first, with her eyes half closed, afraid to look up, afraid to move or speak, waiting for something to happen, for some one to come and stop Vincent. But the scourging voice went on with a relentless brutality, laying bare the secret places of her soul, its unconscious hypocrisy, its vanity, its latent capacity for evil. She answered the closing question with an inarticulate sound like a sob. It might have softened him, if he had not been deaf to everything but his own passion.

"Don't suppose I flatter myself I'm the only victim. How about that young fool Ted Haviland?"

She sprang to her feet. Fear, that had made her lie to Ted, made her tell the truth to Hardy. That fear was deep-rooted; it dated from the days when they were children and Vincent had the mastery in all their play.

"Oh, Vincent, promise me, promise me, you won't do anything to Ted! It's all true about our engagement, but it was more my fault than his."

"I can't believe that, Audrey. I'm very far from blaming him. I've no doubt you treated him as you did me."

He sat down exhausted. Audrey, seeing the change of position, not the sudden collapse that prompted it, was in despair.

"Won't you leave me alone now, Vincent? Haven't you said enough?"

"Not yet. Let me think a bit."

He leaned back and closed his eyes. He had so much to say, and now he had no words to say it with.

Audrey looked at the clock; it was half-past four. Would he begin again? She almost wished he would; it would be better than this silence—better than that frowning forehead, with the terrible accusing thoughts behind it. Would no one come? Would he never go?

Hardy had found words and was beginning to rouse himself, when in answer to her prayer the door was thrown open. Her deliverance had come in the shape of Langley Wyndham.

Hardy's eyes followed her. A moment before she had sat white and trembling, shrunk up into herself before the storm of his accusation;

now, for that instant, her face became beautiful as he had never seen it before. There was something dramatic in her movement as she rose and went forward to meet Wyndham. There was no mistaking her manner and the tremor of her voice as she spoke to him. Hardy knew his rival before he saw him.

"My cousin Mr. Hardy; Mr. Langley Wyndham."

The men looked at each other and bowed stiffly. Wyndham wondered. The scene they had just gone through had left its mark on Hardy's face and Audrey's. The student of human nature congratulated himself on the inspiration which had prompted him to call at this crisis. The cousin suggested interesting complications in his heroine's life: judging by the set of his lower jaw, she must have had a bad quarter of an hour with him. He would have to reconstruct that drama from the fragments preserved.

When Wyndham sat down, Hardy sat down too. He suspected Audrey of having invited this man in order to get rid of himself. She wanted him to go. A savage jealousy made him determined to stay and spoil her pleasure. But Audrey, with Wyndham beside her, had recovered her presence of mind. Unable to endure the situation longer, she was about to risk a bold stroke, by which she would at once revenge herself on Vincent, escape from the torture of his society, and assure herself of Wyndham's friendship.

After the preliminary commonplaces, she watched her opportunity till she could arrest Wyndham's eyes with hers, throwing into their expression all that she knew of pathos and appeal. Then she rose and held out her hand to Hardy, saying with distinct deliberation—

"I'm afraid you must excuse me now, Vincent; I have to take Mr. Wyndham to call on my uncle Dean Craven."

The look that she turned on Wyndham said plainly, "You see I'm desperate. If you haven't enough chivalry to back that up, I'm done for."

Happily for her, this time Wyndham's chivalry was equal to his intelligence. He answered in the most natural manner possible—

"If Miss Craven is ready, I am. As I'm rather late, I think we'd better take a hansom."

They left Hardy stupefied with astonishment.

As they drove towards Charing Cross, she turned to Wyndham and said —

"Forgive my making use of you. Had you any other engagement?"

"I have no engagements."

"I am glad. It was the only thing I could think of to get rid of him. If you had left me, he would have stayed; if I had gone out by myself, he would have followed. But it was good of you to stand by me like that."

"Not at all. I'm delighted to call on Dean Craven, still more delighted to be of service to you."

"Thank you."

They said no more till, as they came in sight of the Hôtel Metropole, he turned to her with a smile —

"Do you remember Mr. Jackson?"

"Mr. Jackson? — Mr. Jackson?" She shook her head. "Oh yes, of course I do. At Oxford, that night? Whatever put him into your head, of all people?"

"Dean Craven, I suppose. Ridiculous association of ideas."

"Mr. Jackson — I wonder why such people exist."

"So do I. Do you know, I've hated Mr. Jackson with a deadly hatred for the last month."

"Why, whatever has he done?"

"Nothing. But if it hadn't been for him I should have known you a year ago."

The hansom drew up. She sank back into her corner and held out her hand.

"I'll say good-bye now. I'm not equal to seeing them, after all. You can tell them you've seen me, and that I meant to call."

"Very well. Is he to drive you straight home?"

"Yes, please. But tell him to go the longest way round, by Fulham—or anywhere."

He said good-bye, got out, and gave the order to the driver. As the hansom turned up Northumberland Avenue, he caught a side view of the pathetic little face through the window. Then she was whirled away from him, towards Fulham—or anywhere. He stood looking after her till the sound of the horse's bells was lost in the roar of Charing Cross.

Then he remembered that he had once said she would be "capable of anything."

CHAPTER XVIII

Hardy left the house five minutes after Audrey and Wyndham. In the doorway of the dining-room he stepped on a small muslin pocket-handkerchief. It was stained here and there with specks of blood. He picked it up, kissed it, and put it in his pocket.

For a long time after that he had no clear sense of anything, except, at times, of the misery that made the only difference between being drunk and sober.

Yes; Hardy was carrying out the threat he had made to Audrey, with a passionate deliberation. He was "giving his whole mind to it," as he had said. He had been used to speak of the sins of his past life with that exaggeration which was part of his character; they had been slight, considering the extent of his temptation. Then he was, as it were, an amateur in evil. Now he had an object in view—he was sinning for the wages of sin.

After all, there was a boyish simplicity about Hardy; otherwise the idea of living for a year alone on the Rockies, to make himself "fit to love Audrey," would hardly have occurred to him. As it was, that guileless scheme proved fatal in its results. The loneliness, the privation, the excitement and fatigue of his sportsman's life—for with all his boasting he was a true sportsman—had roused some old hereditary impulse in his blood, and he found himself worsted by the craving for drink before he was aware of its existence in him. But the thought of Audrey was always present with him; and it kept him up. He fought himself hand to hand, and won the fight ten times for once that he was beaten. He was literally saved by hope. Happily for him, when he had finished the stores he brought out with him, it was almost as difficult to satisfy his craving as it was to annihilate it. When he came home the tendency was sleeping in him still; and though, as long as he had hope, it might have slept for ever, when hope was gone it was there, ready to take possession of him. His love for Audrey was the strongest passion in his nature. It filled the horizon of his life. He looked before and after, and could see nothing else but it. It was of the kind that deepens through its own monotony. Now that Audrey had cast him off, there was no reason for the struggle, because there was nothing more to struggle for, and nothing to live for unless it were to kill life in the act of living. That indeed was something.

After the first month or so of it, he had no further interest in his present course. He chose it now as the form of suicide least likely to be recognised as such.

Perhaps—who knows?—if he had had any friends who would have given him a helping hand, it might never have come to this. But, in the first place, Hardy had no home that could be called a home. His mother was fond of him in her way; but she was now a hysterical invalid, abject under the influence of her second husband, and year by year his step-father's jealousy (the jealousy of a childless man) had driven the mother and son further apart. Of the Havilands, whom he would naturally have turned to, he had seen nothing for the last few months. Ted disliked meeting him, and he on his part was equally anxious to avoid Ted. That was how Katherine remained ignorant of the truth until she was enlightened by Mrs. Rogers.

"It yn't *my* business," said that excellent woman, as she began to dust the studio one morning, in the leisurely manner that Katherine dreaded, it being the invariable forerunner of conversation, "and I don't know who's business it is, but somebody ought to look after that Mr. 'Ardy. 'Is friends ought to be written to, m'm."

Katherine felt a pang of remorse.

"Why? Is Mr. Hardy ill?"

"I didn't say he was ill. But if I was to tell *you*, miss——"

Here Mrs. Rogers pursed her lips, not so much to impress Katherine with her incorruptible discretion, as to excite interest in the disclosures she meant to make.

"Between you and me, m'm, if somebody don't stop 'im, 'ell drink 'imself to death down there some o' these days."

"What do you mean? It's quite impossible—I've known Mr. Hardy all my life."

"I've known 'im three months; and if I wasn't that soft-'earted, I wouldn't keep 'im a day longer, not a day I wouldn't. 'E won't sleep in 'is bed like a Christian—lies on top all of a heap like. Last week, when I was a-cleanin' out his bottom cupboard, the brandy bottles was standin' up like a row o' ninepins. This mornin' they was lyin' down flat as your fyce—empty, m'm, every one of 'em. It did give me a turn. And 'e'll order 'is dinner for eight o'clock, and not come 'ome till two in the mornin'—if 'e comes 'ome at all. 'E's out now Lord knows where."

"I don't want to hear any more. You're very likely mistaken."

"I wish I was, miss. But you'll not deceive me, I'm that upset with it all. And my fear is, miss, 'e'll drive away my old lydy on the first floor, with 'is goings on."

Katherine left the room, too deeply grieved to bear Mrs. Rogers's professional loquacity.

That night she was able to realise the truth of what she had been told. She had gone out to dine with some new acquaintance; Ted had called for her to take her home, and they were walking back along the Embankment, when they came suddenly upon Hardy. He was standing under a gas-lamp, talking to somebody, or rather listening to somebody talking. He turned his back on them as they passed, but there was no mistaking his figure in the glare of the false daylight. As for his companion, Katherine was aware of something in satin skirts which the gaslight ran over like water—something that smelt of musk and had hair the colour of brass. She walked on without a word, sick at heart. This was the first time she had been brought face to face with the hideous side of life. Like many good women, she thoroughly realised the existence of evil in the abstract; but evil incarnate in a person—it was hard to associate that with any one she knew as she had known Vincent. Her artistic nature was morbidly sensitive to impressions taken in through the eye, and nothing could have so forced home the truth as that little scene, suddenly flashed on her out of the London night. But now that she had seen, it was not the horror that she felt, but the pity of it. She remembered Vincent's face when she had shown him Audrey's picture. Her thoughts went further back. She remembered him a boy, playing with her in a lordly manner, as befitted his sex; or a young man, coming and going in her father's home with frank, brotherly ways. She remembered how she had grudged the time she gave him, and the relief she felt when he left off coming. But she could not remember anywhere the least sign of what he had become.

Something ought to be done—she could not clearly say what. Writing to his people, as Mrs. Rogers had suggested, was out of the question. She knew too well the state of things in his home. To be sure, there was his uncle, Sir Theophilus Parker, whom he had expectations from; but for that very reason the old gentleman was the last person whom it would be advisable to inform of Vincent's conduct. Relations failing, there remained his friends; and she only knew two of these—herself and Ted.

All that was most fine and sensitive in her nature cried out against the burden she knew she would have to lay on it. But her humanity was so deeply moved by the tragedy she had twice been an unwilling spectator of, that she never so much as dreamed of asking, "Am *I* my brother's keeper?" Doubtless she could have found plenty of excellent people to tell her she was not. Her only difficulty was with Ted. Nothing could be done till he had got over his nervous dread of meeting Vincent.

Katherine had no precise idea of what had passed between her brother and Audrey, and how far Vincent had been connected with it; but she had gathered from Ted's silence all that she wanted to know. Whatever Audrey had said or done, there was an end of her as far as he was concerned. It was from the boy's silence, too, that she realised the extent of his suffering. Before the inevitable thing had happened, he had done nothing but talk of Audrey, sometimes with melancholy, more often in the jocular strain adopted by self-conscious persons to carry off some ridiculous fatality. Anger following suspense had driven him to think of suicide; but now that it was all over with him, he had no idea of killing himself. Katherine had never been much afraid of that, and as yet none of the other things she had dreaded had happened; but it was evident that the boy's nature had been deeply affected, and that the shock was a moral one. It was not Audrey's unfaithfulness that had hurt him so much as her untruthfulness. Ted thought so little of himself in some ways that he could have understood the one, and therefore forgiven it. The other was the unpardonable sin; it injured what he loved better than himself—his idea of Audrey. Katherine did not know this, but she saw that the present time was the moral turning-point in his life, and that his pain was the sort that shapes character for good or for evil. But, after all, she knew very little of the elements that went to make up Ted's character. His imagination, as she had pointed out to Audrey on a memorable occasion, had been developed long before his heart, and out of all proportion to it. It had so happened that all at once the passionate part of his nature had been roused and shaken before it was half-formed. She asked herself what line would be taken now by those forces of feeling set free so violently and so abruptly checked?

Well, at any rate Audrey's conduct had not had the effect of driving brother and sister apart. It had drawn them closer together if anything. Ted seemed to find relief in Katherine's society from the torment of his own thoughts, and he had shown no desire to look for distraction abroad; indeed the difficulty was to make him go out of doors at all for necessary exercise. He would have fits of work, when nothing would induce him to stir from the easel. Another time, he would spend whole mornings lying on the floor, with his arms clasped above his head, or sitting with a book in his hands, a book which he never seemed to read. He hardly ever spoke; he was always thinking. And worse than all, he had lost his appetite and his sense of humour.

Mrs. Rogers had her own theory on the subject, which she imparted to Katherine.

"Miss, it's them baths as has done it. Anythin' in reason and I'll not sy no, but cold water to that igstent, m'm, it's against nature. It's my belief Mr. 'Aviland would 'ave slept and 'ad 'is dinner in 'is bath, if I 'adn't put my foot down. 'E's chilled 'is blood, depend upon it, m'm." And indeed that seemed very likely.

Katherine said nothing about Hardy at the time; but the next night, when she and Ted were sitting over the fire, she began.

"Ted, that was Vincent we saw on the Embankment last night."

"Yes, I saw him.

"Do you know, I believe he's killing himself with drinking."

"I know he is."

"Do you think we could do anything to help him before it's too late?"

He shook his head.

"Oh, Ted, we might! He never used to be like this. He's got no one to speak to; we've left him by himself all this time in those horrid rooms. The wall-paper alone is enough to send anybody to the bad. We might have thought of him."

"I've done nothing else but think of him for the last two months. We can't do anything. He's bound to go on like that; I don't see how he can help it. As for drinking, nothing can stop *that*; I've seen fellows like him before; and Vincent never did anything by halves."

"It's terrible. But we ought to try—it's the least we can do."

"The least *I* can do is to keep out of his way. He hates the sight of me."

"Why?"

"Don't you know? Didn't it ever strike you that Audrey was engaged to Vincent all the time?"

"No. I thought he liked her, but—what makes you think that?"

"I can't tell you. But any sort of affectionate advances would come rather badly from me. How's Vincent to know that I never knew?"

"You may be sure he knows. He knows Audrey."

Ted sighed, but he said nothing; there was nothing to be said.

"Would you very much mind asking him to supper to-morrow night?"

"No. He won't come. But you'd better write to him yourself, or else he'll think you don't want him."

She wrote a note, and Ted took it downstairs, to be ready for Vincent at such time as he should come in. The boy turned into his own room without going up again to say good-night.

He had left Katherine thinking. She had been struck with his words; they had thrown a new light on his character. His tone was bitter when he told her he had been thinking of nothing but Vincent; but it was not the bitterness of selfish resentment. A shuddering hope went through her. Either there always had been things in Ted's nature which she had never suspected, or he had just begun his education by suffering—by having felt. The latter was the more probable explanation; she knew him to be capable of such absorption in pleasant sensations, that, if all had gone well with him, he might from sheer light-heartedness have remained indifferent to other people's woes. And all along he had been such an irresponsible person, but now he was actually growing a conscience, and a peculiarly delicate one too. Without any fault of his own, he had behaved dishonourably to Vincent; and apart from the blow to his own honour, it was evident that what stung him now was remorse for his infinitesimal share in the causes that had led to Vincent's ruin.

In all that he had said there was no trace of any lingering love for Audrey. Was it possible that the tragic spectacle of Vincent's fate had moved him too with pity and terror, for the purging of his passion?

Hardy did not find Katherine's note till late next morning. He read it twice over with an incredulous air, and put it into the fire. He wrote a short but grateful refusal, saying truly that he was very seedy, and not pleasant company for any one at present.

Not long after, he was alone, as usual, in his dingy ground-floor sitting-room. It was about five o'clock; but he had not lit his lamp yet, and he had let his fire go out, though it was cold and rainy. A gas-lamp from the street shone through the dripping window-panes, bringing a dreary twilight into the room, making it one with the melancholy of the rain-swept streets.

He sat by the table, with his head in his hands, a prey to the appalling depression which was his mood when sober.

For the last three months he had had a curious double consciousness: of himself as an actor in a phantom world, lost in some night of dreams, where the same thoughts—always, the same thoughts—thoughts that were sins—came to him in sickening recurrence; the horror of it being that the act followed instantaneously on the thought: of himself as a spectator, separate from that other self, yet bound to it; looking on at all it did, ashamed and loathing, yet powerless to interfere. And, as happens in nightmares, his very dread suggested the thing he dreaded, and changed his dream to something more hideous than before—horror upon horror, still foreseen, and still foredoomed in the senseless sequence of the dream. Now these two states of mind were divided by a little clear space. The passive self was free for a while and could think. It could think—that was all.

He was waked from his thoughts by a knock and a voice at the door. He answered gruffly, and as he looked up he saw Katherine standing in the open doorway, letting in a stream of light from the lamp she carried in her hand.

He stared at her stupidly, blinking at the light, and hid his face in his hands again.

"I beg your pardon, Vincent. I knocked, and I thought you said 'Come in.' I came to see how you were; I was afraid you were worse."

"I am worse. What's more, I shall never be better."

She put her lamp on the chimneypiece and stood beside him.

"Don't say that; of course you'll be better. Can we do anything for you?"

"No; nothing—thanks."

She moved back a little, and shaded the lamp with her hands. She was afraid to disturb him, but she did not like to leave him in his misery. How ill and wretched he looked in that abominable room! The lamplight showed her all its repulsive details. She had done her best for it; but in the last two months it had sunk back into something worse than its former ugliness, degraded in its owner's degradation. There was no trace now of the clever alterations and contrivances which she had devised for his comfort. The muslin curtains she had lent him were dark with smoke; the rug had slipped from the horsehair sofa; there were stains on the shabby tablecloth and carpet; and on the sideboard there was a sordid litter of bottles and glasses, pipes, tobacco-ash, and Hardy's hats. The floor was strewn with the crumpled papers and shoes that he had flung away from him in his fits of irritation. In the midst of it all she noticed that Mrs. Rogers had brought back all her terrible household goods, the pink vases, the paper screens, and the antimacassars—"To cheer him up, I suppose, poor fellow!"

Hardy looked round as if he had read her thoughts.

"You'd better leave me. This isn't a nice place for you."

"It isn't a very nice place for anybody. You've let your fire go out. Come upstairs and get warm; we haven't seen you for ages."

He shook his head sadly.

"I can't, Sis, I'm much too seedy."

"Nonsense! You will be, if you sit down here catching cold." She took up her lamp, and laid a hand on his shoulder.

"Come; don't keep me waiting, or I shall catch cold too."

His will was in abeyance, and to her intense relief he got up and followed her.

She was shocked at the change in his appearance when she saw him in the full lamplight of the studio. He was pitifully thin; his fingers, as he held out his hands to the blaze, were pale, even with the red glow of the fire through them. His eyes had lost their dog-like pathos, and had the hard look of the human animal. She got ready some strong coffee, and made him drink it. That, with the warmth and the unaccustomed kindness, revived him. Then she sat down in a low chair opposite him, with some sewing in her lap, so that he might talk to her or not, as he pleased. At first he evidently preferred to think; and when he did speak, it was as if he were thinking aloud.

"I was cut by two men I know to-day. I wonder how many women there are in London who would do what you've done for me to-night?"

"What have I done? I walked into your room without an invitation — I don't suppose many women in London would have done that. But is there any woman in London who has known you as long as I have?"

He winced perceptibly, and she remembered that there was one.

"Ah, if you really knew me, Kathy, you'd cut me dead!"

"My dear Vincent, don't talk rubbish. I do know — a good deal — and I'm very sorry; that's all. I should be sorrier if I thought it was going to last for ever; but I don't."

"You are too good to me; but — if you only knew!"

He sat silent, watching as she sewed. Something in his attitude reminded her of that other evening, three months ago, when he had lain back in that chair boasting gloriously, full of hope and the pride of life. He appealed to her more now in his illness and degradation than he had ever done in his splendid sanity. For he had seemed so strong; there was no outward sign of weakness then about that long-limbed athlete.

"Vincent," she said presently, "what's become of the Pioneer-book? You promised to read me some of it — don't you remember?"

"Yes. I shall never do anything with it now."

"Oh, Vincent, what a pity! But if it's not to be printed, do you mind my seeing the manuscript?"

"No; I'll let you have it some day, Sis, and you shall do what you like with it." He sank into silence again.

"Where's Ted?" he asked suddenly.

"He'll be in soon; he wants to see you."

"Does he? How do you know that?" There was a look of suspicion in Hardy's eyes as they glanced up. It was a symptom of his miserable condition that he was apt to imagine slights.

"I've only his word for it, of course."

"Kathy——" he hesitated.

"Well?"

"There's something I wanted to tell him; but the fact is, I don't think I've the pluck to do it."

"Never mind, then. Tell me if you can; though I think I know, and it's all right."

"No, it isn't all right. I suppose you know he was pretty well off his head about—that cousin of mine? I rather think he owed me one for being before him, as he thought. At any rate, he cut me ever since— before I took to the flowing bowl, too. You might tell him, if you think it would be any satisfaction to him to know it, that she cared rather less for me than she did for him; in fact, I believe there was some unhappy devil that she preferred to either of us. At least a third man came into it somewhere. There may be a fourth now, for anything I know."

There was a brutality about his calmness which surprised Katherine; she could not realise the effect of the means he used for blunting his sensibilities.

"You're quite mistaken. Ted hasn't any feeling of the sort. He simply kept out of your way because he was afraid you'd think he had behaved dishonourably; and of course he couldn't explain because of—Audrey. But it wasn't his fault. He knew nothing."

"I never thought he did know. Do you suppose I blamed *him*, poor beggar?"

All the same, Hardy slunk away soon after Ted came in. When Mrs. Rogers came up with supper, she informed them that it was fine now—if you could but trust it. And "Mr. 'Ardy 'ad gorn orf like a mad thing. Temptin' Providence, I call it, without an umbrella."

Ted remarked, as they sat down to supper, that he thought "Providence would have sufficient strength of mind to resist temptation; but he was not so sure about Hardy."

And indeed Katherine had to own that her first experiment with Vincent was a failure. But she struggled on, experience having taught her that it is easier to do good original work of your own than to patch up what other people have spoiled. One week, drawn by some yearning for human sympathy, Hardy would come nearly every evening to the studio; then they would see no more of him for ten days or so. At times she felt that the strain of it was greater than she could bear. She had learnt to manage Vincent in his various moods, varying from humorous irascibility to hysterical penitence; but when he was out of her sight her influence was powerless. Now indeed she asked herself—

"Why am I wasting my precious time and making myself miserable in this way? I've no sense of religion, and I don't love Vincent—he's simply a nuisance. It must be sheer obstinacy."

It was with a feeling little short of despair that she sat down to the pages of the Pioneer-book. She had determined at any cost to read the manuscript through; but she soon became fascinated in spite of herself. "Be tender to it, Sis, it's a part of myself," he had said when he handed it over to her. She thought she had detected a gleam of interest in his face, and felt that she was on the right tack. But Vincent's book was more than a part of himself, it was a fair transcript of the whole. His weakness and his strength were in it. She saw his vanity, his exaggeration; but also his sincerity, his manliness, his simple delight in simple things. Scenery on a large scale stirred a strain of rude poetry in him this was akin to the first rhythmic utterances of man. To be sure, the thing had its faults; for poor Vincent had been anxious that his book should be recognised as the work of a scholar and a gentleman. At times a spirit of unbridled quotation would seize him, and you came upon familiar gems from the classics imbedded in the text. At times, after some coarse but graphic touch, his style became suddenly refined, almost to sickliness. When he was not pointing his moral with a hatchet, he was adorning his tale with verbiage gathered from the worst authors. But if Hardy the literary artist made her laugh till she cried again, Hardy the unconscious child of Nature won her heart. If only she could make him finish what he had begun!

She determined to illustrate the book: that might inflame Vincent's ambition, and would certainly require his co-operation. So now, every evening, in the spare time after supper, she set to work on the drawings, aided by some photographs and rough sketches made by Hardy. After a little stratagem she got him to come up and help her with suggestions, or to sit for her while she sketched him in all the attitudes of the sportsman.

He was enthusiastic over the first few drawings. Perhaps his simple remarks, "H'm, that's clever!" or, "By Jove, that's not half bad!" gave her a purer pleasure than she could have derived from the most discriminating criticism. When his interest showed signs of flagging, she hit on a new means of rousing it. She began to find out that so long as she drew correctly, he looked on with a melancholy indifference, but that when she made any mistake he was always delighted to put her right. So she went on making mistakes, and then Vincent got impatient.

"Look here, Sis, that's all wrong. You don't carry a rifle with the muzzle pointing towards your left ear. Here, give the thing to me!"

Katherine gravely handed him another sketch—

"How's that?"

"That's worse. Why, you little duffer, you don't suppose I'm going to send a bullet into that bear taking aim at *that* angle? I should blow my boots off. I thought you could draw?"

She smiled in secret. "So I can, if you'll show me which way up the things go."

Then they put their heads together over it, and between them they turned out some work worthy of the Pioneer-book. Ted joined in too, and began a black-and-white series of his own, parodying the acts of the distinguished sportsman: Vincent attacked by a skunk; Vincent swarming up a pine tree with a bear hanging on to his trousers' legs; Vincent shooting the rapids in his canoe—canoe uppermost; and so on. Ted was so much entertained with his own performances that he was actually heard to laugh. And when the boy laughed, the man laughed too. As for Katherine, she could have cried, knowing that a returning sense of humour is often the surest sign of hope in these cases.

Laughter, flattery, and feminine wiles may not be the methods most commended by moralists and divines for the conversion of poor sinners; but Katherine seldom consulted authorities—she had the courage of her convictions.

One fine morning in February she appeared in her hat and jacket at the door of the ground-floor sitting-room.

"Vincent, will you come with me to the Zoo? I'm going to do some grizzlies and wapiti—from the life—for the Pioneer-book, and I want you to help me."

He agreed, and they started almost gaily, with Mrs. Rogers peering up at them from the front area-window, putting that and that together with the ingenuity of her kind. It was the first of many walks they had together. Ted generally went with them, but now and again he was left behind. At these times Katherine was touched by Vincent's pride in being allowed to take her about alone. He was grateful for it; he knew it was her way of showing that she trusted him.

At last the series of illustrations came to an end. The two artists had raced each other: Katherine, having had the start, came in first at the finish with a magnificent design for the cover. She brought the drawings to Vincent, together with his manuscript, and showed them to him triumphantly. He remarked—

"Well, they ought to print the thing, if only as a footnote to your drawings, Sis."

"Will you sit down and finish it, if I undertake to find a publisher?"

He promised, and he kept his word. In the mornings now he might be found working slowly and painfully at his last chapter, she helping him.

So the winter wore on into spring; and Katherine, burdened with arrears of work, said to herself, "I perceive that this is going to be an expensive undertaking." But she looked back gladly on the time lost. At last, after many failures, they had succeeded in wakening Vincent to a sense of distant kinship with the life of boys and maidens. Down at the bottom of his nature there had always been an intense craving for affection, and his heart went out to Ted and Katherine. Not that he considered himself fit for their blameless society. Together with the vices he had acquired there had sprung up humility, that strange virtue, which has its deepest roots in the soil of shame. But all his old yearning after goodness revived in their presence. When he was with them he felt that the cloud of foul experience was lifted for a moment from his mind; they gave him sweet thoughts instead of bitter for a day perhaps, or a night.

And what of the days and the nights when he was not with them? Then, as a rule, he fell, nine times, it may be, out of every ten—who knows? And who knows whether Perfect Justice, measuring our forces with the force of our temptations, may not count as victory what the world calls defeat?

CHAPTER XIX

In her appeal to Wyndham Audrey had played a bold stroke, and it seemed that she had won it. She had amply revenged herself on Hardy, and more than assured herself of Wyndham's friendship. All the same, ever since she had left him at the doors of the Hôtel Metropole, a certain constraint had crept into their intercourse. Wyndham was not easily deceived, and he rightly interpreted her abrupt dismissal of him as a final effort to assert herself before the onset of the inevitable. Even if he at times suspected her of playing a part, she had chosen the right part to play, and he respected her for it. He himself was leading a curious double life. He was working hard at his novel, which promised to surpass everything that he had yet done. He was so much absorbed in observing, studying, shaping, and touching up, that it never occurred to him to ask himself if he were indeed creating. The thing had been growing under his hands through the autumn; in the winter it seemed to advance by bounds; but in the spring his work came to a sudden standstill. He did not know what Laura, his heroine, was going to do next. He had drawn her as the creature of impulse, but dragging the dead weight of all the conventions at her back—a woman variously dramatic when stirred by influences from without, but incapable of decisive action from within. How would such a woman behave under stress of conflicting circumstances?—if it came, say, to a fight for possession between the force of traditional inertia and the feeling of the moment? On the one hand the problem was as old as the hills, on the other it was new with every man and woman born into the world. What he called his literary conscience told him that it had to be solved; another conscience in him shrank from the solution. At this point Wyndham did what, as a conscientious artist, he had never done before; he put his work away for a season, and tried not to think about it, devoting himself to Audrey Craven instead. Even he was not always able to preserve the critical attitude with regard to her. As he had told her, criticism comes first, sympathy last of all. And with him—last of all—it had come. He could not go on from day to day, seeing, hearing, and understanding more and more, without acquiring a curious sympathy with the thing he studied. And when the artist tired of her art, the man felt all the influence of her natural magic. He was prepared for that, and had no illusions on the subject.

He tested his present feelings by comparing them with those he had had for Alison Fraser. He had not the least intention of setting up Audrey Craven anywhere near his idol's ancient place,—he would have shuddered at the bare idea of it. This, though he expressed it differently, was what he meant when he resolved once for all that he would never marry, never put himself in any woman's power again. And in the plenitude of his self-knowledge he knew exactly how far he could let himself go without either of these evil results following.

Unfortunately, in these cases the woman is seldom so well equipped for self-defence as the man. Owing to her invincible ignorance of her own nature, she must be more or less at a disadvantage. And if this is true of women in general, it was doubly true of any one so specially prone to illusion as Audrey Craven, who would have had difficulty in recognising any part of her true self under its numerous disguises. She was therefore unaware of the action and reaction which had been going on within her during the last year. Whatever its precise quality may have been, her love for Ted Haviland was of a different quality from her feeling for Langley Wyndham. Under that earlier influence, whatever intelligence she possessed had been roused from its torpor by the tumult of her senses; her mind had been opened and made ready for the attack of a finer intellectual passion, which again in its turn brought her under the tyranny of the senses. For though her worst enemies could not call Audrey clever, it was Wyndham's intellectual eminence which had fascinated her from the first. Herein lay her danger and her excuse. She was aware—hence her late access of reserve—that she was being carried away by her feelings; but how, when, and whither, she neither knew nor apparently cared to know. In the meanwhile, in Wyndham's friendship she not only triumphed over Vincent's scorn, but she felt secure against his infatuation. For she imagined the scorn and the infatuation as still existing together. She knew that he was still in London, presumably unable to tear himself away from her neighbourhood; and the sense of his presence, of his power over her, had been so long a habit of her mind that she could not lose it now. Otherwise she hardly gave him a thought; and having cut herself off from all communication with Devon Street, she did not certainly know what had become of him.

She had yet to learn.

Towards the end of February she received a letter from Vincent's mother which left no doubt on the subject. The news of his downfall had reached his home at last. Mrs. Hardy knew of her son's attachment to his cousin, and had always had fixed ideas on that point. On being told that he had "gone" irretrievably "to the bad," she jumped to a conclusion: it was the right one, as it happened, though she had managed to cover a great deal of ground in that jump. She at once wrote off a long and violent letter to her niece, taxing her with cruelty, fickleness, and ingratitude, laying Vincent's misdeeds on her shoulders, and ending thus: "They tell me you are engaged. I pray God you may not have to go through what you have made my darling boy suffer."

Now, either the poor hysterical lady was an unconscious instrument in the hands of Destiny, or her prayer may have been meant as a modified and lady-like curse; at any rate, if it had not entered into her head to write that letter, it would have saved the writing of one chapter in her niece's history. But, in the first place, the communication had the effect of making Audrey cry a great deal, for her; in the second, it came by an afternoon post, so that Langley Wyndham, calling at his usual hour, found her crying.

He was a little taken aback by the sight, as indeed any man would have been, for most women of his acquaintance arranged things so as not to do their crying in calling hours.

However, he judged it the truest kindness to sit down and talk as if nothing had happened. But it requires considerable self-possession and command of language to sit still and talk about the weather with a woman's tears falling before you like rain; and even Langley Wyndham, that studious cultivator of phrases, found it hard. Audrey herself relieved him from his embarrassment by frankly drying her eyes and saying—

"I beg your pardon. I didn't mean that to happen; but— —"

He glanced at the letter open in her lap.

"Not bad news, I hope?"

"N-no," she answered, with a sob verging on the hysterical.

Wyndham looked frightened at that, and she checked herself in time.

"No, it's nothing. At least I can't speak about it. And yet—if I did, I believe I should feel better. I am so miserable."

"I am truly sorry. I wish I could be of some use. If you thought you could speak about it to me, you know you can trust me."

"I know I can. Oh, if I could only tell you! But I can't."

"Why not? Would it be so very hard? I *might* be able to help you."

"You might. I do want somebody's advice—so much."

"You are always welcome to mine. You needn't take it, you know."

She smiled through her tears, for she had acquired a faint sense of humour under Ted's influence, and had not yet lost it.

"Well, it's about Vinc—my cousin Mr. Hardy. You remember meeting him here once?"

"I do indeed."

"You may remember something I told you about him then. Perhaps I ought not to have told you."

"Never mind that. Yes, I remember perfectly. Has he been persecuting you again?"

"Ye-yes. Well, no. I haven't seen him for ages, but I live in dread of seeing him every day. I know, sooner or later, he will come."

She paused. "I wonder if I really could tell you everything."

"Please do, or tell me as much as you care to. I'd like to help you if you would let me."

She went on in a low voice, rather suggestive, Wyndham thought, of the confessional: "I was engaged to him once—long ago—he forced me into it. It began when we were children. He always made me do everything he wanted. Then—he went away immediately after—for a year. When he came back—I don't know how it was—I suppose it was because he had been away so long—but I was stronger. He seemed to have lost his hold over me, and I—I broke it off."

She looked away from Wyndham as she spoke.

He wondered, "Is she acting all the time? If so, how admirably she does it! She must be a cleverer woman than I thought. But she isn't a clever woman. Therefore——" But Audrey went on before he could draw a conclusion.

"But I know some day he will come back and make it begin all over again, and I shall have no power. And the thought of it is horrible!"

There was no mistaking the passion in her voice this time. He said to himself, "This is nature," and he felt the same cold shiver of sympathy that sometimes ran through him at the performance of some splendid actress. But before he could presume to sympathise he must judge.

"Do you mind telling me one thing? Had you any graver reasons for breaking it off than what you have told me?"

"Yes. He drinks."

"Brute! That's enough. But—supposing he didn't drink?"

"It would make no difference. I never cared for him. He thought I did. I couldn't help that, could I? And then afterwards so many things happened—I was not the same person. If he had not begun to—do that, still it would have been impossible. But he won't believe it, or else he doesn't care. He'll persecute me again, and perhaps make me marry him."

"My dear Miss Craven, he won't do that. People don't do those things in the nineteenth century. You've only got to state clearly that you won't have anything to say to him, and he can't do anything. If he tries to, there are measures that can be taken."

She shook her head dismally.

"Now comes the advice. Shall I tell you the truth? You've been worrying your brain over that wretched animal till your nerves are all upset. You're ill practically, or you couldn't take this morbid view of it. You ought to leave town and go away for a change."

"Where could I go to?"

"The south coast for choice. It's bracing."

"If I only could! No, I can't leave London."

"Why not? There's an excellent service of trains——"

"Because—because I love London."

"So do I for many reasons. There's no place like it, to my mind. But if I'd overworked myself in it, I should tear myself away. You can have too much of a good thing."

"No, not of the only place on earth you care to be in."

"Well, I've given my valuable advice. You're not going to take it—I never thought you would. Personally I hate the people who give me advice. What I should like to give you would be help. But the question is, Am I able to give it? Have I even the right to offer it?"

She looked up at him. Some lyric voice, whether of hope or joy, or both, had called the soul for an instant to her face—a poor little fluttering soul, that gazed out through her grey eyes at Wyndham—for an instant only, and was seen no more. When he spoke, he spoke not to it, but to the woman he had known.

"You don't answer." (She had answered, and he knew it.) "It all comes back to what I said long ago. The most elementary knowledge of life would have saved you all this: if you'd had it, you could not have let these fatuities worry you to this extent. Do you remember my telling you that you ought to love life for its own sake?"

The moment he had said the words, he would have given anything to recall them, but it was too late; she remembered only too well. However she had disguised the truth, Wyndham's passionate defence of realism was not altogether an appeal to her intellect. He ought not to have reminded her of that now.

"Yes," she answered; "how could I forget?"

"I said at the time that you must know life in order to love it, and I say so now. But, Audrey"—she started and flushed—"if I were another man I should not say that."

"What would you say?"

"That you must love in order to know."

"Is there any need to tell me that *now*?"

"Perhaps not. It's what I would have told you then—if I had been another man."

Her lip quivered slightly, and she held one hand with the other to give herself the feeling of a human touch. He went on without the least idea whether he were talking sense or nonsense, interrupted sometimes by his own conscience, sometimes by Audrey's changes of expression.

"Bear with my egoism a moment—several moments, for I'm going to be tediously autobiographical. Once, when I was a young man, I was offered some journalistic work. It was at the very start; I had barely tasted print. Remember, I was ambitious, and it meant the beginning of a career; I was poor, and it meant a good salary. But it meant the production of a column of 'copy' a-day, whether I was in the vein for it or no. I wanted it badly, and—I refused it. I could *not* be tied down. Since then I have never bound myself to any publisher or editor. This anecdote is not in the least interesting, but it is characteristic of my whole nature, which is my reason for inflicting it on you. That nature may be an unfortunate one, but I didn't invent it myself. Anyhow, knowing it as thoroughly as I do, I've made up my mind never to do certain things—never, for instance, to ask any woman to be my wife. Marriage is the one impossible thing. It involves duty, or, worse still, duties. Now, as it happens, I consider duty to be the very lowest of moral motives. In fact—don't be shocked—it isn't moral at all. It is to conduct what authority is to belief—that is, it has nothing whatever to do with it. No. Goodness no more depends on duty than truth depends on authority. Forgive me; I know you are a metaphysician and a moral philosopher, and you'll appreciate this. You're going to make a quotation; please don't. It's perfectly useless to tell me that Wordsworth calls duty 'stern daughter of the voice of God.' It may be; I don't know. I only know that if I believed it was my *duty* to live, I'd commit suicide tomorrow. I don't like stern daughters. But granted that Wordsworth had the facts at his finger-ends, God's voice is freedom, whatever its daughters may be. That's not a doctrine I'd preach to every one; but for me, and those like me, freedom, absolute freedom, is the condition of all sane thinking and feeling. Fancy loving any one because it was your duty! Take a case. Supposing I married: the more I loved my wife, the less a free agent I should be; and when I once realised that I wasn't free, there would be an end of my love. I deplore this state of things, but I can't alter it. So you see, when I most want to give you love and protection, I can only offer you friendship, which you don't want perhaps, and—er—good advice, which you won't take."

But she was looking beyond him, far away.

"As I can't possibly ask you to—accept my conditions, perhaps the cleverest thing I could do would be to go away and never see you again. There's no other alternative."

Her lips parted as if she would have spoken, but no words came. They searched each other's faces, the woman thirsting for life, for love; the man thirsting too—for knowledge. And he knew.

It was his turn to look away from her; and as he fixed his eyes absently on the corner where the Psyche stood motionless on her pedestal, he noticed, as people will notice at these moments, the ironical suggestion of the torso, with the nasty Malay creese hanging over its head. Psyche and—the sword of Damocles.

"I don't want you to go away," she said at last.

"I am going, all the same. For a little while—a fortnight perhaps. I want you to have time to think." He was not by any means sure what he meant by that. He had solved his problem, though not quite as he had intended to, and that was enough for him. And yet his conscience (not the literary one, but the other) would not altogether acquit him of treachery to Audrey. Instead of going away, as he ought to have done, he sat on talking, in the hope of silencing the reproachful voice inside him, of setting things on their ordinary footing again. But this was impossible at the moment. They were talking now across some thin barrier woven of trivialities, as it were some half-transparent Japanese screen, with all sorts of frivolous figures painted on it in an absurd perspective. And behind this flimsy partition their human life went on, each soul playing its part more or less earnestly in a little tragedy of temptation. Each knew all the time what the other was doing; though Wyndham had still the advantage of Audrey in this respect. Which of them would first have the courage to pull down the screen and face the solid, impenetrable truth?

Neither of them attempted it,—they dared not. After half an hour's commonplaces Wyndham left her to think. He too had some matter for reflection. He was not inhuman, and if at times he seemed so, he had ways of reconciling his inhumanity to his conscience. He told himself that his strictly impartial attitude as the student of human nature enabled him to do these things. He was as a higher intelligence, looking down on the crowd of struggling, suffering men and women beneath him, forgiving, tolerating all, because he understood all. He who saw life so whole, who knew the hidden motives and far-off causes of human action, could make allowances for everything. There was something divine in his literary charity. What matter, then, if he now and then looked into some girl's expressive face, and found out the secret she thought she was hiding so cleverly from everybody,—if he knew the sources of So-and-so's mysterious illness, which had puzzled the doctors so long? And what if he had obtained something more than a passing glimpse into the nature of the woman who had trusted him? It would have been base, impossible, in any other man, of course: the impersonal point of view, you see, made all the difference.

CHAPTER XX

From that afternoon Wyndham kept away from Chelsea Gardens; in fact, he had left town. To do him justice, he honestly thought he was doing "the cleverest thing" for Audrey in leaving her—to think. It would have been the cleverest thing if he could have kept away altogether; but as long as she had the certainty of his return, it was about the stupidest. If he had stayed, they would have resumed their ordinary relations; all might have blown over like a mood, and whatever he knew about her, Audrey herself would never have known it. As it was, he had emphasised the situation by going. And what was more, he had thrown Audrey back on her uninteresting self—the very worst company she could have had at present. She had been used to seeing him almost daily through a whole winter; he had made her dependent on his society for all her interests and pleasures; and when she was suddenly deprived of it, instead of being able to think, she spent her time in miserable longing. She could not think and feel at the same time. Feeling such as hers was incompatible with any form of thinking; it was feeling in a vacuum—the most dangerous kind of all. The emptiness of her life, now that Wyndham was gone, made her say to herself that she could bear anything—anything but that. It made her realise what the years, the long unspeakable years, would be like when she had given him up. She looked behind and around her, and there were the grey levels of ordinary existence; she looked below her, and there was the deep; she was going into the darkness of it, swiftly, helplessly, blown on by the wind of vanity. She saw no darkness for the light before her—a nebulous light; but it dazzled her like the sun shining through a fog.

Once, at the fiercest point of her temptation, she felt an impulse to confession—that mysterious instinct which lies somewhere at the heart of all humanity; she had wild thoughts of going to Katherine and telling her all, asking her what she ought to do. Katherine was large-minded, she would not blame her—much; perhaps she would tell her she ought not to give Wyndham up, that she ought to think of him, to be ready to sacrifice the world for his sake. Yes, Katherine was so "clever," she would be a good judge; and Audrey would abide by her judgment. Unhappily, when it came to the point, she was afraid of her judgment—she had always been a little afraid of Katherine. Once she even thought of going to Mr. Flaxman Reed, that "holy anachronism," as she had once heard Wyndham call him. But his judgment was a foregone conclusion; Mr. Flaxman Reed was not large-minded.

Once, too, a gleam of reason came to her. She loved dearly the admiration and good opinion of her world; and she reflected that the step she contemplated meant no congratulations, no wedding-dress, no presents, and no callers. Wedding indeed! As she had read of a similar case in "London Legends," it would be a "social funeral, with no flowers by request." But these considerations had no weight after an evening spent with cousin Bella. And though she played on her piano till the lace butterflies on Miss Craven's cap fluttered again (why would cousin Bella wear caps in defiance of the fashion?), it was no good. If she had had a fine voice, she would have sung at the top of it; failing that medium of expression, she longed to put her fingers in her own ears and scream into cousin Bella's. And as they yawned in each other's faces, and she realised that something like this might be the programme for an indefinite time, she remembered how Langley had called her a metaphysician and a moral philosopher. It was on statements like these, apparently borne out by the fact of his friendship, that she based the flattering fiction of her own intellectuality. Without that fiction Audrey could not have supported life in the rare atmosphere she had accustomed herself to breathe. The conclusion of it all was that, come what might come, she could not give Langley up.

One afternoon she crossed the river for a walk in Battersea Park. It was a warm spring, and down the long avenue the trees were tipped with the flame of bursting buds, like so many green lights turned low. The beds and borders were gay with crocuses and hyacinths, and the open spaces were beginning to look green again. Audrey cared little for these things, but to-day she was somehow aware of them; she felt in her the new life of the spring, as she had felt it a year ago. She walked rapidly from sheer excitement, till she had tired herself out; then she sat down on one of the benches, overlooking the waste ground where the children played. Except for a bright fringe under the iron railings, it was still untouched by spring, and the sallow grass had long been trodden into the dust. Some ragged little cricketers were shouting not far off, and near her, by the railings, was a family group—a young father and mother, with their children, from two years old and upwards, crawling around them. They were enjoying a picnic tea in the sunshine, with the voluptuous carelessness of outward show that marks the children of the people. Audrey looked at it all with a faint disgust, but she was too tired to move on to a more cheerful spot. She turned her back on the picnic party, and began to think about Wyndham. He had been away ten days; he said he was going for a fortnight; in another week at the longest she would see him. She was roused by a tug at her petticoats. The two-year-old, attracted like some wild animal by her stillness, had scrambled through the railings, and was trying to pull its fat little body up by one hand on to the bench beside her. Its other hand grasped firmly a sheaf of fresh grass. It was clean and pretty, and something in its baby face sent a pang to Audrey's heart. She loosened its chubby fingers, hoping it would toddle away; but it gave a wilful chuckle, and stood still, staring at her, reproaching, accusing, in the unconscious cruelty of its innocence. And yet surely the Divine Charity had chosen the tenderest and most delicate means of stirring into life her unborn conscience. Moved by who knows what better impulse, she stooped suddenly down and touched its face with the tips of her gloved fingers. Startled at the strange caress, like some animal stroked too lightly, the little thing made its face swell, and asserted its humanity by a howl. Then it fled from her with a passionate waddle, scattering blades of grass behind it as it went.

Even so do we chase away from us the ministers of grace.

She leaned back, overcome by a sort of moral exhaustion. Her self-love was hurt, as it would have been if a dog had shrunk from her advances; for Audrey was not accustomed to have her favours rejected. She was further irritated by the ostentatious affection of the child's mother as she helped it through the railings with shrill cries of "There then, blessums! Did she then, the naughty lydy!" And when baby echoed "Naughty lydy!" it was as if the two-year-old had judged her.

She sat a little while longer, and then went away. As she rose she looked sadly back at the family group. The man was lying on his back and letting the children walk about on the top of him. Baby had found peace in sucking an orange and stamping on her father's waist. The woman was strewing paper bags and orange-peel around her in a fine disorder, while she thriftily packed the remains of their meal in a basket. Audrey shuddered; their arrangements were all so ugly and unpleasant. And yet—they were married, they were respectable, they were happy, these terrible people; while she—she was miserable. She had no sense of justice; and she rebelled against the policy of Nature, who leaves her coarser children free, and levies her taxes on the aristocracy of feeling.

The sordid domesticity of the scene had glorified by contrast her own dramatic mood. Poor Audrey! She hated vulgarity, and yet she was trying to lay hold on "the great things of life" through the vulgarest of all life's tragedies.

Langley would be in town again in a week. He would ask if she had made up her mind; and she knew now too well the answer she would give him.

But Langley was not in town again in a week, nor yet in a fortnight. And when, at the end of six weeks, he did come back, he came back married—to Miss Alison Fraser.

Nobody ever knew how that came about. Miss Gladys Armstrong, who may be considered an authority, maintained that as Wyndham had the pride which is supposed to be the peculiar property of the Evil One, he could never have proposed to the same woman twice. Consequently Miss Fraser must have proposed to him. Perhaps she had; there are ways of doing these things, and whatever Alison Fraser did she did gracefully. As for her private conscience, in refusing him with conscious magnanimity she had done no good to anybody, not even herself; in marrying him finally she had saved the situation, without knowing that there was a situation to be saved.

The news threw Audrey into what she imagined to be the beginning of a brain fever, but which proved to be a state of nervous collapse, lasting, with some intermissions, for a fortnight. At the end of that time—whether it was that she was so fickle a creature that even Fate could make no abiding impression on her, or that she was no longer burdened with the decision of a momentous question—to all appearances she recovered. So much so that, when some one sent her an invitation to the private view at the New Gallery, she put on her best clothes (not without a pang) and went.

Alas! the place was full of associations, melancholy with the sheeted ghosts of the past. This time last year she had been to the private view with Ted. They had amused themselves with laughing at the pictures, and wondering how long it would be before one of his would be hanging there. And as she listlessly turned the pages of her catalogue, the first names that caught her attention were, "Haviland, Katherine, 232"; "Haviland, Edward, 296." She turned back the pages hastily to No. 232 and read, "The Witch of Atlas." That picture she knew. No. 296 gave her "Sappho: A Study of a Head."

Of a head? Whose head?

She found the picture (not exactly in the place of honour, but agreeably well hung and with a small crowd before it), and recognised Katherine's striking profile raised in the attitude of a suppliant who implores, the cloud of her dark hair flaming into bronze against a sunset sky. Ted was rather too fond of that trick; but the study was not a mere vulgar success—he had achieved expression in it. It was marked "Sold." There were some lines of verse on the square panel at the base of the frame. Ted could not have afforded such a setting for his picture, but the frame was contributed by Mr. Percival Knowles, the purchaser of the canvas. The same gentleman was also the author of the verse, specially written for the portrait. Knowles, by-the-bye, was an occasional poet—that is to say, he could burst into poetry occasionally; and Audrey read:—

> "Oh Aphrodite, queen of dread desire!
>   By all the dreams that throng Love's golden ways,
>   By all the honied vows thy votary pays,
> By sacrificial wine, and holy fire!
> Thou who hast made my heart thy living lyre,
>   Hast thou no gift for me, nor any grace?
>   Why hast thou turned the light of Love's sweet face
> From me, the sweetest singer of Love's choir?"

> "For songs that charm the long ambrosial years
>   The gods bring many gifts, and mine shall be—
>   Immortal life in mortal agony—
> Vain longing, fanned by wingèd hopes and fears
> To inextinguishable flame—and tears
>   Bitter as death, salt as the Lesbian Sea."

Her breast rose and fell with the lines; by this time she was educated up to their feeling.

"Who was Sappho, and what did she do?—I know, but I've forgotten," asked a voice in the crowd.

"Oh, the woman who threw herself at the other fellow's head, you know, who naturally didn't appreciate the compliment."

Audrey was not intelligent enough to refrain from the inward comment, "How singularly inappropriate! I should have said Katherine was about the last person in the world to——" She turned round and found herself face to face with the poet. Knowles had been wandering through the crowd with evasive eyes, successfully dodging the ladies of his acquaintance, while his air of abstraction took all quality of offence from the unerring precision of his movements. But when he saw Miss Craven he stopped. He had an inkling of the truth, and respected her feelings too much to slight her while Wyndham's marriage was still a topic of the hour.

"Not bad for the boy, that!" said he, smiling gently at Sappho. "He's coming out, isn't he?"

"So are you, I think—in a new line too!"

"Ah—er—not quite a new one. I've been taken that way before."

She was about to make some pretty speech when they were joined by Ted, who had not noticed Audrey. His forehead puckered slightly when he saw her, but that was no doubt from sympathy with her probable embarrassment. For the first time in their acquaintance he was indifferent to the touch of the small hand that had tried to mould his destiny. If the truth must be told, in the flush of his success Ted had found out that his passion for Audrey was only the flickering of the flame on the altar dedicated to eternal Art. He listened to her compliments without that sense of apotheosis which (however low he rated it) her criticism had been wont to produce.

"Don't let's be seen looking at it any longer," he said at last; "let's go and pretend to get excited about some other fellow's work."

So they left Audrey to herself. She turned back and went down the room to see "The Witch of Atlas," the lady robed in her "subtle veil" of starbeams and mist. Her view of this picture was somewhat obstructed by a stout gentleman who, together with a thin lady, was taking up the whole of the available space before it. His companion, a badly-dressed young woman with a double eye-glass, was trying to decipher the lines quoted in her catalogue. As Audrey paused she looked up and stared, as only a woman with a double eye-glass can stare, at the same time attracting the stout gentleman's attention by a movement of her elbow.

"Look, uncle, quick! That's her! That's the person!"

"What's that, Nettie?" (The stout gentleman swung round as if on a pivot, as Audrey moved gracefully by.) "You don't mean to say so? Where's Ted?"

She walked on through the rooms, depressed by the meeting with Knowles—it suggested Wyndham. She would be meeting *him* next.

And indeed she met him in the first gallery, where her aimless wanderings had brought her again.

His wife was with him. Audrey knew that she must meet her some time, and she had expected to see in Alison Fraser an enlarged edition of herself; she had even feared an *édition de luxe*, which would have been intolerable. She was prepared for distinction; but she saw with a finer agony the slight figure, the sweet proud face with its setting of pale gold hair, and worse than all, the indefinable air of remoteness and reserve which made Mrs. Langley Wyndham more than a "distinguished" woman. Wyndham lifted his hat and would have passed on; but Audrey, to show her perfect self-possession, stopped and held out her hand. He felt it trembling as he took it in a preoccupied manner; and Mrs. Langley Wyndham became instantly absorbed in picture No. 1.

"Have you seen young Haviland's performance?" asked Wyndham. (He had to say something.)

"Yes; it's a very fine study."

"So Knowles tells me. But everything's a fine study in this collection. There ought to be 'a fine' for the abuse of that expression."

"But it really is; go and see for yourself."

"It's his sister, isn't it?"

"Yes."

"Ah, that accounts for it. He could give his mind to it in that case." Wyndham was surprised at his own fatuity; his remarks sounded like the weird inanities that pass for witticisms in dreams.

"Perhaps. But never mind Mr. Haviland; I want you to introduce me to your wife."

Wyndham looked round; his wife had turned an unconscious back.

"Oh—er—thank you, you're very kind, but—er—we're just going."

He had not meant them so, but his words were like a whip laid across Audrey's shoulders. He moved on, and his wife joined him.

Audrey came across them half an hour later, stooping over some designs in black and white. She saw Mrs. Langley Wyndham look up in her husband's face with a smile, raising her golden eyebrows. The look was one of those intimate trifles that have no meaning beyond the two persons concerned in it. For Audrey, smarting from Wyndham's insult, it was the flick of the lash in her face.

CHAPTER XXI

In the autumn of that year Audrey woke and found herself the classic of the hour, a literary queen without a rival. Wyndham's great work was finished, and it stood alone. Not another heroine of fiction could lift her head beside Laura, the leading character of "An Idyll of Piccadilly." He himself owned, almost with emotion, that it was the best thing he had ever done. He had not touched the surface this time; he had gone deep down to the springs of human nature. He had not merely analysed the woman till her character lay in ruins around him, but he had built her up again out of the psychic atoms, and Laura was alive. She showed the hand of the master by her own nullity. In her splendid vanity she was like some piece of elaborate golden fretwork, from which the substance had been refined by excess of workmanship.

The voice of criticism was one voice; there arose a unanimous hymn of praise from every literary "organ" in the country. It was Mr. Langley Wyndham's masterpiece, a work that left the excellence of "London Legends" far behind it on a lower plane. Though there was no falling off in point of style, the author had found something better to do this time than to cultivate the flowers of perfect speech. "Laura" was a triumph of intimate characterisation. And the brutal touches that disfigured his former work were absent from this; he had shown us that the boldest, most inflexible realism is compatible with a delicacy worthy of the daintiest of esoteric ideals.

The book, dedicated "To my Wife," appeared early in October. By November the question of the sources was opened out, and it began to be whispered (a whisper that could be traced to the private utterances of Miss Gladys Armstrong) that the prototype of Laura was a Miss Audrey Craven. In the person of her ubiquitous double, Miss Audrey Craven became a leading figure in London society. Then bit by bit the news got into the papers, and Wyndham's *succès d'estime* was followed by *succès de scandale* which promised to treble his editions.

Thus Audrey, unable to achieve greatness, had greatness thrust upon her; and the weight of it bowed her to the earth. The earth? As she read on, the earth seemed to crumble away from under her feet, leaving her baseless and alone before that terrifying apocalypse. Wyndham had trained her intelligence till it could appreciate the force of every chapter in his book of revelations. At last she saw herself as she was. And yet—could that be she? That mixture of vanity, stupidity, and passion? To be sure, he had been careful to give her brown hair instead of tell-tale red, and skillfully to alter the plot of her life with all details of time and place; but—what had he said? "Light as air, fluent as water, a being mingled of fire and a little earth; fickle as the wind that blew her in a wavering line across the surface of things." "Modern, and of stuff so fine that it chafed under the very breath of disapproval; and yet with a little malleable heart in it compounded of the most primeval of affections." She turned over the pages; everywhere she came upon the same thing. Now the phrases were spun out fine, they were subtle, they seemed to cling round her and stifle her; now they were short and keen, and they cut like knives. "Women may be divided into three classes—the virtuous, the flirtuous, and the non-virtuous. The middle class is by far the largest. It shades off finely into the two extremes. Laura belonged to it." "The moon was up, and Diana, divine sportswoman, was abroad, hunting big game." "Laura had made a virtue of necessity. She said that proved the necessity of virtue."

Oh, the cruelty of it! Would Ted, would Vincent, have done this if they had had it in their power? True, they had reproached her; but it was to her face, alone in her own drawing-room, where she had a chance of defending herself. *They* would not have held her up to public scorn. And they had some right to blame her,—she saw that now. But what had she done to deserve this from Langley? How had he found it in his heart to speak against her? She had loved him. Yes, she had known many a passing pain, but she had never really suffered until now. That was a part of her education that had been neglected hitherto. Only an accomplished student of human nature could have coached her through the highest branches of it.

Having set the scandal successfully afloat, the society papers began to utter a feeble protest against it—thus increasing their own reputation for a refined morality. But they had no power to turn the tide, and the scandal floated on. In society itself judgment was divided. Whether "Laura" was or was not a work of the highest art, was a question you might have heard discussed at every other dinner-table. Perhaps the criticism that was most to the point was that of Miss Gladys Armstrong, who proclaimed publicly that Langley Wyndham laboured under the disadvantage of not being a woman, and having no imagination to make up for it. Meanwhile the tone of the larger reviews remained unchanged. The reviewers, to a man, had committed themselves to the position that the book was Wyndham's masterpiece; and nobody could be found to go back on that opinion.

But in all that concert of adulation one voice was silent—the only voice that Wyndham cared to hear, that of Percival Knowles. The others might howl in chorus, and it would not be worth his while even to listen; he was looking forward to Knowles's long impressive solo. But that solo never came, neither could the note of Knowles be detected in the intricate chorus. It was strange. Knowles had been the high priest of the new Wyndham worship, and to him the eminent novelist had looked for sympathy and appreciation. But Knowles had made no sign. They had avoided the subject whenever they met; Wyndham was not so hardened by authorship as to have lost the instinctive delicacy felt by the creator at the birth of his book. Knowles seemed only too much inclined to respect that delicacy. Finally, Wyndham resolved to go and see his friend alone, and tentatively sound him on the subject of "Laura." He proposed to himself a pleasant evening's chat, in which that lady would be discussed in all her bearings, and he would enjoy a foretaste of the praise ere long to be dealt out to him before an admiring public. On his way to Knowles's rooms he heard in fancy the congratulation, the temperate flattery, the fine discriminating phrase.

He found Knowles amusing himself with a blue pencil and Miss Armstrong's last novel. "Laura: An Idyll of Piccadilly" lay on the table beside him, its pages cut, but with none of those slips of paper between them which marked the other books put aside for review. Knowles greeted his friend with an embarrassed laugh, and they fell to discussing every question of the hour except the burning one for Wyndham. By the rapidity of his conversational manœuvres, it was evident that the critic wanted to steer clear of that topic. Wyndham, however, after ambling round and round it for some time with no effect, suddenly brought up straight in front of it with—

"By-the-bye, have you condescended to read my last fairy-tale?"

"What, the Mayfairy tale?" said Knowles, with deft pleasantry. "Yes, of course I've read it."

"What do you think of it?"

Knowles suddenly looked grave. "Well, at the moment, I had much rather not tell you."

"Really? Well, I suppose I shall know some day."

Knowles looked as if he were struggling with an unpleasant duty, and it were getting the better of him.

"Not from me, I'm afraid. It will be the first work of yours I have left unnoticed. As I can't review it favourably, I prefer not to notice it at all."

"You surely don't suppose that I came here to fish for a review?"

"I do not."

"Thanks. I don't deny that I should have appreciated the public expression of your opinion, favourable or unfavourable. But I respect your scruples as far as I understand them. The only thing is——"

He paused; it was his turn to feel uncomfortable.

"Is what?"

"Well, after the way you've delivered yourself on my other books, which are feebleness itself compared with this one, I must say your present attitude astonishes me."

"I've given you my reasons for it."

"No; that's what you've not done. Surely we've known each other too long for this foolishness. Of course, it's considerate of you not to damn me for the entertainment of the British public; but you know you're the only man in England whose judgment I care about, and I confess I'd like to have your private opinion—the usual honest and candid thing, you know. I'm not talking of gods, men, and columns."

Knowles sat silent, frowning.

"Oh, well, of course, if you'd rather not, there's nothing more to be said."

"Not much."

But Wyndham's palpitating egoism was martyred by this silence beyond endurance, and he burst out in spite of himself—

"But it's inconceivable to me, after the way you've treated my first crude work. You must have set up some new canons of art since then. Otherwise I should say you were inconsistent."

But Knowles was not to be drawn out, if he could possibly help it.

"Do you mind telling me one thing—have you anything to say against its form?"

"Not a word. I admit that in form it's about as perfect as it well could be. I—er—" (he was beginning to feel that he could not help it) "object to your use of your matter."

"What on earth do you mean?"

"I mean what I say."

"Please explain."

"Very well. Since you so earnestly desire my honest and candid opinion, you shall have it. You remind me that I praised your earlier work, and suggest my inconsistency in not approving of your latest. My praise was sincere. I thought, and I have never changed my opinion, that the originality of your first books amounted to genius. Your last, however great its other qualities, has not that merit. It is, *I* think, conspicuously destitute of imagination."

"Do you deny its vitality—its faithfulness to nature?"

"Certainly not. I object to it as a barefaced plagiarism from nature."

"Then at least you'll admit that my heroine lives?"

"She does, unfortunately. Wouldn't it have been better taste to wait till she was decently dead?"

"Oh—I see. You mean *that*."

"Yes; I mean that. If you had no respect for your own reputation, you might have thought of Miss Craven's."

"Excuse me, this is simply irrelevant nonsense, and most unworthy of you. Miss Craven, as you perfectly well know, is one manifestation of the eternal flirt. I seized on the type she belongs to, and individualised it."

"You did nothing of the sort. You seized on the individual and put her into type—a very different thing. Do you imagine that life will ever be the same to that poor woman again? I never liked Miss Craven, but she was harmless, even nice, before you got hold of her and spoilt her, by making her think herself clever. Isn't that what happens to Laura?"

"That—among other things."

"Other things, also slavishly copied from Miss Craven. I recognise the faithfulness of your portraiture in all its details; so does she and everybody else."

"Knowles, you talk like the lay fool. Surely you know how all fiction, worthy of the name, is made? I took what lay nearest at hand, as hundreds of novelists have done before me; though as for that, there's not an incident in the book that is not the purest fiction. You don't give me credit—I won't say for originality, but—for ordinary reconstructive ability."

"I give you credit for having made the most of quite exceptional advantages. You best know how you obtained them."

Wyndham reflected a moment, then looked Knowles in the face.

"I assure you solemnly there was never any question of Miss Craven's honour."

Knowles raised his eyebrows. "I didn't suppose for a moment there was. How about your own, though? Your notions of honour strike me as being quaintly original—rather more original than your Piccadyllic heroine."

Knowles was not bad-tempered, but he was a frequent cause of bad temper in other people. It was with the utmost difficulty that Wyndham controlled himself for a final effort to evade the personal, and set the question at large on general grounds.

"Then I suppose you would deny the right of any artist to make use of living material?"

Knowles yawned. "I don't attempt to deny anything. I'm debating another question."

"What is that?" Wyndham smiled an uneasy muscular smile.

"Whether it isn't my duty to kick you, or rather to *try* to kick you, out of this room."

"Really; and what for? For the crime of writing a successful story?"

"For the perpetration of the most consummate piece of literary scoundrelism on record."

As that statement was accompanied by a nervous twitching of the lips which Wyndham was at liberty to take for a smile, he held out his hand to Knowles before saying good-night.

"My dear Knowles, if *your* notions of literary honour held good, there would be an end of realism."

"The end of realism, my dear Wyndham, is the thing of all others I most desire to see."

They had shaken hands; but Wyndham understood his friend, and he knew as certainly as if Knowles had told him so that Audrey Craven, the woman whom neither of them loved, had avenged herself. She had struck, through Laura, at the friendship of his life. He was also informed of one or two facts about himself which had not as yet come within the range of his observation. He consoled himself with the reflection that the temptations of genius are not those of other men. And perhaps he was right.

Knowles sat down to his review of Miss Armstrong's book with unruffled urbanity. He wrote: "This authoress belongs to a select but rapidly increasing band of thinkers. There may be schisms in the new school with regard to details, but on the whole it is a united one. The members are unanimous in their fearless optimism. One and all they preach the same hopeful doctrine, that the attainment of a high standard of immodesty by woman will in time make morality possible for man."

He went to bed vowing that of all professions that chosen by the man of letters is the most detestable.

CHAPTER XXII

That winter was a hard one for the Havilands; they were at the very lowest ebb of their resources, short of being actually in debt. The reclaiming of Hardy had been an expensive undertaking for Katherine in more ways than one. And naturally the more successful her efforts were the more time they consumed. She had been so busy all summer finishing off old work that she had not been able to take up anything fresh. She had even been obliged to send away sitters, and they had betaken themselves elsewhere. The "Witch" had not sold, though she had won a big paragraph all to herself in "Modern Art." In her first enthusiasm over Ted's success Katherine had encouraged him to give up his pot-boilers. She had taken over some of his black-and-white work herself. And in the midst of it all she was engaged on a portrait of Vincent. They were so dependent on what they earned that these serious interruptions to work threatened an inroad on their small capital. Now, they might any day have applied to Mr. Pigott for a loan, and rejoiced that worthy gentleman's heart; but such a step was the last indignity, not even to be contemplated by Ted and Katherine. And even if their pride had not stood in their way, that source of revenue seemed closed to them now. Ted and his uncle had had an unfortunate encounter in the New Gallery. The fact that he was indebted to Katherine for an invitation to the private view had not prevented Mr. Pigott from speaking his mind freely to her brother on the subject of the Witch. He said he could have forgiven Ted for painting such a picture. He could have forgiven Katherine too, if it had not been for her ability— that made her doubly responsible. Ted tried to soothe him; he led him gently away from the spot; he promised to do all he could to induce Katherine to cultivate the grace of stupidity; but it was useless. The old gentleman stood to his ground, and Ted left him there. He received a letter from him the next morning:—

"DEAR EDWARD,—I parted from you yesterday more in sorrow than in anger. I need not tell you how deeply shocked and grieved I was to learn from a literary young friend that the subject of your sister's picture is taken from the works of the atheist Shelley—a man whose unprincipled life, I am told, is an all-sufficient commentary on his opinions.

"Your cousin Nettie is earning a modest competence by poker-work, and the painting of flowers, birds, and other innocent and beautiful objects. Why cannot Katherine do the same?

"When she is willing to give up her present pursuits for some becoming occupation, let her be assured of my ready encouragement and help. Till then, no more.—From your affectionate uncle,

"JAMES PIGOTT."

Mr. Pigott had written his last sentence advisedly. "Some day," he said to himself, "those young people will have to put their pride in their pocket." He might have known that the Haviland pride was not of the kind that goes conveniently into any pocket, even an empty one.

But Katherine worked her hardest, and gave little heed to these things. She saw her own chances of success dwindling farther into the distance, and was surprised to see how little she cared, for a curious callousness had come over her of late. Selfish ambition—selfish, because it often persists in living when all other things are dead—seemed to have died in her at last. Had she overcome it? Or was it that she had really ceased to care? She had too much to think of to be able to settle that question just now.

After all, she had another source of pride. Vincent had begun by looking to her as a protection against his worst self; and when his mother died suddenly that winter, his last link with home being broken, he became more and more dependent on Katherine. And now, though the tie of comradeship between them was closer than ever, he had no longer any need of her. He could go alone. His will was free, his intellect was awake. He read hard now. All his old ardours and enthusiasms returned to him; he worked on the Pioneer-book, recasting his favourite parts, beating the whole into shape, and hunting down the superfluous adjective with a manly delight in the new sport. Katherine had shown the revised manuscript to Knowles, and he had found her a publisher and worked him into the right frame of mind. Katherine had suppressed part of that publisher's verdict: it was to the effect that, though the text was up to the average merit of its kind, the illustrations would form the most valuable portion of the work.

Hardy had submitted the final revision of his proofs to Katherine. But on one point he was resolute: "I want the dedication to stand as it is, Sis." And Katherine nodded her head and was silent.

He often talked about Audrey now. He was no longer bitter and vindictive, as he had been in the days of his degradation. His old feeling for her had returned to him, unchanged, except for the refining process he himself had undergone. His love was ennobled now by an infinite pity. Not that he had lost sight of what she had done for him; but now that his eyes were clearer, he saw her as she was, and felt to the full the pathos of her vanity.

Wyndham's book was severely criticised in Devon Street. One day, about four months after its appearance, Hardy had returned to the subject nearest his heart, and was discussing it with Katherine as he sat to her for his portrait, now nearly finished. He had just pleasantly told her that he wished he had managed to fall in love with her instead of with Audrey; she would have made something very different of him—a remark to which Katherine made no answer, treating it, as Hardy thought, with the contempt it deserved. Then he broke out, as he had done many a time before.

"I don't know how it is. When I was away from her, I used to think of her as a sort of amateur angel leading me on." (Katherine smiled; it was very evident that Audrey had "led him on.") "When I was with her she seemed to be a little devil, encouraging everything that was bad in me. I don't know how she did it; but she did. And yet, Kathy, whatever they may say, I don't believe she's bad. I don't swear, of course, that she's a paragon of goodness——"

"Isn't there a medium?"

"But she was a sweet little thing before she met that scoundrel Wyndham. Wasn't she?"

But Katherine was giving the whole of her attention to Vincent's nose.

"Putting Audrey out of the question, I don't think much of Mr. Langley Wyndham. I don't like his books; I can't breathe in his stuffy drawing-rooms. Why can't the fellow open his windows sometimes and let in a little of God's fresh air? As you know, I believe he's even a shadier character than I am."

"He hasn't got a character; it's all run to literature."

"H'm—I'm not so sure about that."

Katherine had laid down her brushes, and was examining her work with her head on one side. "Well, he can't draw a character, anyhow; Laura's simply impossible."

"I don't know. Laura is Audrey, and Audrey's a funny person."

"I used to think that Audrey wasn't a person—that she was made up of little bits of people stuck together."

"That's not bad, Sis. She *is* made up of bits of people stuck together."

"Yes; but the thing is, what makes them stick? Mr. Wyndham doesn't go into that, and *that's* Audrey. His work is clever—too clever by half—but it's terribly superficial."

Hardy meditated on that saying; then he began again.

"You've done a great deal for me, Kathy. I sometimes think that if you'd given your mind to it, you could have made something of Audrey. You know, poor little thing, she used to think she was very strong-minded; but she was more easily twisted about than any woman I know. That's what made her so fickle. If there's any truth in that stupid story of Wyndham's, she must have been like a piece of putty in her hands. I believe, if you could have got hold of her, you could have done her some good."

"I don't believe in doing people good."

"I do. I'm a case in point."

"No, you're not."

"I am. You did *me* good."

"I'm very glad to hear it. If I did, it's because I never thought about it. Now, if I tried my hand on Audrey, I should set to work with the fixed intention of doing her good; therefore I should fail miserably. It's a different thing altogether."

"I see no difference myself."

Katherine was silent. Her charity had covered the multitude of Vincent's sins. Why had she not been able to spare a corner of it for Audrey's?

"Come," said Hardy, "it's not as if she was really very bad."

"No, it's not; there'd be some chance then. There is a medium, and the medium is hopeless. The wonder is you never found that out."

"I did. I knew it all the time; yet I loved her. It made no difference— nothing ever will. I've tried to kill my feeling for her, but it's no use—I can't. I should have to kill myself first; and even then I believe I should find it waiting for me in Hades when I got there."

"After all, why should you try to kill it, Vincent?"

"It's the shame of it, Sis."

Katherine might have thought that on the contrary he seemed rather proud of the permanence of his affections, but she was too much preoccupied to be aware of his moral absurdity.

"Well, I don't know much about these things; but it seems to me that even if she doesn't love you, even if she isn't everything you thought she was, there's no reason to be ashamed of loving her."

"Ah, Kathy, you never loved any one like that."

Her colour changed. "No. It isn't every one who can love like that."

"What would you do if you were in my case—if you'd given yourself away like me? Supposing you went and lost your little heart to some man-fiend who was, we'll say, about as bad a lot as I am, and who had the execrable taste not to care a rap for you, — wouldn't you feel ashamed of him and yourself too?"

Katherine's white face flushed; she looked away from him, and answered steadily —

"No, I wouldn't."

He thought he had hurt her feelings, and was about to change the subject when she turned a beaming face to him.

"But then, you see, I don't love anything much."

"Good as you are, you'd be a better woman if you did."

"Of course there are exceptions. I've some sort of affection for the Witch and Ted."

"Ted is a very fine boy, and the Witch is a very fine picture, but — well, some day you'll have an affection for something else; it won't be a boy, and it won't be a picture. Then, Sis, you'll know what it is to feel, and your art will go pop."

"Oh, I hope not. But it's not true; look at Ted."

"Ted's a man, and you are a woman. Ten to one, a really great passion improves a man's art: it plays the deuce with a woman's."

"I don't believe it!" said Katherine, with rather more warmth than the occasion demanded.

"Shall I tell you what you've been doing, Sis? First of all, you've tried to live two lives and get the best out of each. That was tempting Providence, as Mrs. Rogers would say. You found that wouldn't work, so you said to yourself, 'I give it up. Here goes; I'll be a woman at all costs. I'll know what it is to love.'"

Katherine took up her brushes again, and in spite of herself moved one foot impatiently. Hardy went on, well pleased with his own lucidity.

"And you gave up the only thing you really cared about, and played at being the slave of duty, the devoted sister."

She sighed (was it a sigh of relief?).

"You're wrong. I'm anything but a devoted sister."

"Yes, you're anything but a devoted sister. I'm going to claim one of the privileges of friendship—that of speaking unpleasant truths in the unpleasantest way possible."

"Go on. This is getting interesting."

"I repeat, then, you're not a truly devoted sister. A truly devoted sister would give her brother a chance of developing some moral fibre on his own account. Ever since you two lived together you've been making noble sacrifices. Now two can't play at that game, and the boy hasn't had a chance. The consequence is, he won't work; he prefers taking it easy."

"That was Audrey's fault, not mine."

"Yes, but you encouraged him; and now he does what he likes, young monkey, and you do all the pot-boilers. And you're making yourself ill over them. So much for Ted. I've given him a hint, and he took it very well. Now for the Witch. I believe in your heart of hearts you love her better than everybody else put together. And now you're off on the other tack; you're trying to sit on the artist in you that you may develop the woman. I mean the other way about; you're sitting on the woman that you may develop the artist."

"Aren't you getting a little mixed?"

"That plan works worse than all. Let me implore you not to go on with it. If you only knew it, there's nothing that you will ever do that's lovelier than your own womanhood. Whatever you do, don't kill that. Don't go on hardening your heart to everything human till there's no sweetness left in your nature, Kathy. I want my little sister to make the best of her life. Some day some good man will ask you to be his wife. If, when that day comes, you don't know how to love, little woman, all the success in the world won't make up to you for the happiness you have missed."

"Oh, Vincent, if you only knew how funny you are!" She laughed the laugh that Vincent loved to hear, and when she looked at him her eyelashes were all wet with it.

"All right, Sis. Some day you'll own that your elder brother wasn't such a fool as you think him."

"I—I don't think you a fool. I only wish you knew how frightfully funny you are! No, I don't, though," she added below her breath.

But Vincent was quite unable to see wherein lay the humour of his excellent remarks. He considered that his experience gave him a right to speak with authority on questions of feeling. But it had not made him understand everything.

The next morning Katherine was sitting before her easel, waiting for Vincent to come up for the last sitting. It was a raw, cold day, and her fingers felt numbed as they took up the brushes. Ted had made a promise to Hardy to do his fair share of the more remunerative work. Before keeping it, he was giving a few final touches to one of the figures in his Dante study of Paolo and Francesca, swept like leaves on the wind of hell. He was in high good humour, and as he worked he talked incessantly, quoting from an imaginary review. "In the genius of Mr. Edward Haviland we have a new Avatar of the spirit of Art. Mr. Haviland is the disciple of no school. He owes no debt either to the past or to the present. He works in a noble freedom from prejudice and preconception, uncorrupted by custom as he is untrammelled by tradition. If we may classify what is above and beyond classification, we should say that in matter Mr. Haviland is an idealist, while in form he is an ultra-realist. We dare to prophesy that he will become the founder of a new romantico-classical school in the near future——"

"Oh, Ted, do be quiet, and let me think for a minute."

"What's the matter, Kathy?"

"I don't know. I think I'm tired, or else it's the cold."

Ted looked at her earnestly (for him) and then came over to her and stroked her hair. "There's something wrong. Won't you confide in your brother?"

"I'm all right—only lazy."

"Can't—can't I do anything?"

"Well, perhaps. I don't want you to give up much of your time to it; but if you'd finish some of those black-and-white things—I don't feel equal to tackling them all single-handed."

"Oh," said the boy, turning very red, "why didn't you say so before?" He sat down and began at once on the pile of manuscripts waiting to be illustrated. But he continued to talk. "I saw Vincent the other day, and he told me his opinion of you pretty plainly."

"What did he say?"

"Why, that you've sacrificed your poor brother to your desire to cut a moral figure; that you've been cultivating all sorts of extravagant virtues at my expense. I might have been playing the most heroic parts, and getting any amount of applause, if you hadn't selfishly bagged all the best ones for yourself. You've taken up the whole of the stage, so that I haven't had room even to exercise the minor virtues. Just reach me that sheaf of crayons, there's a good girl. Thanks." Ted put on a judical air, and chose a crayon. "Look there! you've taken the most uncomfortable chair and the worst light in the studio, when I might have been posing in them all the time. I haven't had half a chance. Vincent said so. No wonder he's disgusted with you. Ah! that's not so bad for a mere tyro. No, Kathy, he's quite right. You're an angel, and I've been a lazy scoundrel. But you'll admit that during my painful mental affliction I wasn't quite responsible. And afterwards—well, how was I to know? I thought we were getting on very nicely."

"So we were, Ted—up till now."

Her last words were so charged with feeling that Ted looked up surprised. But he said nothing, being a person of tact.

The sitting that morning was not a long one. Hardy seemed tired and depressed. After posing patiently for half an hour, he gave it up.

"It's no good this morning. I must go out and get a little warmth into me. You people had better come too."

"It's such a horrid day," pleaded Katherine. "You'll get exceedingly wet, and come back no warmer. It's going to rain or snow, or something." As she spoke, the first drops of a cold sleet rattled on the skylight.

But Vincent was obstinate and restless.

"I must go, if it's only for a turn on the Embankment. What with my book and your picture, I haven't stretched my legs all week. Come along, Ted. You'll die, Kathy, if you persist in wallowing in oil-paint like that, and taking no exercise."

They set out before a cutting north-easter and a sharp shower of rain that froze as it fell. Katherine watched them as they crossed the street and turned on to the Embankment. The wind came round the corner, as a north-easter will, and through the window-sash, chilling her as she stood. "There's nobody more surprised than myself," she said. "And yet I might have known that if I went in for this sort of thing, I should make a mess of it." She went back to the fire, and settled herself in the attitude of thought. There was no end to her thinking now. Perhaps that was the reason why she was always tired. Hitherto she had triumphed over fatigue and privation by a power which seemed inexhaustible, and was certainly mysterious. Much of it was due to sheer youth and health, and to the exercise which gave her a steady hand and a cool head—much, doubtless, to her unflinching will; but Katherine was hardly aware how far her strength had lain in the absence of temptation to any feminine weakness. Hitherto she had seen her object always in a clear untroubled air, and her work had gained something of her life's austere and passionless serenity. Now it was all different, and she was thinking of what had made that difference.

Ted came back glowing from his walk; but Vincent was colder than ever. He sat shivering over the Havilands' fire all afternoon, and went to bed early.

"We'll finish that sitting to-morrow, Sis," he said, wearily. Ted went out again to dine with Knowles, and Katherine was left alone.

It might have been her own mood, or the shadow of Vincent's, but she was depressed with vague presentiments of trouble. They gathered like the formless winter clouds, without falling in any rain. Then she realised that she was very tired. She wrapped herself in a rug and lay down on the couch to rest. And rest came as it comes after a sleepless night, not in sleep deep and restorative, but in a gentle numbing of the brain. She woke out of her stupor refreshed. The cloud had rolled away, and she could work again. She sat down to the last pile of Vincent's proofs.

When she had finished them, she turned over the pages again. The reading had brought back to her the last eighteen months, with all the meaning that they had for her now. She looked back and thought of the years when she had first worked for Ted, of the precious time that Audrey had wasted. The fatalism that was her mood so often now told her that these things *had to be*. And it was better, infinitely better, for Ted to have had that experience. She looked back on the year that Vincent had wasted out of his own life, and saw that that too had to be. There had been vicarious salvation even there. Ted had once told her that there was a time when, as he expressed it, he would have walked calmly to perdition, if Vincent had not gone before him and shown him what was there. She looked back on that year of her own life, "wasted," as she had once thought—the year she had given up so grudgingly at the beginning, so freely at the end—and she was content.

And now she was giving up, not time alone, and thought, and labour, but love—love that could have no certain reward but pain. And she was still content. At first she had been astonished and indignant at her own capacity for emotion; it was as if her nature had suddenly revealed itself in a new and unpleasant light. Then she had grown accustomed to it. Yesterday she was even amused at the strangeness and the fatuity of it all. She described herself as a bungling amateur wandering out of her own line and attempting the impossible. Clearly she should have left this sort of thing to people like Audrey, to whose genius it was suited, and who might hope to attain some success in it; but for her the love of art was quite incompatible with the art of love. She could have imagined herself entertaining these feelings for some one like Percival Knowles, for instance, who was clever and had an educated sense of humour, who wrote verses for her and flattered her artistic vanity; but to have fixed upon Vincent of all people in the world! She must have done it because it was impossible. That was what she had said yesterday; but to-day she understood. Had she not helped to make Vincent a man that she could love without shame? He was the work of her hands, that which her own fingers had made. It was natural that she should love her own work. Was she not an artist before everything, as he had said? Her tears came, and after her tears a calm, in which she heard the beating of a heart that was not her own, and felt the pulse of the divine Fate that moves through human things.

Then she asked herself—Was Vincent right? What effect had this curious experience really had on her painting? She felt no personal interest in the answer, but she got up and went to the easel. Her portrait of Vincent was finished—all but the right hand, that was still in outline. It was strange. Ted's best work had begun with his head of Audrey. What about her own? She saw through her tears that in all her long and hateful apprenticeship to portrait-painting, nothing that she had ever done could compare with this last. There was a new quality in it, something that she had once despaired of attaining. And that was character. She had painted the man himself, as she saw him. Not the Vincent of any particular hour, but Vincent with the memory of the past, and the hope of the future in his face. All the infinite suggestion and pathos, the complex expression that life had left on it, was there. If she had not loved Vincent—loved him not only as he was, but as he might have been—would she have known how to paint like that? Although her womanhood would never receive the full reward of its devotion, that debt had been paid back to her art with interest. The artistic voice told her that Vincent was wrong; that for her what women call love had meant knowledge; that her strength would henceforth lie in the visible rendering of character; and that work of such a high order would command immediate success.

And the voice of her womanhood cried out in anguish—"All the success in the world won't make up to you for the happiness you have missed."

There was no sitting the next day; for Vincent was in bed, ill, with congestion of the lungs.

CHAPTER XXIII

There is a little village in North Devon, sheltered from the sea by a low range of sand-hills that stretches for miles on each side of it. The coast turns westward here, and no cliff breaks that line of billowy sand; northward and southward it goes, with the rhythmic monotony of the sea. The sand-hills are dotted with tufts of the long star-grass, where the rabbits sit; inland they are covered with fine blades bitten short by the sheep. Seaward lies the hard ribbed sand, glistening with salt, and fringed with the white surf of the Atlantic.

On the coast, about a mile from the village, there is a long one-storyed bungalow, built on the sand-hills. The sand is in the garden, where no flowers grow but sea-pinks and the wild horn-poppy; it lies in drifts about the verandah, and is whirled by the Atlantic storms on to the low thatched roof. The house stands alone but for a few fishermen's huts beside it, huddled close together for neighbourhood.

Here, because it was the most man-forsaken spot she knew, Audrey had come, exchanging the roar of London for the roar of the Atlantic. She thought she would find consolation in the presence of Nature. London had become intolerable to her. Everywhere she turned she was reminded of the hateful Laura. Laura stood open in the window of every book-shop; Laura lay on every drawing-room table; there was no getting away from her. And yet Audrey's notoriety had won her more friends than she had ever had before. Everywhere people were kind to her; they made much of her; they said it was "hard lines," it was "a shame," "execrable," "unpardonable," and they assured her that nobody thought a bit the worse of her for all that. Some even went so far as to declare that they saw not the remotest resemblance between her and the popular heroine. But it was no use. Nothing could raise her in her own esteem. She fled. She longed to be alone with Nature. She took the bungalow for the winter; and once there, she wished she had never come.

She arrived in a storm that lasted some days. She thought she would have gone mad simply with hearing the mad wind and sea. It was the same whether she sat indoors listening to them, or she walked out, battling with the wreaths of whirling sand. After the storm came the dull, grey, heaving calm,—always the rolling clouds, the rolling sand-hills, and the rolling sea. That was infinitely worse. And to add to her depression, Audrey had never been so rigidly confined to the society of her chaperon; there was nobody else to see or hear, and the boundaries of the poor lady's intellect were conspicuous in the melancholy waste. There was no escape from her except into the cold monotony without.

Then February set in warm though grey. One morning Audrey was able to sit out in a sunny hollow of the sand-hills, where the rabbits had flattened a nest for her. Then she could think.

She was in the presence of Nature. Art was nothing to this. Art, in the time of her brief acquaintance with it, had baffled her, and given her a hint of her own feebleness; but Nature was the great Incomprehensible—and she was alone with it. Alone, in a lonely land, peopled mostly by the wild creatures of sea and shore, by peasants and fishermen, men and women who looked at her with strange eyes and spoke a strange language; whose ways were dark to her, and their thoughts unfathomable. She was face to face not only with primitive human beings, but with the primeval forces of the world—the stern, implacable will of the wind and sea. Not that she could feel these things thus, for they lay beyond the range of her emotions; but at the same time they tortured her. At first it was only by a dull sense of their presence, annihilating her own. Then, because they were things too great for her to grasp, they cruelly flung her back upon herself. They had no revelation for her. But left to herself, bit by bit her own character was revealed to her,—not as it had appeared to her before—not even as Wyndham had revealed it to her—but in the nothingness that was its being. It was stripped bare of all that had clothed it, and ruled it, and made it seem beautiful in her eyes. Left to herself, all the influences that had lent colour and consistency to this blank, unstable nature, had passed out of her life. The men whose destiny she had tried to mould, who had ended by moulding hers, twisting it now into one shape, now into another, had done with it at last; they had flung it from them unshapen as before. There was no permanence even in destiny. Vincent, whose will had dominated her own; Ted, whose boyish passion had touched her heart and made her feel; Langley, whose intellect had kindled hers, and made her able to think,—they were all gone, and she was alone. That was Langley's doing—Langley, whom alone of the three she had really loved—ah, she hated him for it now. And hating him, she remembered the many virtues of the two whom she had not loved well. Vincent—that was a revelation of love—why had she shut her eyes to it? Ted too, poor boy, he might have been hers still if she had chosen. She might have been moulding his destiny at this moment—instead of which, his destiny was doubtless moulding itself admirably without her.

Then her mood changed. She revolted against the cruelty of her lot. Her sex was the original, the unpardonable injustice. If she had only been a man, she could have taken her life into her own hands, and shaped it according to her will. But woman, even modern woman, is the slave of circumstances and the fool of fate.

"Audrey, Audrey, my dear!" called a wind-blown voice across the sand-hills. Solitude had frightened Miss Craven out of the bungalow, and she was picking her way in and out among the rabbit holes.

North Devon was hateful to cousin Bella. She hated the wastes of sand and sea, the discomforts of the bungalow, the slow hours uncertainly measured by meal-times that seemed as if they would never come. Her brain was wild with unsatisfied curiosity. Yet she had tact in the presence of real suffering. She had forborne to question Audrey about the past, and their present life was not fruitful in topics. She did nothing but wonder. "I wonder when it will be tea-time? I wonder if there was anything between Audrey and her cousin? I wonder which of those three gentlemen it was? I wonder when it will be tea-time?" That was the monotonous rondo of her thoughts to which the sea kept time.

"Audrey, my dear, come in! I think it must be lunch-time," she wailed. But no answer came from the hollow. She meekly turned, and picked her way back again across the sand-hills.

Audrey lay hidden till the forlorn little figure was out of sight; then she got up and looked around her. She shuddered. Her life was as bleak as the bleak landscape smitten by the salt wind—cold and grey and formless as the winter sea.

What was that black silhouette on the sands? She strained her eyes to see. Another figure was making its way towards her from the bungalow. When it came near she recognised the unofficial rustic who brought telegrams from the nearest post-town. She waited. The man approached her with an inane smile on his face.

"Teleegram vur yü, Mizz," he drawled.

She tore open the cover, and read: "Come at once. Vincent dying. Wire what train you come by.—Katherine."

She crumpled the paper in her clenched hand. The landscape was blotted out; she saw nothing but the envelope lying at her feet, a dull orange patch against the greyish sand.

"Any awnzur, Mizz?"

"No." She shut her eyes and tried to realise it. "Yes—yes, there is! Wait—I must look out my trains first."

She made out that by driving to Barnstaple, and catching the two-o'clock train, she would reach Waterloo about eight. She sent the man back with a telegram saying that she would be in Devon Street by nine that evening at the latest.

It was past one then, and she had yet to pack. It was hopeless—she could never catch that train. It did not matter; there was another to Paddington an hour later: it was a slow train, but she would be with Vincent by eleven.

But she was faint, and had to have some luncheon before she could do anything; and there was so much to do. She flew hither and thither, trying to collect her clothes and her thoughts. Her grey cloak and her bearskins—she would want them, it would be cold in the train. And her best hat—where was her best hat? Cousin Bella had hidden her best hat. Ah! she *must* think, or everything would go wrong. What was it all about? Vincent dying—dying? Audrey knew little about dying, except that it was a habit people had of plunging you suddenly into mourning when you had just ordered a new dress. Death was another of those things she could not understand.

By the time she had had luncheon, and decided what clothes she would take, and packed them; by the time the one old fly in the village had been ordered, and had made its way at a funereal pace to Barnstaple,—Audrey was just in time to see the three-o'clock train steaming out of the station. By taking the next train and travelling all night, she would only reach Paddington at four in the morning.

As she was at last borne on towards London, lying back on the cushions and trying to sleep, the facts became more clear to her. Vincent was dying; and he had sent for her. She was exalted once more in her own eyes.

It seemed to her then that her love for Vincent had been the one stable and enduring thing in her nature, the link that bound her to a transfigured past, that gave coherence to a life of episodes.

CHAPTER XXIV

Vincent had been ill for six weeks before Katherine sent off her telegram. For a month of that time he had been struggling with death. Then, when the mild weather set in, he had taken a sudden turn for the better, and it seemed to himself and the Havilands that he had won the victory. Only the doctor and Mrs. Rogers looked grave,—the doctor because of his science, which taught him to be cautious in raising people's hopes; Mrs. Rogers, because of a deep theological pessimism. She unburdened herself to Katherine.

"I knew 'ow it 'ud be when 'e gave up them 'abits of 'is, miss. 'E's been as good as gold for the last year. 'E 'yn't given me no trouble nor anybody; a goin' about so soft, and bilin' of 'is corffee in 'is little Hetna. I said to *myself* then, 'e's going to be took. It was the same with my pore 'usban', miss."

"Don't talk nonsense, Mrs. Rogers. Mr. Hardy hasn't the least intention of dying; he's getting better as fast as ever he can."

"Oh, miss! don't you sy so! It gives me a turn to 'ear anybody talk so presumptuous. Don't you do it, m'm. If 'e is a little better, it's enuff to make the Almighty tyke 'im, jest to 'ear you, miss."

Katherine forgave Mrs. Rogers, for the affectionate woman had helped to nurse Vincent with a zeal out of all proportion to her knowledge. Katherine had engaged a night-nurse during the crisis of his illness; after that, she and Ted nursed him themselves by turns—one sitting up all night, while the other slept on a bed made up in the sitting-room, to be within call. Katherine learned to know Ted better in those six weeks than in all his life before. The boy seemed to be possessed by a passion of remorse. He was as quiet as Katherine in Vincent's room, and could do anything that had to be done there with the gentleness and devotion of a woman. She would willingly have kept on the trained nurse, in order to give Vincent every advantage in the fight for recovery; but it was impossible.

For all three of them had come to the end of their resources at the same time. The Havilands were in debt at last. Vincent had sunk nearly all his capital in his British Columbian farm, where the agent, in whose integrity he had guilelessly trusted, worked the land for his own benefit, and cheated him out of the returns. His mother had left everything to her second husband. Worse than all was the reprehensible conduct of Sir Theophilus Parker. The old gentleman had died well within the term his nephew had given him, but had made no mention of him in his will, and "Lavernac and three thousand a-year" went to a kinsman of irreproachable morals, but a Radical, and many degrees more distant than Vincent from the blood of a Tory squire.

So, after the struggle with death, came the struggle with poverty. Work was impossible for hands busy with service in the sick-room, and young brains worn out with watching and anxiety. The most expensive luxuries were poor Vincent's necessities; for everything depended now on keeping up his strength.

One morning, after a long night's watching, instead of turning into the next room to sleep, Katherine put on her hat and cloak and went up to the deserted studio. She left the house with the "Witch of Atlas" under her cloak, and carried her to every picture-dealer in Piccadilly and New Bond Street. It was all in vain. Everywhere the Witch was pronounced to be beautiful, but unsalable. She was bowed out of every shop-door with polite regret, expressed in one formula: "The demand for this kind of work is really so small that we could only offer you a nominal sum, madam." Finally, Katherine turned into a small shop in Westminster, only to receive the same answer. But this time she was desperate. "What do you call a nominal sum?" The dealer looked the picture up and down; he noted, too, the shabby cloak and worn face of the artist.

"Frame included, five guineas. Not a shilling more, miss."

"I'll take that," she said, almost greedily. And the Witch was handed over the counter in exchange for the tenth part of her value.

But five guineas were a mere drop in the ocean of their necessities.

Two days later Katherine set out again, no longer alert and eager, but with a white face, a firm mouth, and a bearing so emphatically resolute that it suggested a previous agony of indecision. She took a 'bus from Lupus Street to the City. Getting out at Leadenhall Street, she walked on till she came to a building where an arrow painted on the doorway guided her to the offices of Messrs. Pigott & Co., on the third floor. On and on she went, up the broad stone stairs, with a sick heart and trembling knees, the steepest, weariest climb she had ever made in a life of climbing. When she reached the third floor she almost turned back at the sight of the closed door marked "Private." Then the thought of Vincent lying in his wretched room, a sudden blinding vision of his white face laid back on the pillows, overcame the last rebellion of her pride. She knocked; a well-regulated voice answered, "Who is there?" She brushed her eyelashes with her hand and walked in.

"It's me, uncle."

Mr. Pigott almost started from his seat. "You, Katherine? Bless me! Dear me, dear me!" He put on his spectacles, and examined her as if she had been some curious animal. And he, too, noticed not only her frayed skirt and the worn edges of the fur about her cloak, but the sharp lines of her face and the black shadows under her eyes.

"Sit down, my dear."

She obeyed, putting her elbow on the office table and resting her head in her hand. She looked defiantly, almost fiercely, before her, and spoke in a cold, hard voice—

"I've come to ask you if you'll lend us some money. We're in debt——"

"In debt? Tt-t-t-tt—that's bad."

"I know it is. But we've had illness in the house, and expenses that we had to meet."

"Bless me! Is the boy ill?"

"No; it's not Ted——" But as she tried to explain who it was she broke down utterly, and burst into tears. Then uncle James took off his spectacles and wiped them. He waited till she could speak coherently; and when he had heard, he took his cheque-book out of his drawer, asking no questions and making no comments—for which Katherine respected him.

"How much will clear you, Katherine, and see you to the end of this business?"

"Twenty pounds would clear us; but——"

Uncle James looked very grave, and he wrote with a slow and terrible deliberation. But he smiled lavishly as he handed her a cheque for a hundred guineas. He had made it guineas.

"Remember, there's plenty more where that came from."

"I—I don't know how to thank you, uncle; we'll repay it gradually, with the interest."

"Interest, indeed; you'll do nothing of the kind. And we won't say anything about repayment either, this time. Only keep out of debt—keep out of debt, and don't make a fool of yourself, Katherine."

Katherine hesitated, and her voice trembled. "I—I'm not——"

"No, I don't say you are. I ask no questions; and, Katherine!" he looked up, but she was still standing beside him.

"Yes."

"Always come to me at once when you want money; and go to your aunt Kate when you want advice. She'll help you better than I can, my dear."

"Thank you—thank you very much indeed. You are too good to me." She stooped down and kissed him on the forehead, pressing his hand in hers, and was gone before he could see her tears. Perhaps they would have gratified him. But he was amply rewarded by her kiss and the compliment paid him by his own conscience, which told him that he had not forced his niece's confidence, as he might have done, nor yet chuckled, as he might have done, over her fallen pride. It was a remarkable fulfilment of prophecy, too.

When she got back to Devon Street, Vincent was asleep, with Mrs. Rogers watching over him, and Ted was waiting for her to come to lunch. He looked terribly depressed.

She showed him her cheque in silence.

"You never asked *him*, that stern old Puritan father?"

"Don't, Ted. Yes, I did. I thought it would kill me; but it didn't. Oh, Ted, we *have* done him an injustice. He was kindness itself. I had to tell him about Vincent, too, and he never said a word—only gave me the cheque, and said we weren't to pay it back."

"H'm, that wasn't half bad of him, poor old thing." That admission meant a great deal from Ted.

"There's a letter there for you,—from Knowles, I think."

"What's he writing about?" She tore open the envelope. To her intense surprise she found a cheque for fifty guineas in it, and this note:—

"DEAR MISS HAVILAND,—Forgive my saying so, but when you want to sell your pictures, why don't you consult your friends instead of going to a thieving dealer? I found the Witch in the hands of such an one, and rescued her, for I won't say how little. As I could not possibly keep my ill-gotten gains on any other terms, please accept the enclosed, which with what you probably received will make up something like her real value. I need not tell you how delighted I am to possess so exquisite a specimen of your best work."

"Ted, what am I to do? Send it back again?"

"No, you little fool! Keep it, and never do *that* again—for any one."

For any one? What was there that she would not do for Vincent? But Ted, having said that, looked more depressed than ever. He went to the fireplace, and leaned against the chimneypiece, shading his face with his hand.

"What is it, Ted?"

He made no answer. A terrible fear clutched at her heart, and he saw it in her eyes.

"He's all right now; he's sleeping. But— —"

"But *what*? Tell me, Ted."

"Well, Crashawe was here this morning, and he says he isn't really better."

"But he *is* better. He said so himself when he examined him yesterday."

"Yes, so he is, in a way. That is, you see, his lungs are all right. It's his heart that's bad now. Crashawe says it must always have been more or less weak. And now— —" He stopped short.

"Ted— —" she implored.

"It may stop beating any minute."

She said nothing; she only took off her hat and cloak and put on her artist's overall,—it was her nurse's apron now. She must go to Vincent. But a thought struck her before she reached the door.

"Does he know?"

"No; but I think he has some idea. He told Crashawe this morning not to interfere with the course of nature." Ted smiled a dreary smile at the recollection.

Katherine dismissed Mrs. Rogers and took up her post at Vincent's bedside. He was still sleeping, with his face turned towards hers as she sat. And as she looked at him she had hope. She was still young, and it was inconceivable to her that anything she loved so much should die. It was not, she pleaded, as if she had been happy, as if her love had any chance of a return, or had asked for anything better than to spend itself like this continually.

And as she sat on watching, it seemed to her that it was better as it was. Better that love should live by immortal things, by things intangible, invisible, by pity, by faith, by hope, breaking little by little every link with earth. She tried to make herself believe this pleasant theory, as she had tried many a day and many a night before, her heart having nothing else to warm it but the fire of its own sacrifice. It was better as it was.

And yet, she said again, in this last six weeks he had been hers in a way in which he could be no other woman's, not even Audrey's. He was hers by her days of service, her nights of watching, by all that had gone before, by her part in his new life. After all, that could never be undone. She was almost happy.

Ted took her place for an hour in the evening, but that was all the rest she gave herself. She meant to sit up with Vincent again to-night.

"Do you know, Kathy, your eyes are very pretty."

It had struck midnight, and Vincent had been awake and looking at her for the last two minutes. She smiled and blushed, and that made her whole face look pretty too. And as he looked into her eyes the blindness fell from his own, and he saw as a dying man sometimes does see.

"Come here, Sis." He stretched out his arm on the counterpane, and as she knelt beside him he put back her hair from her forehead.

"I wonder if I was wrong when I thought you couldn't love anybody?"

Then she knew that he was dying.

"Yes, very wrong indeed. For—I loved you then, Vincent." Her face was transfigured as she spoke. He had to be spared all sudden emotions, but she knew that *her* confession would do him no harm. And indeed he took it quite calmly, without the least change of pulse.

"I'm not ungrateful——"

"There's nothing to be grateful for. I couldn't help it."

"I would have loved you more, Kathy, if it hadn't been for Audrey."

He spoke without emotion, in the tone of a man stating a simple matter of fact. Then he remarked in the same matter-of-fact voice that, as it happened, he was dying, so it made no difference. Perhaps he wanted her to know that a grave was ready for the secret she had just told him. There was no need to remind her of that,—she was sure of it before she spoke.

Her kneeling attitude, and hands outstretched on the counterpane, suggested an order of ideas that had never been very far from him during his illness. For Vincent had been wide awake and thinking difficult thoughts many a time when he lay with his eyes closed, and Katherine had thought he was asleep.

"I want you to read to me," he said at last.

"What would you like?"

"Well—the New Testament, I think, if it's all the same to you."

She rose from her knees and looked helplessly round the room. There was a Bible somewhere upstairs, but—

"You'll find one in the drawer there, where my handkerchiefs are."

She looked, rummaging gently among his poor things. She came on a small muslin pocket-handkerchief, stained with blood, also a loop of black ribbon of the kind that little girls tie their hair with. Some fine reddish hairs were still tangled in the knot. At last she found a small pocket Testament mixed up with some of his neckties. It was old and worn. Katherine wondered at that, though she could hardly have said why. Then she saw written on the fly-leaf, in a sprawling girl's hand, "Vincent, with Audrey's best love," and a date that went back to their childhood. It was the only present that Audrey had ever made him, and one that had cost her nothing.

"What part shall I read?"

She was afraid that Vincent would lay the burden of choice on her.

But he did not—he had very decided ideas of his own.

"The eighth of Romans, if you don't mind."

An eagle's feather floated out from between the pages at the eighth of Romans. It had been picked up on the snows of the Rocky Mountains. If she had wondered at first, she soon saw why Vincent had chosen that chapter of all others.

"Therefore, brethren, we are debtors, not to the flesh, to live after the flesh.

"For if ye live after the flesh, ye shall die: but if ye through the Spirit do mortify the deeds of the body, ye shall live." Vincent was dying.

She read on, and as she read she saw behind the edges of the veil that divides the seen from the unseen.

"For the creature was made subject to vanity, not willingly, but by reason of him who hath subjected the same in hope;

"Because the creature itself also shall be delivered from the bondage of corruption into the glorious liberty of the children of God."

Her heart beat faster and her breast heaved, but the words lifted her above pathos and tears, and prepared her for the consolation of the close.

"Do you believe all that?" he asked suddenly, when she had finished. She had not expected that.

"I didn't, but I do now."

"Why?" His eyes were fixed on hers, scrutinising, pathetic.

"Because I *must*."

That reason seemed to be hardly enough for Vincent. He was still hesitating and uncertain, as if he were looking for something that she could not give him. Then he lay back again with his eyes closed.

It was Katherine's turn to think. But Vincent's peace of mind was of more importance to her than the truth or falsehood of a creed. She had realised that there were things that even her love could not do for him. With a sudden flash of recollection she thought of the young priest she had once met at Audrey's house. If any one could help

Vincent now, it might be Mr. Flaxman Reed. She was probably mistaken (nobody is very wise between twelve and one in the morning), but at least she could try.

"Vincent," she whispered, "would you like to see a clergyman?"

She smiled, for after all it might be the very last thing that he wanted. He smiled too, a little consciously. His mood had changed for the time being—he had come back again to earth.

"No; thank you, Sis. But I should like——"

"What? Tell me."

"To see—Audrey."

The three words gave her a shock, but they told her nothing new.

"You shall. I'll send for her first thing in the morning."

He turned round with his face away from her, and settled himself again to sleep. And Katherine watched. He would be Audrey's to-morrow. He was hers at least for that one night.

No—never, never again. To-morrow had come, and the image of Audrey was between them. It always had been there.

Was it better so?

The next day Audrey had to be found. Ted went to Chelsea Gardens early in the morning, supposing her to be there. The house was shut up, and the caretaker had mislaid her address. He went back to Devon Street. Katherine and Ted were in despair; Vincent alone was equal to the emergency. His mind was on the alert—it had grasped all the necessary details. He gave them Dean Craven's address, and told Ted to wire to Oxford for Audrey's. That was how Audrey never got the telegram till one o'clock.

That morning the doctor pronounced Vincent decidedly better. The change, he said, was something miraculous. He took Katherine out of the room to tell her so.

"Keep him quiet, and he *may* pull through yet. I don't say he will, but he may. Only—he mustn't have any excitement."

"He's had a great deal this morning. If it lasts all day, and if—he has any more of it to-night, will it hurt him? It's pleasant excitement, you know."

The doctor looked keenly at her. To judge by her white face she was not sharing in the pleasant excitement.

"Well, I can't say. Pleasure does less harm than pain, sometimes. Don't let him have any suspense, though. Suspense will kill him."

But suspense was what he had to bear.

Katherine knew that he was living on in the hope of Audrey's coming. Well, she would be with him by nine at the latest, as she had said.

At half-past eight Vincent began to listen for every bell. At nine he asked to have the door set ajar, that he might hear the wheels of her cab in the street. But though many cabs went by, none stopped.

"She's missed her train. We didn't give her much time. Look out the next, Kathy."

Katherine looked it out. "She'll be here by eleven if she catches the three-o'clock. It gets to Paddington at ten."

Vincent closed his eyes and waited patiently till ten. Then he became excited again, the nervous tension increasing with every quarter of an hour. By eleven the street was still, and Vincent strained his ears for every sound. But no sounds were to be heard.

It was half-past eleven. A look of fear had come over his face.

Katherine could bear it no longer. She went into the next room, where Ted was standing at the window. She laid her hands on his shoulder, clinging to him.

"Oh Ted, Ted," she whispered, fiercely. "She'll kill him. He'll *die* if she doesn't come. And—she isn't coming."

Ted had never known his sister do that before. It was horrible, like seeing a man cry. He put his arms round her (he had almost to hold her up), and comforted her as best he could. But she put him from her gently, and went back to her post.

"She'll come to-morrow, Vincent," she said.

"No. If she were coming, she would have wired."

But that was just what Audrey had forgotten to do. By the time she had reached Barnstaple, she was too much taken up with her own tragic importance to think of any small detail of the kind.

Vincent had turned over on his side. He had no more hope, and nothing mattered now. He had done his best, but was not going to carry on a trivial dispute with death.

But though his spirit had given up the struggle, his body still fought on with its own blind will, a long, weary fight that seemed as if it would never end. Towards morning he became to all appearance unconscious.

At seven o'clock the front-door bell rang; there was a stir in the hall and the sound of Mrs. Rogers' voice whispering.

Then the door opened and closed softly. Audrey was standing there, a strange figure in the dim white room, wrapped in her bearskins, and glowing with life and the fresh morning air.

At first she could distinguish nothing in the shaded light. Then she made out Ted, sitting with his back to her at the foot of the bed, and Katherine standing at the head of it. But when she saw the motionless figure raised by pillows, and vaguely defined under the disordered bedclothes, a terror seized her, and she hid her face in her hands.

"Come here, Audrey," said Katherine, gently. And she came—gliding, trembling, as she had come to him that afternoon at Chelsea, a year and a half ago. But she kept her eyes fixed on Katherine. She was afraid to look *there*.

"Take his hand. Speak to him."

Audrey looked round, but Ted had left the room. Her small white hand slid out of her muff, warm with the warm fur, and rested on Vincent's hand; but no words came. She was sick with fear.

The touch was enough. Warm and caressing, the little fingers curled into the hollow of his hand and Vincent woke from his stupor. He opened his eyes, but their look was vague and wondering; he was not conscious yet. Katherine moved aside and drew up the blind, and the faint daylight fell on Audrey's face, as her eyes still followed Katherine.

For one instant his brain seemed to fill suddenly with light. It streamed from his brain into the room, and he saw her standing in the midst of it.

"Audrey!" The loud hoarse voice startled Katherine, and made Audrey shake with fright. His hand closed tightly on hers, and he sank back into unconsciousness.

For two hours the two women kept watch together by his bed: Katherine at the head, holding Vincent in her strong arms; Audrey sitting at the foot with her back turned to him, pressing her handkerchief to her mouth. At nine o'clock she shivered and looked round, as Vincent's head sank forward on his breast.

Katherine, standing at the back of the bed, first saw what had happened by the change on Audrey's face. The corners of her mouth had suddenly straightened, and she started up, white and rigid.

"He's dead! Take me away, Katherine—take me away!"

But this time Katherine neither saw nor heard her.

"No; he was bound to die. What else could you expect after the life he led, poor fellow?"

It was all over. Audrey had dragged herself out of the room, she scarcely knew how—dragged herself up to Katherine's room and thrown herself on the bed in a passion of weeping; and Katherine, kneeling for the second time by Vincent's side, could hear the verdict of science through the half-open door. Dr. Crashawe was talking to Ted.

Neither Audrey nor Katherine knew how they got through the next three days. Audrey was afraid to sleep alone, and Katherine had her with her night and day. Audrey would have gone back to Chelsea but for her fear, and for a feeling that to leave Devon Street would be a miserable abandonment of a great situation. All those three days Katherine was tender to her for Vincent's sake. Happily for her, Audrey disliked going into his room; she was afraid of the long figure under the straight white sheet. Katherine could keep her watch with him again alone; she had no rival there.

Once indeed they stood by his bed together, when Katherine drew back the sheet from his face, and Audrey laid above his heart a wreath of eucharis lilies, the symbol of purity.

They stood beside him, the woman who loved him and the woman he had loved; and they envied him, one the peace, the other the glory of death.

CHAPTER XXV

It was early one morning about a week after the funeral. Hardy had gone to his grave, followed last by his friends, and first by his next of kin, Audrey, and the man who had Lavernac. Audrey was still (as she always had been) his affectionate cousin. The fact was expressly stated on the visiting-card attached to the flowers wherewith she had covered his coffin.

It was in Katherine's bedroom. Katherine was still in bed, waiting for Audrey to be dressed before her. Audrey was sitting at the dressing-table brushing her hair, twisting it into the big coil that shone like copper on the surface, with a dull dark red at the heart of it. She had on Katherine's white dressing-gown and Katherine's slippers. She had laughed when she put them on, they were so ridiculously large for her tiny feet.

Audrey was rebounding after the pressure that had been put on her during the last ten days. The weight was lifted now. After all, she had not felt herself an important actor in that drama of death. Death himself had come and waived her coldly aside. She had been nothing in that household filled with his presence. Here again she had been overpowered by one of those unseen, incomprehensible things that she could not grasp, but that crushed her and made her of no account. At times, in her misery, she had even felt a vague, faint jealousy of the dead. But since the day of the funeral her supple nature had unbent. She could talk now, and she talked incessantly, generally about Vincent.

She had begun by monopolising his memory, making it a sacred possession of her own, till not even that consolation was left to Katherine. Audrey stood between her and every scene connected in her mind with Vincent; the figure of Audrey seemed to draw nearer and grow larger, until it covered everything else. Her stream of talk was blotting out the impressions that Katherine most longed to keep, giving to the past a transient character of its own. She was killing remembrance; and there came upon Katherine a fear of the forgetfulness where all things end.

And now, as she lay there watching Audrey, she recalled the truth that she had lost sight of since Vincent's death—the truth that he had told her. He would have loved her—if it had not been for Audrey. She had begun to realise the intensity of the duel which had been between Audrey and her from the first.

It had begun in the days when Audrey had stood in the way of Ted's career; it had gone on afterwards, when it was to be feared that she had done him still more grievous harm; and it had ended in separating Katherine from Vincent, and even from his memory. Rather, that duel had neither beginning nor end. There was something foregone and inevitable about it, something that had its roots deep down in their opposite natures. It had to be. It had been from the hour when she first met Audrey until now, when the two women were again thrown together in a detestable mockery of friendship, forced into each other's arms, lying by each other's side.

Audrey had been quiet for some time, and Katherine was nervously wondering when she would begin.

"Katherine," she said at last, "I want you to come back with me to Chelsea to-day." The fact was, Miss Craven was in Devonshire, and Audrey was still afraid to be in the house by herself.

"I couldn't, possibly. I can't leave Ted."

"That doesn't matter. Ted can come too."

What *was* Audrey's mind like? Had it no memory?

"I think not, Audrey."

Audrey said no more. She gave the last touches to her hair, put on her black dress, and turned herself slowly round before the looking-glass. She was satisfied with the result.

It was her last day in Devon Street, so the Havilands had to be nice to her. Ted went out soon after breakfast; he was incapable of any sustained effort. Audrey did not know it, but the boy hated the house now that she was in it. Katherine had dreaded being left alone with her that morning. She knew that last words would come. And they came.

They were sitting together by the studio fire, talking about indifferent subjects, when suddenly Audrey left her seat and knelt down by Katherine's knees in at attitude of confession.

"Katherine," she began, and her grey eyes filled with tears, "before I go, I want to tell you something——"

"What is it?"

"I want you to know that I really loved Vincent all the time."

She waited to see the effect of her words, but Katherine set her teeth firmly and said nothing. Audrey went on, still kneeling. "I don't know what made me get engaged to Ted,—I liked him, you know, dear boy, but—I think it was because Vincent would not understand me; and he wanted to hurry things so. And you see I didn't know then how much I loved him. Then afterwards——" She stopped; she had come to the difficult part of her confession.

"Well?"

"Then, you see, I knew Mr. Wyndham, and he——" Another pause.

"What did Mr. Wyndham do?" It was better that she should talk about Mr. Wyndham than about Vincent.

"I don't know what he did, but he made me mad; he made me think I cared for him. He was so clever. You know I always adored clever people; and, well—nobody could call poor Vincent clever, *could* they?"

In spite of herself, Katherine's lip curled with scorn. But Audrey was too much absorbed in her confession to see it.

"I suppose that fascinated me. Then afterwards when Vincent took to those dreadful ways—whatever my feelings were, you *know*, Katherine, it was impossible."

Katherine could bear it no longer, but she managed to control her voice in answering. "Why do you tell me these things? Do you suppose I care to hear about your 'feelings'? — if you do feel."

"If I *do* feel? Kathy!"

"Well, why can't you keep quiet, now it's too late?"

"Because — because I wanted you to know that I loved him."

There was silence. Presently Audrey put one hand on Katherine's knee.

"Kathy — —"

"I'd rather you didn't call me that, if you don't mind."

"Why?" Audrey stared with large, incomprehensive eyes.

"I can't tell you why."

"Katherine, then — it *is* prettier. Do you know, I sometimes think it's better, oh, infinitely better, that he should have died."

Katherine rose from her seat, to end it, looking down on the kneeling figure, as she answered bitterly —

"It was indeed — infinitely better."

But irony, like so many other things of the kind, was beyond Audrey.

"I suppose I ought to go now," she said, rising. Katherine made no answer.

Audrey went away to get ready, a little reluctantly, for she had so much more to say. It had never occurred to her to be jealous of Katherine. That may have been either because she did not know, or because she did not care. She had been so sure of Vincent.

Presently she came back with her hat on. She carried her bearskins in her hand, and under the shade of the broad black beaver her face wore an expression of anxious thought.

"Katherine,"—she held out her cape and muff, and Katherine remembered that they were those which Vincent had given her,—"I suppose I can wear my furs still, even if I *am* in mourning?"

There was neither scorn nor irony in the look that Katherine turned on her, and Audrey understood this time. As plainly as looks can speak, it condemned her as altogether lighter than vanity itself; and while condemning, it forgave her.

"*He* gave them to me, you know," she said at last. Audrey's pathos generally came too late.

She drove away, wrapped in her furs, and for once unconscious of her own beauty, so dissatisfied was she with the part she had played in the great tragedy. Somehow her parts seemed always to dwindle this way in retrospect.

That afternoon a parcel arrived, addressed to Hardy by his publishers. Katherine opened it. It contained early copies of the Pioneer-book, the book that after all Vincent was never to see.

She saw with a pang her own design blazing in gold on the cover, and her frontispiece sketch of the author. Then she turned to the dedication page, and read—

TO HER
WHO HAS INSPIRED
ALL THAT THERE MAY BE OF GOOD IN IT
THIS BOOK IS DEDICATED
BY HER AFFECTIONATE COUSIN,
VINCENT HARDY.

It was an epitaph.

CHAPTER XXVI

One day's work among the poor of St. Teresa's, Lambeth, is enough to exhaust you, if you are at all sensitive and highly strung, and Audrey had had three days of it. No wonder, then, that as she leaned back in a particularly hard wooden chair in the vicar's study every nerve in her body was on edge.

It was a year after Vincent's death. With lapse of time that event had lost much of its oppressive magnificence, and it affected Audrey more in looking back than it had done in reality. Time, too, had thrown her relations with Wyndham into relief; and as she realised more and more their true nature, the conscience that had been so long quiescent began to stir in her. Its voice seemed to be seconding Wyndham's and Katherine's verdict. She became uneasy about herself. Once more, this time in serious sincerity, she felt the need of a stronger personality upholding and pervading her own. Absolute dependence on somebody else's character had become a habit of her nature: she could no more live now without some burning stimulus to thought and feeling than the drunkard can satisfy his thirst with plain water. Naturally she thought of Mr. Flaxman Reed, as Katherine had thought of him the midnight before Vincent's death, or as she had thought of him herself in the day of her temptation. This time she had ended by going to him, as many a woman had gone before, with her empty life in her hands, begging that it might be filled. For all cases of the kind Mr. Flaxman Reed had one remedy—work in the parish of St. Teresa's; as a rule it either killed or cured them. But he had spared Audrey hitherto, as he would have spared some sick child a medicine too strong and bitter for it. Finally, much to his surprise, she asked him for the work of her own accord, and he gave it to her.

And now she had had three days of it. It was enough. It made her head ache yet to think of all she had gone through. For the first two days she had been sustained by a new and wholly delightful sensation, the consciousness of her own goodness; on the third day that support had suddenly given way. A woman's coarse word, the way a man had looked at her as she lifted her silk petticoats out of the mud, some bit of crude criticism such as Demos publishes at street corners in the expressive vernacular, had been sufficient to destroy all the bright illusions that gilded the gutters of Lambeth — reflections of a day that was not hers. And yet, she had come into a new world with new ideas and new emotions; if not the best of all possible worlds, it was better than any which had once seemed probable, and she wanted to stay in it. She was dazzled by the splendour of religion. The curtain had risen on the great miracle-play of the soul; she, too, longed to dance in the masque of the virtues and the graces. Every fresh phase of life had presented itself to Audrey in spectacular magnificence; she could not help seeing things so, it was the way her mind worked. The candles burning on the high altar of St. Teresa's were only footlights in the wrong place; and the veil that Mr. Flaxman Reed had lifted a little for her was the curtain going up before another stage. Meanwhile while she had to consider his possible criticism of her own acting. Sitting in the hard ascetic chair, she looked round the room and tried to understand a little of its owner's life. Every detail in it was a challenge to her intelligence. She perplexed herself with questions. Why didn't Mr. Flaxman Reed have a proper carpet on the floor? Why didn't he hang a curtain over that ugly green baize door? It led into the room where he held his classes and entertained his poorer parishioners; that room was also his dining-room. How could he eat his meals after all those dreadful people had been in it, poor things? Why only common deal bookcases, a varnished desk, and that little painted table underneath the big crucifix? Why these painfully uneasy chairs, and — yes — only one picture, and that of the most emaciated of Madonnas? Could not her old favourite Botticelli have supplied him with a lovelier type? Or there was Raphael. Sometimes, on a Sunday evening after service, she had come in here from the rich, warm, scented church, with the music of an august liturgy ringing in her ears, and the chill place had struck like death to all her senses. And this was the atmosphere in which his life was spent — this, and the gaunt streets and the terrible slums of Lambeth.

She was not left long alone, for Mr. Flaxman Reed never kept any one waiting if he could help it. As he seated himself opposite to her, the set lines of his face relaxed and his manner softened. Her eyes followed the outline of his face, which stood out white and sharp against the dark window-curtain. She noted the crossed legs, the hands folded on his knees, the weary pose of the whole wasted figure. It ought to have been an appeal to her pity. The poor man was suffering from many kinds of hunger, and from intense exhaustion. He had just dismissed a tiresome parishioner, and, vexed with himself for having kept Audrey waiting, had left his dinner in the next room untouched, and came all unnerved to this interview which he dreaded yet desired. He listened quietly to the story of her failure; it was not only what he had expected, but what he had wished.

"It's no good my trying any more," she urged in the pleading voice that she could make so sweet. "I can't do anything. The sight of those poor wretches' misery only makes me miserable too. I dream of it at night. I assure you it's been the most awful three days I ever spent in my life."

"Has it?"

"Yes. I feel things so terribly, you know; and it's not as if I could do anything—I simply can't. What *must* you think of me?"

"I think nothing. I knew that you would tell me this, and I am glad."

"Are you? Glad that I failed?"

"Yes; glad and thankful." He paused; his thin sensitive lips trembled, and when he spoke again it was in a low constrained voice, as if he were struggling with some powerful feeling.

"I wanted you to learn by failure that it is not what we know, nor what we do, but what we are that matters in the sight of God."

"Yes, I know that." She sat looking up, with her head a little on one side, holding her chin in one hand: it had been her attitude in her student days at Oxford when trying to follow a difficult lecture, and she reverted to it now. For Mr. Flaxman Reed was very difficult. His style fascinated and yet repelled her, and in this case the style was the man.

"What am I?" said Audrey, presently. It was a curious question, and none of her friends had answered it to her satisfaction. She was eager to know Mr. Reed's opinion. He turned and looked at her, and his eyes were two clear lights under the shadow of the sharp eyebone.

"What are you? With all your faults and all your failures, you are something infinitely more valuable than you know."

"What makes you say so?"

"I say so because I think that God cares more for those that hunger and thirst after righteousness than for those who are filled at his table. Believe me, nothing in all our intercourse has touched me so much as this confession of your failure."

"Has it really? Can you—can you trust me again in spite of it?"

"Yes; you have trusted me. I take it as one of the greatest pleasures, the greatest privileges of my life, that you should have come to me as you have done—not when you were bright and happy, but in your weakness and distress, in what I imagine to have been the darkest hour of all, when refuge failed you, and no man cared for your soul."

"No; that's the worst of it,—that there's nobody to turn to—nobody cares. If I thought that you cared—but——"

"Indeed I care."

"For my soul—yes." Her "yes" was a deep sigh.

"Why not? It is my office. A priest is answerable to God for the souls of his people."

He spoke with a touch of austerity in his tone. Something warned him that if this conversation was to be profitable to either of them, he must avoid personalities. His position in the Church was a compromise. His attitude towards Audrey Craven was only another kind of compromise,—so much concession to her weakness, so much to her appealing womanhood. He had begun by believing in her soul,—that was the plea he made to the fierce exacting conscience, always requiring a spiritual motive for his simplest actions,—and he had ended by creating the thing he believed in, and in his own language he was answerable to God for it. But hitherto with his own nature he had made no compromise. He had sacrificed heart, senses, and intellect to the tyranny of his conscience; he had ceased to dread their insane revolt against that benevolent despotism. And now the question that tormented him was whether all the time he had not been temporising with his own inexorable humanity, whether his relations with Audrey Craven did not involve a perpetual intrigue between the earthly and the heavenly. For there was a strange discrepancy between his simple heart that took all things seriously—even a frivolous woman—and the tortuous entangled thing that was his conscience. He went on at first in the same self-controlled voice, monotonous but for a peculiar throbbing stress on some words, and he seemed to be speaking more to himself than her.

"You say you can do nothing, and I believe it. What of that? The things that are seen are temporal, the things that are unseen are eternal. Our deeds are of the things that are seen; they are part of the visible finite world, done with our hands, with our body. They belong to the flesh that profiteth nothing. It is only the spirit, only the pure and holy will, that gives them life. That will is not ours—not yours or mine. Before we can receive it our will must die; otherwise there would be two wills in us struggling for possession. You have come to me for help—after all I can give you none. I can only tell you what I know—that there is no way of peace but the way of renunciation. I can only say: if your will is not yet one with God's will, renounce it—give it up. Then and then only you will live—not before. Look there!" he pointed to the crucifix. "The great Pagan religions had each their symbol of life. For us who are Christ's the symbol of life is the crucifix. Crucify self. When you have done that, you will have no need to come and ask me what you must do and what you must leave undone. Your deeds are—they *must* be pure."

His excitement moved her, her eyes filled with tears; but she followed his words slowly and painfully. He was always making these speeches to her, full of the things she could not understand. How often she had felt this sense of effort and pain in the old "art" days with Ted, or when she had been held helpless in the grasp of Wyndham's relentless intellect. She had chafed when the barriers rose between her mind and theirs. But between her and this nineteenth century ascetic there was an immeasurable gulf fixed; she could not reach the hand he stretched out to her across it. Even his living presence seemed endlessly far from hers, and the thought of that separation filled her with a deep resigned humility. Now, though his thoughts were poured into her consciousness without mixing with it, cloudy, insoluble, troubling its blank transparency, something in the rhythmic movement of his words stirred her, so responsive was she to every impression of sense. They recalled to her that other gospel of life preached to her by Langley, and though she understood imperfectly, she felt the difference with shame. The young priest went on, still as if speaking to himself.

"There are only two things we have to learn—the knowledge of self and the knowledge of God, and they hang together. If there is any sin in us, unconfessed and unrecognised as sin, there is no knowledge of God and no union with him possible for us."

She rose, moved a step forward, and then stood looking at him irresolutely. Truly a revelation was there for her; but she was in that state of excitement in which we are more capable of making revelations than of receiving them. He had risen too, and was holding out his hand. "Well," he said more gently, "there is something you want to say to me. Please sit down again."

She shook her head and still stood upright. Possessed with the thought of the confession she was about to make, she felt that she needed all the dignity that attitude afforded. At last she spoke, very low and quickly, keeping her eyes fixed on the floor.

"You say you know me, but you don't. You don't know what I am—what I am capable of. But I must tell you,—the thought of it is stifling me. Once, only two years ago, I had a terrible temptation. It came to me through some one whom I loved—very dearly. I was ready to give up everything—*everything*, you understand—for him; and I would have done it, only—God was good to me. He made it impossible for me, and I was saved. But I am just as bad, just as guilty, as if he had let it happen."

It was done. The unutterable thing was said. For once Audrey had been absolutely truthful and sincere. The soul that he had evoked had come forth as it were new-born out of the darkness.

At first neither of them spoke. Then he sat down and thanked her, simply, for what she had just told him. But to his own shame and grief he had nothing more to say. He had heard many a confession, and from many a guiltier woman's lips, but none so piteous, because none so purely spontaneous, as this. And to all he had given pity, counsel, and help.

But now he was dumb.

She was thirsting for help, for help that she could understand. She clasped her hands imploringly and looked into his face, but it had no pity for her and no deliverance. She could see nothing there but grief—grief terrible and profound.

"I see. Then you too judge me—like the rest."

"God forbid. I judge no man." Which was true, for it was the woman he had judged.

She looked at him again, a long look full of wonder and reproach; then she went quietly away.

She had reached the end of the narrow passage leading from the study to the front hall, when she recollected that she had left behind her a small manual of devotion. He had given it to her not long ago. She went back for it, and knocked softly at the study door. There was no answer, and supposing that he had gone through into the room beyond, she opened the door and looked in.

He was kneeling in the far corner of the study, with his hands stretched out before the crucifix. From the threshold where she stood she could see the agony of his uplifted face and hear his prayer. "O wretched man that I am! who shall deliver me from the body of this death?"

Audrey knew then that for one moment the love she had hungered and thirsted after, more than after righteousness, had been actually within her grasp, and that she had lost it. The shadow of an uncommitted sin stood between her and the one man by whom and for whom she could have grown pure and womanly and good. For Flaxman Reed had loved her, though up to that evening he had been in complete ignorance of the fact, being already wedded to what the world considers an impossible ideal.

Such is the power of suggestion, that Audrey's confession of her weakness had revealed to him his own. If she had been all that he believed her to be, he might not have regarded his feeling for her as in itself of the nature of sin; but his sensitive soul, made morbid by its self-imposed asceticism, recoiled from the very thought of impurity in the woman he loved. Hence his powerlessness to help her. He knew, none better, that a stronger man would not have felt this difficulty. He had trembled before his own intellect; now he was afraid of his own heart.

Audrey—it was for such that his Christ had died. And he could not even speak a word to save her.

He became almost blasphemous in his agony. Christ had died on *his* cross. He, Christ's servant, had crucified self—and it could not die. Was this the ironic destiny of all ideals too austere for earth, too divine for humanity?

Not long afterwards Flaxman Reed was received into the communion of the Church of Rome. He had done with compromise.

CHAPTER XXVII

It was Audrey's fate to be condemned by those whom she had most cared for. Ted and Vincent, Langley and Katherine, and lastly Mr. Flaxman Reed, they had all judged her—harshly, imperfectly, as human nature judges. Of the five, perhaps Vincent, because he was a child of Nature, and Katherine, because she was a good woman, alone appreciated the more pathetic of Audrey's effects. She presented the moving spectacle of a small creature struggling with things too great for her. Love, art, nature, religion, she had never really given herself up to any one of them; but she had called upon them all in turn, and instead of sustaining, they had overwhelmed her.

And it seemed that Mr. Flaxman Reed, as the minister of the religion in which she had sought shelter for a day, had failed her the most unexpectedly, and in her direst necessity. And yet he had done more for her than any of the others. She had lied to all of them; he had made it possible for her to be true. Flaxman Reed would certainly not have called himself a psychological realist; but by reason of his one strength, his habit of constant communion with the unseen, he had solved Langley Wyndham's problem. It would never have occurred to the great novelist, in his search for the real Audrey, to look deeper than the "primitive passions," or to suspect that the secret of personality could lie in so pure a piece of mechanism as the human conscience.

Soon after her confession Audrey left town for the neighbourhood of Oxford. She may have perceived that London was too vast a stage for her slender performances; or she may have had some idea of following up a line slanting gently between the two paths pointed out to her by Langley Wyndham and Flaxman Reed, who had been the strongest forces in her life. She had come to herself, but she was not the stuff of which renunciants are made.

It was about three years later that Mr. Langley Wyndham, looking over his "Times" one morning, had the joy of reading the announcement of Miss Audrey Craven's marriage with Algernon Jackson, Esq., of Broughton Poggs, in the county of Oxfordshire.

It was true. After all, Audrey had married a nonentity: it was the end of her long quest of the eminent and superlative.

Mr. Jackson was certainly not an eminent person, and he was superlative only in so far as he passed for "the biggest bore in the county"; but he had the positive merit of being a gentleman, which in these days of a talented democracy amounts almost to genius. Since that night when, as a guileless undergraduate, he had interfered with Audrey's first introduction to Langley Wyndham, Mr. Jackson's career had been simplicity itself. He had tried most of the learned professions, and failed in all he tried. He then took up model goose-farming on a large scale, and achieved success amidst the jeers of his family and friends. The echo of that derision was soon lost in the jingle of Algernon's guineas. Not every one can attain a golden mediocrity; and it was a great step for a man who had hitherto ranked as a nonentity. On the strength of it he asked the beautiful Miss Craven to be his wife, and no one was more surprised than himself when she consented. She was his first and last love—of a series of loves. For Mr. Jackson had never read "Laura"; indeed he read but few books, and if you had told him of Langley Wyndham's masterpiece to-day, he would have forgotten all about it by to-morrow; he would certainly never have thought of identifying its heroine with his wife.

Nobody ever understood why Audrey made that marriage. For any one who had enjoyed the friendship of such men as Langley Wyndham and Flaxman Reed, there was bathos in the step; it seemed an ugly concession to actuality. It may have been; for Audrey was nothing if not modern, the daughter of an age that has flirted with half-a-dozen ideals, all equally fascinating, and finally decided in favour of a mature realism. She may have learned that hardest lesson of the schools, the translation of life's drama from fancy into fact; found out that all the time the grey old chorus has been singing, not of love and joy, as she once in her ignorance imagined, but of unspeakable rest on the great consoling platitudes of life, where there is no more revelation because there is no mystery, and no despair because there is no hope. The text of that chorus is often corrupt, but the meaning is never hopelessly obscure. In other words, she may have married Mr. Jackson in a fit of pessimism.

Or perhaps—perhaps she had profited by the more cheerful though equally important lesson of the playground; learned that whether the game of life be fast or slow, dull or amusing, matters little when you are knocked out in the first round (she herself had had many rounds, not counting Mr. Jackson); that in these circumstances one may still find considerable entertainment in looking on; and that in any case the player is not for the game, but the game for the player. The player—who may be left on the ground long after all games have been played out. But this is to suppose that Audrey was a philosopher, which is manifestly absurd.

Perhaps! More likely than not her revelation came when she was least looking for it, stumbling by the merest accident on one of "the great things of life," the eternal, the incomprehensible; for of these some say that the greatest is love. It is certainly the most incomprehensible. She may have loved Mr. Jackson. If she did not, she has never let him know it.

THE END